Rex Bromfield

This book is a work of fiction. Names, characters, places, and incidents are a product of the author's imagination or are used fictitiously. Any resemblance to actual events, locales, or persons, living or dead, is coincidental.

Copyright © 2020 by RbF Inc.
Cover Art by Fred Gonder copyright © 2020 by RbF Inc.

Scanning, uploading, and distribution without the author's permission is a theft of the author's intellectual property

August 2020

ISBN: 9781693787423

Contents

A death In The Family....................1
What was going on 9
Nobody's Home............................18
Sara...25
That Woman..................................29
The Last Supper.............................56
The Great Escape...........................68
The Pursuit of a Decent Burger....90
Sanctuary.....................................128
The Man Who Fell To Earth.......133
Fat's...145
Back In The Saddle Again..........156
Strange Fruit................................169
The Wrong Man..........................180
Coming Out.................................200
Somewhere Over The Rainbow..206
The Revolutionary.......................222
Zero hour.....................................251
Best Laid Plans 254
Wilson's Map 257
A Moveable Feast.......................268
The Kraken Wakes......................278
The Standoff................................293

The Accidental Tourist...............303
In Memoriam..............................306
Invasion of the Body Snatcher....311

The Dominican Republic

August 2016

A Death In The Family

Ed Miller peered from the window of the cut-rate airline 737 that was taking him back to Toronto, far to the north. He didn't really want to go. He had no choice. As the plane tilted away, he got a last look at the idyllic beach village of Punta Cana; the only real home he'd ever cared for.

Life in the Dominican Republic had been easy, but since his father's death, Ed lost everything bequeathed to him, and now even his own mother had cut him off without a word of explanation. All he had left was a few loud Hawaiian shirts, some Bermuda shorts, and a few odds and ends, all of which he carried with him in two ragged suitcases.

Crawling back to his mom on bended knee to beg for cash wasn't an easy thing for Ed. He would have to admit that at thirty-four he had failed in life, failed at everything and become an overweight, lazy, flabby, weak excuse for a man... no, he wouldn't say all that, just the part about being broke. Mom was no Scarlett Johansson herself.

Ed didn't really watch the in-flight movie, he just kind of stared at the silent images flickering on the screen and thought back across his life. How had he come to this point? Ed wasn't the sort of guy who ever really thought much about the important things, so he wasn't very good at it. A mediocre student at a suburban Toronto high school, he excelled at schoolyard social politics, double-talking and joking his way out of frequent academic failures. He was a cute, amiable kid, easily attracting the attentions of girls in his sexy little souped-up yellow Beemer—until he smashed it up showing off in rush-hour traffic. Good thing he managed by sheer luck to avoid the people waiting at the bus stop.

His dad, Sid, had connections with the police and got him out of that one. Ed didn't know exactly how, but he knew he owed him. Ed and his dad were solid pals, so when his parents finalized the divorce and Sid took off to tropical climes, Ed went with him.

In the Dominican Republic, in nothing more than a shack on the beach, Ed's dad brought his sharp business sense into play and opened *Sid's Cabana On The Beach*. Sid had done his homework. There wasn't a decent cheap bar and eatery for miles. The two hotels nearby had stuffy restaurants that served mediocre fare, so Sid put a gaudy sign on the roof, cranked up the Reggae and served huge portions, undercutting the competition's prices by thirty percent.

Sid's Cabana was a shabby little affair, but it was an instant success. The only thing that threatened this perfect little situation—and what caused Dad's sudden demise—was his alcoholism. When Ed was just ten his mom told him, as if it were something he didn't know, that his dad was a bad alcoholic. But even at that early age Ed knew she was wrong. He was actually quite a *good* alcoholic. He drank almost constantly during his waking hours and seemed to hold it well as long as others were around. But when the party was over, there were unpredictable outbursts of outrageous behaviour, and blackouts. How many times had Ed had to leave him to sleep it off wherever he passed out?

Ed was the *bad* alcoholic. He hardly ever took more than one drink and rarely finished that one. As a result, Ed could savour a good glass of Medoc and a rare steak done to a turn with a steaming baked potato slathered in butter and sour cream, finished with a double cut of his favourite freshly baked blueberry pie with French vanilla ice cream. Throwing up and falling down never came into it.

Ed did well in the Dominican Republic. He was in reasonable shape, though starkly white in a bathing suit in a population of mainly black folks, but he was good looking and the local women liked his jovial, laid-back manner.

Now, after almost fifteen years of Caribbean cuisine and little or no exercise, his weight fluctuated around two-sixty. It wasn't a *bad* two-sixty, but it was two-sixty just the same.

Ed worked the slow day shift at the Cabana, until Sid breezed in around four to get the party rolling. Secretly, Ed wished he could be more like his dad. He was impressed with the way Dad could hold his own with a group of vacationing day traders, then cross the room and liven up a gathering of dockworkers with a crude joke and a round on the house. Sid thrived in his little underworld. Ed saw the slight winks and nods as Sid brokered secret arrangements between police officials, neighbourhood strongmen, and even a few known Santo Domingo felons. On two occasions, Ed saw his dad make change for a one thousand dollar bill from his shirt pocket. Though Sid kept most of this away from his son, Ed picked up many techniques.

Sid's real problems lay hidden and silent. His cholesterol could clog a big city sewer system. His heart, constantly fighting to shunt blood to his extremities, was weaker than a newborn's fist. He weighed over three hundred pounds, and he wasn't doing a thing about it. Ed could still remember the day it caught up with him as clearly as if it had happened that morning. Sid was standing on the bar in his stocking feet holding one end of a big cloth banner with the unoriginal slogan HAPPY HOUR ALL DAY. Ed stood similarly at the other end of the bar where he had just finished banging a nail through the corner of the banner into a beam in the ceiling. He handed the hammer down to Carlito, the large bartender who handed it up to Sid. Sid, reached down, took the hammer, then stretched on tiptoes to nail the other end of the banner to the ceiling beam. It was precisely then, as he was about to strike the nail, that a shot of adrenaline was released in response to physical activity unseen by Sid's body in twenty-seven years. Because of very low levels of potassium and magnesium in his diet, the electrical signals in Sid's heart became all scrambled and the lower chambers of the tortured organ fibrillated wildly. A sharp pain shot through Sid like lightening. His eyes bulged, and his breathing stopped. He looked down the bar at his son Ed, who now appeared to be in negative. There was a blinding flash of green light seen only by Sid, and down he went. Sid might have survived his fall from the bar that morning if he hadn't landed on his head.

The only doctors Sid Miller ever saw were the ones who frequented his establishment to self-medicate with alcohol and who knows what prescription drugs.

Sid's death was a surprise to no one except Ed, who went along all these years as if nothing would change, as if the bright soft sunny days would come and go forever. But as he waited for the coroner to arrive, Ed sat on a bar stool staring at his dad, now covered with the happy hour banner, and wondered what it all meant.

Ed was suddenly the new owner of *Sid's Cabana On The Beach*. For months everyone asked after his father and raised innumerable toasts to Sid's memory, but, in his absence, business dropped off.

The only good thing that came from Sid Miller's death was that Ed re-established contact with his mom. When Ed called her to inform her of her ex-husband's passing, she seemed surprised that he had lasted as long as he did. Ed sensed some vague satisfaction in her tone. She wouldn't be attending the funeral, but she encouraged Ed to visit her. He gave some lame excuse.

Later, when he got into financial trouble, she sent him some bail-out money and renewed her campaign to get him to abandon the Cabana On The Beach and return to Toronto. Ed guessed correctly that it was an attempt to claw back some slices of joy that Sid and Ed had stolen from her when they ran off. But so far, the only thing she kept from the marriage was the one hundred plus pounds she had gradually packed on to her petite frame. She was fat too, and that made her resent Sid even more. *He* had made her that way and secretly she wished he would show up on her doorstep, crawling back in need of her compassion. But now Sid was gone and it was Ed who was crawling back. If only he could have kept up the mortgage payments on his own. But he missed one payment, then another. Sometimes there wasn't a soul in the place all day, but

Ed kept telling himself that things would pick up soon.

It was not to be.

He fell further behind with the mortgage. And then the dreaded call came that finally ended the barefoot days and balmy nights, the four hour work days, the two nubile topless volleyball girls he'd watch frolic every morning on the sand court across from the cabana. The call was from the bank that held the mortgage.

The stern male voice on the other end was Spanish accented and official. "Mister Miller, Victor Valesquez of the Banco Central de la Republica..."

Ed brightened. "Hey Vic, we never see you down here anymore. What's the matter, you gone on the wagon or something?"

"Mister Miller, I regret to inform you that the bank has no choice but to foreclose on your mortgage," Victor blurted. He was never any good at delivering bad news. It was probably one reason for his excessive drinking, which he was now doing elsewhere.

"Come on Vic, there's no sense getting all tense over a few missed payments. I'll call my mom and..."

"You have returned none of my calls," Vic said. "I've already left many messages for your mother. She doesn't return my calls either. We require you to vacate within forty-eight hours," Vic said finally, and the line went dead.

"The prick hung up on me," Ed said to Carlito, then immediately dialed his mom in Toronto.

No answer.

Ed stared out the window at the two volleyball girls for a while, then tried to call Vic back. He was "too busy to take the call."

Trembling and tearing up, Carlito had figured out what was happening. Ed sat with him as he downed three double whisky sours and cried. Then Carlito took off his apron and went home for the last time.

--

Now, Ed's plane was making its final approach into Toronto. He would go straight to Mom, convince her that saving the Cabana On The Beach was the right thing to do, then get out of there before winter hit. Taking his mom with him wasn't out of the question.

Customs was tricky. They confiscated his bag of macadamia nuts—very hard items to come by in Canada and expensive as hell. Ed thought they were done until they donned rubber gloves and pulled back a layer of shirts to discover the two candied hams and a vacuum-sealed nut cake he had brought along. If he'd known they would take these he would have eaten them instead of the two skimpy meals he got on the plane.

Skipping the cost of a cab, Ed boarded an airport bus.

--

By 8:15 P.M. Toronto time, Ed was standing on the sidewalk across from Union Station on Front Street.

His mom had a small condo ten blocks away and Ed considered walking, but he wondered what she might have in her fridge and hailed a cab.

He tossed his bags into the back seat and climbed in, greeting the surly cabby. "Nice evening." No response. Toronto used to be a place where folks spoke politely to everyone. "Seventy-five Dalhousie Street," Ed said and the cabby headed north on University Avenue, then turned left onto Richmond Street. Ed realized they were going the wrong way. If he didn't turn soon, he'd say something. Meanwhile, the tip was diminishing proportionately.

The cab turned north and Ed finally spoke up. "Say, isn't Dalhousie on the east side?"

"Construction" the cabby muttered and turned onto Queen Street behind a streetcar, then stopped.

"Pain in the ass these streetcars eh?" Ed said trying to sound Canadian, but the cabby didn't so much as look at him in the rear-view mirror.

After creeping along for five minutes Ed said, "Look, it's not far, I think I'll walk." He handed the guy ten bucks and got out. Heading east on foot, he felt like an idiot. He'd paid ten bucks to be driven five blocks further away from his destination. As he hoofed it along Queen Street, he saw the cause of the delay.

Fire trucks blocked the entire street and a blaze in a shop on the south side was just coming under control. Police were keeping people back, but as Ed crossed the street, he noticed that the main fire raged in one shop: "WENDY'S LARGE GALS' BOUTIQUE." Ed could barely make out some graffiti on the front of the store:

DON'T SHOW IT HERE!

Ed sensed that something strange was going on.

What Was Going On

The good Reverend Father Allen wheeled his twelve-year-old Cadillac through the clogged traffic toward the warehouse district.

He didn't drive a Cadillac because it was a luxury car. Father Allen didn't really believe in luxury. It was because General Motors was the only manufacturer willing to replace a broken driver's seat back every year for the full length of the warranty. That was in the old days when the Father was at the height of his powers and sporting a domineering three-hundred pound plus physique. Stress had taken its toll, and he now hovered around two-seventy.

That night something weighed on the good Father's mind as he sought to avoid a street blocked by fire trucks. Though he felt more comfortable in jeans and a sweatshirt, he had taken to wearing his clerical collar almost all the time now since things had gotten worse. Still, sixty-eight was no age for a dedicated man of the cloth to be playing street crusader. By now he should be delivering the word on television, but this work took him into the streets. Saving souls was what he knew.

Father Allen had seen his share of hardship. He'd never really gotten over the loss of his loving wife, Elspeth, four years earlier in a freak airline accident. If it hadn't been for his daughter Sara, Father Allen would have given up long ago. But people needed him now more than ever, and they...

A horn blared, and he realized that he'd driven straight through a red light. He checked his mirrors and slowed down. A police stop was the last thing he needed.

Finally, down an alley to a dark mews flanked by featureless warehouses, Father Allen pulled his car over to the curb. Shutting off the engine and the lights, he looked slowly around, waiting for everything to settle down, making sure no one was watching. You couldn't be too careful these days. He pulled himself from the car, then ever so gently pressed the door closed with a substantial right hip. Again he waited for the envelope of silence to close in. He didn't notice the thirteen police officers watching him from the darkness of a transport vehicle parked in the shadows.

It was so quiet down here that the Father could hear the snap of each individual grain of grit under his shoes echo off the brick walls as he made his way across the street to an apparently empty warehouse.

Lieutenant Bill Lardner, his partner Detective Ray Bailey, and the eleven uniformed cops with them could hear each of the good Father's footfalls, too. They watched as he strode up to a plain wooden door, looked up and down once more, then knocked twice, waited, then knocked three times more.

Father Allen knew the routine well. So did Lt. Lardner. The police had been staking out this location for almost a month, waiting for a certain evening when there would be enough "big fish" in attendance to justify a full-scale raid. They watched as the door opened and a nervous little man in coveralls admitted the Father, then closed the door quietly behind them. Lardner turned back to his men. "Okay, we're going in."

Bailey rubbed his hands together, eager to get going. This bothered Lardner about his partner. He was always champing at the bit, eager to do his job. He once heard Bailey bragging to two patrolmen about staying single so he could get the dangerous cases, but Lardner believed that he was single because he couldn't find a woman who liked to talk about special weapons and tactics before, after, and possibly during sex.

"Okay, now pay attention," Lardner said to the men. "This is where it gets tricky. Don't get caught up in the way it looks. These people may or may not be committing a crime. Chances are they're not." It was important to impress the men with procedure. If they acted with care and compassion, later, when the shit hit the fan, their collective nose would be clean.

Bailey chimed in as if Lardner's instruction needed clarification. "The point is, this will take them by surprise."

"So, just go easy," Lardner added. Lardner was playing it safe. He didn't want any slip up that might attract the press. "This is as much for your protection as it is for theirs," he explained. "Things will get a whole lot worse if somebody gets hurt." Lardner created a long pause and made the facial expression that said he was now looking each man in the eye, though, in the darkness, he couldn't really see them in any detail and they couldn't see him either. But the men all knew he was serious. Each man nodded an unseen "yes" back at him.

Bailey couldn't stand waiting another second. "Just remember, these folks can be dangerous," he said. "Never position yourself between two of them when making an arrest or between one of them and a wall. Don't even try to push and shove. And whatever you do never go down stairs ahead of them, always behind.

Keep your eyes open for this, it's a killer."

Everyone but Lardner and Bailey laughed. Bailey stressed the point. "It's not funny. I know what I'm talking about."

Lardner cut back in. He didn't want the men taking any of this lightly. "We gotta have nice orderly arrests. No profanity and keep your firearms holstered."

--

Father Allen strode between rows of high shelves ahead of the little man who admitted him. "I don't know Father," The man yammered, scrambling to keep up. "We try to keep track of everyone, but it simply isn't possible to...."

"Oh, come on, Rick!" Father Allen said. "How could you miss him? He's the biggest spender in the place!" Father Allen pulled open a hidden panel and stepped into Jacque's midnight eatery. Virtually unknown and secreted in the back of the dull, dusty warehouse, Jacque's was the underground epitome of elegance and good taste. The place was packed with mostly overweight gourmands. The creme de la crème de la crème of affluent society. A Brahms concerto seeped gently into the crowded, noisy room, fabulous exotic dishes were swept in from the kitchen by a hurried crew of thin but capable waiters. There was everything from Venison Steak St. Hubert to Softshelled Crabs Almandine, Pakistani Pigeon and Pilaf to Viennese Noodle Pudding. No ordinary lasagna here. Tonight Jacque's chefs were serving Cannelloni a la Nerone, a mouthwatering handmade pasta stuffed with a secret mixture of chicken, prosciutto and parmesan, smothered in a rich sauce and broiled to perfection.

Once a legitimate eatery in the theatre district,

Jacque's was driven into this backstreet darkness by the incremental stiffening of regulations restricting the preparation and portioning of food products.

But Jacque was an artiste, an epicurean genius who believed that the right to create great art transcended all boundaries and restrictions. That's why he saw no infraction in importing, for example, Italian white winter truffles via the black market to please patrons as discerning as himself. Many of his most ardent followers were the wealthy and politically well-connected cognoscenti who knew that without high art and culture, a society shrivels and dies. And they loved great cuisine.

In the old days one had to make reservations weeks in advance. But when picket lines appeared in front of Jacque's thirty-eight table restaurant, his thin customers abandoned him. Eventually the phones fell silent. Soon his clientele consisted solely of "that all too visible minority" as one critic put it, and in no time Jacque's became known as a hangout for the well-to-do obese. After eight months, beset by health and safety inspectors, representatives of the Provincial and Federal Revenue Agencies and the RCMP, Jacque closed his doors, and financed by wealthy lifelong patrons, took his operation underground. The police knew about the place from the start, but resisted targeting Jacque's and it's privileged clientele.

Until now.

Father Allen scanned the crowded room. An effeminate maître d' scurried over, wringing his hands with mixed emotions and a fake French accent. "Why Father Allen... what a surprise! What brings you to our modest establishment this fine evening?"

Ignoring him, Father Allen spotted one particularly rowdy table in the corner and waded through to where the outsize Alderman Adams was enthusiastically celebrating his fifty-sixth birthday.

The Alderman was genuinely pleased to see him. "Father Allen! Sit down." He pulled an unused chair from the table behind him. "You're just in time to help us wish me a happy..."

Father Allen spoke softly at first. "Ken, you of all people should know better... there could be undercover agents in here right now writing down names... taking photographs!"

Alderman Adams remained jovial. "Hogwash! Nobody knows about this place. Besides," he laughed to the others, "it's not a felony to celebrate your birthday... not yet anyway."

Father Allen waved a hand at the room. "*All* of this is against the law! Haven't you been reading the papers?"

Alderman Adams got serious. "What the hell's a person to do Father, give up their livelihood just because some freaky little fitness fanatics decide everyone should weigh less than one-ten? I'm sick of it, for Christ's sake!"

"Don't drag *Him* into it." Father Allen countered. "This isn't any of *His* doing. We created this situation all by ourselves."

"Sorry..." The alderman took a sip of wine. "But be reasonable, Father. How can anyone in their right mind honestly believe that eating two desserts is substance abuse?"

The Father grasped the alderman's shoulder, scrunching the corner of his suit jacket. "I'm telling you Ken, this is..."

Suddenly the alderman was less than amused. "Calm down, will you? I'm a city official. They can't do anything to me." Alderman Adams yanked himself free, patted down his crumpled shoulder pad and poured Father Allen a glass of wine.

"Here, this is a nice full-bodied Chardonnay which, believe it or not, goes beautifully with the roast leg of veal. And to finish there's Grand Marnier pots de crème that the waiters say are too rich for one person to eat. Imagine. You should see the fabulous butter cream cake they have on the pastry cart it's all...."

"Kenneth!" Father Allen said emphatically.

"What?" Alderman Adams grabbed a plate and sliced a thick piece of veal roast for the Father.

Father Allen placed a hand on his arm, stopping him. "Is any of your family here with you?"

"Not yet, but I expect them momentarily...."

"Good, you and your friends have to get out of here..."

But before Father Allen could finish his plea, the now no-longer-secret panel banged open and Lardner, Bailey and the squad of cops burst in.

Bailey held a loudhailer to his mouth. "Ladies and gentlemen, this is a raid." He pointed to a wall. "No one is in any danger. Put down your food and line up in an orderly fashion on that side of the room with your identification ready."

The merriment quickly gave way to screams of horror and panic. Some tried to escape. Others tried to hide, but the police seemed to be everywhere. Some of Jacque's customers continued to stuff food into their mouths as they were rounded up and led out of the room. The police weren't looking for Jacque. He was already in custody, having been arrested several weeks earlier for income tax fraud. The eatery was now run by his two sons, who never showed their faces in the place for fear of becoming caught up in exactly what was now taking place.

As everyone at the alderman's table stood up, Father Allen finally sat down and buried his face in his hands. This was pretty well going to do it. With the "bulk" of his congregation under arrest and the rest afraid to attend services, who was left?

Detective Bailey saw the Father sitting alone at the table and came over. "Come on, move it!" he barked.

Lardner, constantly on the alert for anything the media could blow out of proportion, stepped in. "Uh Father," Lardner said, "we don't want to take you in." Though he wasn't very religious, nothing short of a smoking gun could make Lardner arrest a man of the cloth. "I think you'd better be on your way."

Father Allen pulled himself slowly to his feet. His eyes met Lardner's. For an instant the two men shared an affinity, some compassion, an understanding of the "big" picture. Father Allen, adept at seeing into people's souls, knew Lardner meant him and his people no harm.

"You're just letting him go?" Bailey protested.

"He just came in here. We saw him." Lardner said, "He's only trying to help." Bailey grimaced, then moved off to attend to the growing melee.

Lardner cast Father Allen an abstract but reassuring nod. Father Allen knew there was nothing he could do at this point. He turned and shuffled towards the door in clerical immunity and left.

By the time they had herded the alleged felons into out-sized paddy wagons, everyone had more or less resigned themselves to the situation. All except for Alderman Adams, who continued to rant loudly at the cops. "This is an absolute outrage!" he bellowed. "You don't have the slightest idea how much trouble there will be when your superiors learn who I am!"

Lardner looked up and down the street. 'Good,' he

thought. 'No reporters around.'

They didn't get any of the employees. Kitchen and wait staff seemed to have vanished in the confusion. It was more than half an hour after the last cop left. The street outside Jacque's was quiet once more. Slowly, the crew of employees emerged naked and shivering from the very back of the deep freeze locker at the back of the kitchen. The cops searched the locker but couldn't endure the cold. In their quick survey they saw nothing out of the ordinary. They didn't notice the little piles of white clothing here and there on the floor or the naked chefs and waiters hanging camouflaged in their state of nature among the huge sides of meat. At one point one cop swung the head waiter aside to shine his flashlight between him and a side of veal. His light fell on the maître d' who barely suppressed a sneeze. Luck was with him; he was mistaken for contraband and left swaying in that artificial winter.

Without a word between them the staff put on their coats and went their separate ways via a small window on the second floor at the other end of the building and down a fire escape to disappear into the night.

Nobody's Home

Ed remembered his mom's neighbourhood as a notorious rat and cockroach-infested cluster of low-rise low-rent walk ups. Now there was proper street lighting, security, the works. Ed wondered where the homeless, the addicts, the prostitutes and pimps had gone. He'd soon find out they were still there, just hidden behind and between the glittering new facades.

The doorman interrogated Ed as if he were requesting entry to the White House. In Ed's time you could just walk into an apartment building, go upstairs and knock on the door. Not anymore. It was a good thing he still had the card key his mom had sent years ago after he tentatively agreed to visit her one Christmas.

The third-floor hallway was dark. Good way to cut down on the cleaning costs, Ed thought as he made his way to apartment 304 where someone had scrawled "CHUBBOS MUST GO!" in heavy felt marker on the door. It was spray-painted over, but the words showed through well enough to read even in subdued lighting. Ed knocked, but no one answered. He inserted the key card and opened the door a crack.

"Hello?"

No answer.

"Mom? You home? It's me, Ed."

Still no answer. He stepped into the dingy living room. Tried the lights. Didn't work. Luckily there was enough light coming in through the large floor-to-ceiling windows and he could move about without stumbling over anything. It smelled of something rotten, but it was faint. Could be the long-dead plants that drooped on end tables. Ed opened a window that opened onto a useless four-and-a-half-inch balcony. Fresh night air wafted in, raising a mist of dust that took a few minutes to settle. Mom wasn't just out shopping. And she hadn't left in a hurry either; she'd carefully covered all the furniture with bed sheets before going... where?

The kitchen light worked and cast an eerie glow back into the rest of the apartment. Good, the power wasn't out. Ed checked the fridge. A jar of strawberry preserves and a wedge of mouldy cheese in Saran Wrap. He tossed it into the trash, then stooped to search the back of the fridge. A plastic squeeze container of chocolate sauce. He took it out, twisted the lid off and gave it a sniff. Rancid. "Aw shit."

He retrieved the cheese from the trash, unwrapped it and gave it a sniff. He thought, "cheese is rotten milk isn't it?" It looked normal for cheese, but he decided against tasting it, re-wrapped it and placed it carefully on the counter. You never know. When he pulled open the microwave door, a lone fly spiralled out, made a direct left turn, flew straight into the wall and drop dead on the counter.

Then something... a sound, faint but inside the apartment. Sounded like breathing or high-pitched moaning. It was so faint that Ed's growling stomach almost drowned it out. He moved back to the living room and listened. It was coming from the bedroom. The door was ajar, and it creaked loudly when he pushed it open. He looked about in the gloom. The closet. The door was open about three inches and Ed put his ear to the opening. Definitely in here, a low small wheezing kind of... whimpering. Slowly Ed pulled the door open wider. The sound stopped, and he opened the door right up letting some light seep in and there it was, looking up from a clearing in a small forest of women's shoes was the tiniest, skinniest, bedraggled-looking, miserable little cat he'd ever seen. It looked like someone had run it over with a car, then pissed on it and run it over again. It tried to meow, but only a gasping gurgle came out.

"Hey there, what the hell are you doing here?" was the only thing Ed could think of to say but he choked up a bit when he realized that the animal had come into this little corner to die, as cats do. This time the cat managed a weak, stuttering meow. Ed reached down and carefully lifted the sad animal out of the dark. It was like holding a sock full of broken chopsticks.

His mom couldn't have been gone long or the pitiful creature would surely be dead. Then he noticed the tiny stash of mouse skeletons, bleached white with age and lined along the floor at the back of the closet. He stroked the poor animal's head, but some grey and orange fur stayed in his hand, so he stopped.

"You know, you're not in good shape." he said as if he expected the animal to understand. "Where's Mummy? You know where Mummy is, girl?" If the cat could have understood, it would have informed him that Mummy went out the front door long ago and that would have been the extent of its knowledge.

Now the sad animal found her voice and began to yowl in a faltering way.

"Jesus, I don't know baby, there's nothing for either of us to eat here." He said then remembered the mouldy cheese on the kitchen counter. Maybe she would eat that.

The cat sniffed the cheese, then gave it a lick.

Maybe if he scrapped some of the green stuff off. Then Ed noticed a plastic bowl on the floor with the name PORKY on the side.

"Hey Porky, I found your bowl."

He went to pick it up and saw that the cupboard nearby had been relentlessly clawed almost all the way through. Pulling open the door, Ed found about a dozen individually wrapped packets of Tender Vittles cat food. "Good for you girl, you almost made it."

Porky went nuts, meowed a long meow of delight as Ed tore a packet open and dumped it into her bowl. Porky attacked the bowl of food with such a ferocity it vanished in an instant. Ed opened and poured only half of the next packet into the bowl so the desperate animal might eat more slowly. It was no use. The second lot went faster than the first. "That's all you can have, girl," Ed said. "Gotta go slow so you don't bust a gut."

Ed knew how she felt. He was starving too. There *was* the jar of strawberry preserves. Not exactly food, but what the hell? He wondered if there were any grocery stores nearby as he fetched a tablespoon from a drawer and took the bottled confection into the living room to see if he could spot anything from the window.

Couldn't see any stores in either direction up and down the street. But there, across the way, went a woman carrying a plastic bag of groceries. Now there went two gay guys carrying environmentally friendly reusable bags overflowing with baguettes, fresh flowers, a celery stalk and what may have been a leg of lamb. There had to be a market nearby.

Good.

"There will be dinner on the table tonight," he said to Porky. And to celebrate, he popped open the jar of strawberry preserves, dug a heaping spoonful of the contents out and stuck it in his mouth. It took about three-tenths of a second for the utterly foul taste to hit him, but he held the terrible substance in his cheeks long enough to get to the small sink at the bar and spit it out. Quick. He located a bottle of Glenfiddich and swilled big chugs straight until the vile taste was gone.

That's when he noticed two framed photos on shelves above the bar: Ed's dad, Sid, proudly holding baby Ed and Sid and Ed's mom on their wedding day. Mom had turned two other pictures to the wall, and Ed turned them back to see that they were both of his mom. At first he didn't recognize her. In one, she posed smiling in front of a generous smorgasbord. It shocked Ed to see that she had become extremely overweight. In the other photo, she lolled on a sofa beside a large man. Both held daiquiris aloft.

Ed's head spun and his stomach growled fiercely as the alcohol hit its emptiness. His thoughts went immediately to the seventy dollars he had tucked safely in his wallet, and in seconds he was waiting for the elevator on his way out to do some grocery shopping.

--

Ed drifted hypnotized through the Metro Foods store, still tipsy from the alcohol. There weren't many people in the place, but he felt eyes on him. He'd go straight for the essentials and be on his way: two Hungry Man dinners, a gallon of maple walnut ice cream, two things of frozen cookie dough, a pound of butter, two loaves of raisin bread, a small Taster's Choice instant coffee and a pint of whipping cream for the coffee. That would hold him over.

There were only two checkout desks open. Ed got in line at the "twelve items or less" desk.

He shouldn't have.

Right away a small, elderly, pointy-faced woman in front of him eagerly counted his items. Ed smiled at her but got nothing in return. Then he spotted the display of candy bars and unconsciously added a generous handful to his order on the conveyor belt.

"This man has more than twelve items," the birdlike woman squawked at the cashier.

What business was this of hers? Ed thought. She was in front of him in line.

The cashier, a pretty girl in her late teens, looked at his items and tried her best to be pleasant. "I'm sorry Sir, you must move to another desk..."

He pointed to the candy bars and said, "Oh, I just picked these up here in line," but the two women just stared at him. He grabbed up a few bars from the conveyor. "Here, I'll put some back..."

"He's still got thirteen items," the old woman crowed pointing at the *TWELVE ITEMS OR LESS* sign and glaring at Ed. "Can't you read?"

Ed was tired. He'd been on a long flight, he didn't know what had become of his mom, and his patience was running out. "Okay," he said curtly. "Fine." And he put all the candy bars back and shoved the rest forward towards the cashier. "Now there's only..." He tried to count the items but lost count. "Oh, who gives a damn?"

"There's no need to raise your voice, sir." the cashier said nicely but didn't move to check his items through. The bird lady crossed her arms in front of her scrawny chest and smiled grotesquely at him. Ed failed to notice that the ruckus had attracted the attention of the security guard who was now making his way slowly across the front of the store towards him.

"Who's raising their voice?" Ed asked, raising his voice. "Look," he spotted the guard and tried to calm down, "I've been on a plane for hours so just cash me out and I'll be on my way."

He pushed his stuff closer to the cashier. The two cookie doughs rolled off the counter and fell at her feet but before he could say another word, the security guard grabbed him firmly by the arm.

Ed pulled his arm free.

Surprised at this reaction, the guard stepped back and stumbled into two abandoned shopping carts. The clatter reverberated through the store. The cashier picked up her phone and dialed 911.

The ride to 51 Division was short. Ed wasn't too worried. He'd be able to glad hand his way free of this without trouble.

--

Ed persuaded the cops to reduce the initial charge of common assault to drunk and disorderly. Then, by agreeing to a Breathalyzer test and with some humiliating self-deprecating jokes about his weight, got it further reduced to disorderly public conduct and creating a disturbance. The cops were all right once he got them laughing. He figured the bail would be less than a thousand dollars. He could put up ten percent to the bondsman and walk out of there.

But just in case, he asked for and got one phone call. He flipped through a Yellow Pages that looked like it had been used to mop the floor, and dialed an outfit called Cocke, Tift, Little and Boyes. An answering machine sang "If you're blue and locked in jail, call back when we're in and we'll arrange your..." but right then a tough, humourless member of the Marshall's Service appeared and tugged on his arm. He never got to leave a message.

Sara

Father Allen sat in his car in the parking lot of The Church of the Safe Way for half an hour before his daughter, Sara, spotted him from the kitchen window of the rectory. The curve of his back and his downcast gaze told her that the situation was grave. Usually when he sat in the car like this, he'd look at the sky, perhaps in silent prayer, seeking answers to whatever was troubling him. But now he looked down at nothing. Not moving.

It reminded her of the night she got the call that dispassionately delivered the worse news ever. The airline situation representative said, "I'm so sorry, Ma'am. Your mother's flight had to make an emergency landing at Aurora, Colorado. We have confirmed that..." and he faltered here, then went on, "due to your mother's brave actions, disaster was averted." He left out the most important part, making the distasteful task that much more difficult.

"Is she all right?" Sara asked.

"I'm afraid she didn't survive the incident." he said blurting it out awkwardly, then added, "Everyone else aboard the flight survived only because of your mother's uh... brave actions."

The press hailed her as a hero, but her passing was an immense blow to Sara, her father and their modest congregation. Elspeth Allen was the strict overseer of all organizational management, logistics, and fiscal affairs of The Church of the Safe Way. But with her passing, Sara saw it as her duty to step into her mother's shoes as best she could.

At her mother's funeral, one tipsy parishioner inappropriately placed his glass of dry red on the lid of Elspeth's closed coffin and asked that gathering, "How the hell—pardon my French—can young Sara here, a mere slip of a thing, fill the shoes of a theological giant like Elspeth Allen?" Little did he know that his glass of French Haut-Medoc was, in reality, an Argentinian Malbec that this "mere slip of a thing" had aggressively negotiated away from the distributor at sixty dollars a case. Sara's intelligence hid quietly behind her simple beauty; a radiant "girl-next-door" look that advertising agencies scour the planet for. Sara was so much smaller than everyone around her, it was easy to see her as a 'mere slip of a thing'. But Sara had become her own woman. She graduated high school with honours and, though she joined the church and supported her parents in their work, she continued to school herself in philosophy and religion, and anything else of interest she could get her hands on. She understood the basics of genetics, worried over the mysteries of quantum mechanics, and learned that we humans know astonishingly little about the huge universe we live in. She'd seen the pathos of human existence and came to believe that humans were nothing more than empty-headed primates littering a grand Darwinian garden. In the back of her mind she secretly entertained the notion that we may be more than just the litterers of the planet. We may be the damned litter itself.

Sara read nothing about Jesus Christ; she already possessed more than adequate knowledge on the words he was alleged to have spoken. Besides, according to her father, Jesus had visited him personally in visions occasionally and he always recounted these rare events to her verbatim. She loved her father but thought his fantasies would be more convincing if Jesus spoke to him in Aramaic. Greek even, but certainly not in modern vernacular English.

That night, as she headed across the parking lot to her father slumped in his car, she had the feeling they were about to enter a new time of trials.

Without a word, she brought him into the house, sat him on the sofa in the living room, hung up his coat in the hall closet, and while he changed into his night robe, she fixed him a cup of hot cocoa.

"Daddy, tell me what happened." Her voice was soft and reassuring. Father Allen sipped the sweet dark brew and the surreptitious but generous double shot of Khaluha that blessed it.

"That woman, that woman," was all he kept muttering.

"Tell me." She swept back a lock of the thinning grey hair that fell across his forehead. "What has she done?"

Father Allen gave her a look that said it all and sipped the steaming confection. "Alderman Adams, Mrs. Kingston, the Hutchinson Brothers, by tomorrow afternoon that woman will have them all. Even the Pomeroy family..."

"Not the whole family." Sara sighed.

"All seven of them." He looked to her through swollen eyes. "I saw others of the flock there too. It's almost our entire congregation now... It's over, there's nothing we can do." Father Allen cast a tearful gaze to the framed mail-order picture of Christ frozen in perpetual prayer on the wall above the fireplace.

"We'll think of something," Sara said with a certainty that sounded naïve, but wasn't. Sara was not a vindictive or vengeful person but she knew that when social injustice reaches a certain level in a community it bursts, like an abscess, spreading discontent through society. Something had to be done before chaos, or even violence, erupted.

Sara always tried to see both sides of a problem. This was her particular gift. She could think about something more than one way—something few people can imagine, let alone do. And that's what she did that night until he was nodding off, then she quietly took him upstairs and tucked him into his bed.

That Woman

"That woman" was Ruth Bracket, forty-something CEO of an organization known as Rightweigh Incorporated. Early the next morning she could be seen surveying her domain from the big window in her office on the second floor. She liked the way the morning mist hugged the ground, giving an ethereal look, while the old-growth trees sheltering the buildings suggested permanence—though the drywall newness smell that lingered everywhere in the building was annoying.

The product of an upwardly mobile, church-going, dysfunctional family, a teenage Ruth Bracket wrote in her diary, "I will ride my Harley Davidson every day to law school and *if* I get married, my husband will ride on the back behind me." Her longest romance lasted a mere forty-three days, and her only serious marriage proposal came from a woman. It didn't work out. They were too alike.

Ruth authored two books. The first, *"Doing Battle In The Sexist Workplace"* sold nine hundred and eleven copies worldwide. The second, a bitter review of her first experience in publishing and a scathing attack on the men involved entitled *"Don't Park It Here Buster"* sold well, though critics said it "lacked the humour promised by the title".

She knew most of the men at the top were "an out of shape, simple-minded, insecure, bigoted, lying pack of..."

If she could sideline them, life would improve, and

since sloth and obesity was their most common trait, this became her goal in life.

"A man's necktie is a clear wardrobe signal that he has never once leaned over to clean a toilet," she would say to her growing following, "though the tie clip may be the suggestion that they are thinking about it," and she would revel in the peals of female laughter. "It is left to us, the women, to clean up this toilet of society!" She was not wrong. And her audience wasn't just women. She was smart enough to raise her appeal to right-minded young businessmen and politicians proposing that the government should institute tax shelters and guarantee loans to get it all under way. Whether you agreed with her or not, most of what Ruth Bracket said made some sense.

Bracket put her money where her mouth was. Well, not *her* money exactly. She found a wealthy real estate entrepreneur who owned a useless acreage on the outskirts of the city and made him a proposal. If he deposited, interest free, one-point-five million dollars into her corporate account she would let it sit, untouched, until she had used it to convince venture capitalists that they were not the first ones in on the project. Eventually, she would return the money, with interest, and take the land off his hands at a discount.

It was fraud.

"Ma'am?" Bracket's young assistant William stood at the door. Though William had stated his age as twenty-eight on his job application, Bracket knew he probably wasn't a day over twenty-four. She hired him because he could lie without blinking. He was organized and efficient. And he had a great ass. He held up a file. "We're expecting a, uh, large consignment of new clients today," he announced. "There was a raid last night at..."

"Yes, I know." Bracket always handled William with fake disregard. "Just put them there," she ordered, nodding to her out-sized desk then watched his ass until he was gone. Bracket knew about the raid on Jacque's because it was her idea.

She returned to gaze out the window. Swirling in her head were fantasies of celebrity, of going down in history as one of the great women who delivered civilization from a horrendous blight. The woman who brought enlightenment to the world and single-handedly... then she spotted some movement across the yard and grabbed a pair of binoculars from on top of the filing cabinet.

Down by the small footbridge that crossed a narrow artificial creek, one man, easily in the three hundred plus pound range stood lookout as another big man with a spray paint can was just finishing scrawling a message on the side of the footbridge so it could be seen from the road. It read:

LET US EAT CAKE!

Bracket trembled in a spasm of rage, then got on the phone. Within seconds, guards apprehended the two graffiti artists and hauled them off to holding cells in the basement.

To the casual visitor, Rightweigh Incorporated was a quiet country retreat. The main floor of the gleaming administration building was a pastel-hued visitor's "Welcome Centre" where friendly pitches were made and agreements signed. Wide curving stairs led to the second floor and the main offices, a wellness clinic and a research lab. Through a basement tunnel, one found a large prison-style cafeteria and eating gallery, and a gymnasium. Government subsidized sleeping quarters, described in advertising as 'Generous Client Accommodations', were on the main floor: twenty-four sleeping halls in two sections: Fourteen for men, and ten for women. Internees slept on rows of sturdy bunks, forty-six to a room. Inmates called it 'The Barracks'. Past a central twenty-four-hour security desk and up the stairs to the second floor, were an array of comfortable private rooms reserved for paying customers. Here, windows looked out upon a large open grassy area and jogging track. Beyond that, trees concealed the fourteen-foot steel wire-mesh fence that surrounded the entire compound. During the day, one got the impression of quiet serenity. But by Ruth Bracket's blunt aesthetic, at night the place was more like a secret military penal lockup in some South American jungle where the incarcerated were kept at the back of a dark and difficult terrain. No one dared attempt escape.

--

Ed got about twelve minutes of fitful sleep in a grimy holding cell before being jolted awake at dawn to join a large group of prisoners. As they were loaded onto two Court Services buses, he noticed that his fellow jailbirds were all overweight. Probably a coincidence.

Ed wasn't worried. All he had to do was explain his situation to the judge, undoubtedly a reasonable and qualified magistrate. He'd probably be released with a warning.

During the short trip to the courthouse, everyone was treated to a loud diatribe by Father Allen's friend Alderman Adams on the injustices of Municipal by-laws and the inability of the police to distinguish their duties from the political and financial ambitions of their corrupt bosses.

As bailiffs shuffled them into the courtroom, Ed thought, 'Jesus, I feel like I'm from a third-world country!' He may have said this out loud. Technically, he *was* from a third world country.

Because of his name, Alderman Adams was first up and everyone had to sit through his angry tirade again. He hoisted himself to his feet and laced into the scrawny sixty-eight-year-old Judge Conroy. "I go on record at the outset by stating that this proceeding is an unmitigated outrage!" he bellowed. "We are private citizens, unconstitutionally detained simply because we must seek our entertainment away from the prying eyes of bigots and, and.... and *sizeists*!"

The Judge ignored the impropriety of protocol and looked the alderman coolly in the eye. "So you admit that this establishment.... this..." he shuffled through a small assortment of papers. "... this Jacque's," and he made a grimace as he said the name, "*was* engaged in the distribution of food products in contravention of the public health act and justifiably investigated by the police. Anyone in attendance was duly detained as found-ins at a crime scene."

"No doubt at the behest of fitness fanatics with substantial interests in the sporting goods and diet industries," Alderman Adams added.

Judge Conroy rolled his eyes at the ceiling and palmed his forehead. "Alderman Adams," he went on, "I'm trying to be fair here. The entire judicial system has bent over backwards to help you people, but you continue to conspire to..."

"What the devil are you talking about?" Alderman Adams raged. "There was no conspiracy! It was a party, *my* birthday party!"

"Oh, really? Well, happy birthday."

Alderman Adams let out a percussive "harrumph!"

and looked around at the others in the room. For once he was speechless.

Judge Conroy took a slip of paper from his pocket and scribbled a note that had nothing to do with the case. After long days in this court, food was the last thing on his mind, so he kept a list of grocery items. Since he'd taken charge of these cases, he'd lost thirty-seven pounds. His doctor warned him that his blood pressure was rising and his weight was getting dangerously low. The note in his pocket was from his wife. He was to pick up two small pork chops, a head of lettuce and half a dozen eggs on the way home. It was still early, and he had just added a bottle of Glendronach single malt to the list.

Ed noticed that some uniformed officers in the place were not real cops. Flashes on their jackets identified them as security staff from Rightweigh Inc. Then he spotted Bailey biting his nails and remembered that he hadn't had breakfast yet.

Alderman Adams looked at where his Rolex would have been if they hadn't taken it from him the night before. "Where the hell's my counsel?"

"For all we know he's in the fat farm, which is where you're going too." Judge Conroy sighed.

Everyone under one-ninety laughed. Alderman Adams trembled with anger.

"Now," Judge Conroy said, banging his gavel, trying to wrap it up, "since you seem to have no credible defence, I have no choice but to..."

The alderman pointed a large finger at the judge. "You of all people should know better than to use the 'F' word like that here in a public court of law!"

"The 'F' word? When did I use the 'F' word?"

"Just now."

"Did I use the 'F' word?" Judge Conroy asked the

stenographer who frantically searched the record and shrugged. "I don't use the 'F' word," Judge Conroy explained calmly.

"The 'F' word," Alderman Adams shouted. "The FAT word dammit, the FAT word!"

Judge Conroy smiled. "Oh that, well Mister Adams, we only speak the plain truth here."

"I would remind you, with all due respect, that my title is Alderman, not Mister. *Alderman* Adams!"

Judge Conroy glared at him. All present knew the judge's next words would set the tone for the day.

Ed was worried. He wouldn't glad-hand and joke his way through this. But he brightened right up when he saw Sara Allen slip quietly in through the doors at the back and make her way steadily and directly through the crowded space to sit down right beside him.

"Hello" he said faintly. She ignored him and leaned over to comfort a large mother and son sitting in the row ahead and he caught a whiff of her. She smelled faintly of plain soap.

There was a distinct purity, a virginal quality about this woman that Ed could not resist.

He swooned.

Most of the female companions Ed had known were outgoing, brash, often drunk, but nonetheless beautiful women who slathered themselves with too much of whatever scent they could lay their hands on. Sara Allen looked and smelled as if she had just showered, dressed simply and come out into the world without makeup, pure and wholesome. Fact is, she'd been up most of the night consoling her father.

The hearing faded into a background din. All Ed heard was Sara's voice as she instructed the two in front of her to answer the questions in as few words as possible, to ask for leniency but not cower. "You'll be up soon," she advised them. "The judge isn't tired yet so you've got a good chance."

When she sat back Ed said, "Your friends will do better if the alderman there doesn't calm down."

"Shh!" Sara warned without affording him more than half a glance.

This didn't deter Ed. He *had* to know this woman.

Judge Conroy banged his gavel, "For your own good, *Mister* Adams, this court is sending you to Rightweigh where you will serve out a very lenient sentence in the lap of luxury, lose weight and become healthy." He cast the alderman what appeared to be a genuinely compassionate smile. "At least a little healthier than you appear to be right now. What more could you want?"

"I want justice," Alderman Adams said and added, "This is *not* proper judicial procedure."

Judge Conroy went red. "We're not here to debate the pros and cons of the law, sir. We are here to determine the extent of your non-compliance with it." With that, he picked up his pen and wrote. Aside from a few murmurs and the odd cough, the courtroom was silent.

"Judge Conroy," the alderman said, "I admonish you..."

"Don't admonish me, I'm rendering judgment."

Ed heard a rustling to his right and looked over to see that the big man beside him had reached all the way up his own shirt sleeve and was extracting one of those big three-dollar Mars bars! He gave Ed a conspiratorial smile, then carefully unwrapped the confection as quietly as possible.

Ed guessed correctly that the police hated strip searching the big people.

The man balled the wrapper up tightly and stuck it

down inside his sock. Then, keeping it low so no one else could see, he broke the bar in two and offered half to Ed. Ed took the half-bar and the two engaged in a chocolaty hand shake.

"Ed," Ed introduced himself.

"Sidney," the other man said, and Ed realized that this guy had the same name as his beloved father Sid.

"This is completely fucked up, you know," Ed said.

"Language!" Sara said and looked to see that Sidney was about to take a bite of the bar and she smoothly and quietly snatched it away from him. "What do you think you're doing?" she said, then spotted Ed's half and grabbed it away too. "Don't you realize where you are?" She pulled out a pink hanky, rolled the illicit confections up in it, and slid them into her bag.

Now Ed smelled her breath. It was rose petals floating on a raspberry pond. Once again the rest of the world disappeared and the only thing he could think of to say was "Are you busy tonight?"

"Yes," she said, "and so are you."

He dared to lean a little closer. "What are you doing for dinner?"

She finally glanced at him. "Eating," she said flatly. "You on the other hand will probably be appearing with the rest of these people to receive the grey uniform in which you will spend the next..." She looked him up and down. "... I'd guess, three months in Rightweigh."

Her gaze held on Ed's big moon face. He managed a small benign smile.

She saw the glimmer of a good person there in that moment and softened, but not too much. This was no time for fraternization with suspects. Who knew what crime got him into this situation. "Do you know what the word 'glib' means?" she asked.

"Isn't that something you wear to eat lobster?"

She suppressed a smile, then realized that perhaps he didn't understand the seriousness of his situation, saw him as the innocent victim he was. She placed her hand on his. "Do you have any idea how much trouble you're in?"

Ed trembled at her touch. He could not speak.

"It behooves you to concentrate," Sara whispered softly. "If you wish, I can arrange for us to talk later."

"I wish." Ed said, wondering if she noticed his voice had cracked.

She gently slipped her hand away and returned her attention to the proceeding, then glanced back at him. "What's your name?"

But before Ed could answer, Judge Conroy picked up his gavel and fixed the alderman with an anorectic gaze. "I've heard enough from you, Mister Adams. I have found you guilty as charged. I'm putting you in the custody of Rightweigh Inc. until such time that you have been able to shed..." He looked at the alderman's paunch. "Let's say twenty kilos shall we?" and he banged the gavel bringing the alderman's hearing to a close. A buzz ran through the crowd.

"TWENTY KILOS!?" the alderman yelled.

"Yes." Judge Conroy glanced at the bailiffs and they advanced on cue. "You could probably stand to lose twice that much. You, as a city employee... a public servant, should know better. But, since you can't seem to locate your counsel, I think twenty kilograms is.... well, dare I say, *big* of me."

Lardner was the only cop in the room who didn't burst out laughing at the judge's pun. Judge Conroy immediately regretted the disruption and banged his gavel.

Ed wasn't familiar with the metric system, but his

new friend Sidney could do the conversion in his head. He whispered to Ed, "Jeez man, that's forty-four pounds!"

"What about bail?" the alderman exclaimed.

"Listen to me," Conroy waved his gavel at the crowd, "all of you. When I started hearing these cases, the seating capacity of this courtroom was seventy-five. But you people continue to get bigger and bigger. Today I can barely stuff fifty of you in here." He looked at the clock on the wall. "Now, let's move on to the next case, *please*."

Three bailiffs surrounded the alderman, but he stood his ground. "This court is a sham, a flagrant denial of human rights." He went to point a finger in the air, but two bailiffs grabbed his hands, pulled them back and cuffed him. The double exit doors swung shut on his final words to Judge Conroy. "I'll see you removed from the bench if it's the last thing I..." and that was it for Alderman Adams.

"Next?" The judge looked around. "Who's next here?"

"Jesus, not nice," Ed said to Sara.

"You won't do well with that language," she cautioned him. "Judge Conroy is a very religious man." She was like a grade school teacher explaining manners to an unruly five-year-old.

Ed found it sexy.

The prosecutor stepped forward. "Your honour, we've got one here, unrepresented, who refuses to speak. She has no ID."

Judge Conroy sighed. "Okay, bring her forward."

The prosecutor wagged his finger and bailiffs escorted a very large and extremely pretty young woman in a flower-print dress forward. As she moved, the accumulated girth beneath her voluminous dress made its printed flora ebb and flow as if alive.

In a perverse display of appreciation, the thin cops all turned to ogle her as she passed then exchanged noisy comments. Someone whistled. When the Judge asked her to state her name, she stared shyly down at her feet.

"Young lady, I need to hear you say your name if I am to hear your case." Judge Conroy said.

"Marilyn" the embarrassed woman muttered.

"What? You must speak up."

"Marilyn, sir."

Judge Conroy wrote it down. "Marilyn... Marilyn what?"

Marilyn flushed a bright pink. "Mari... Marilyn.... Small." The cops erupted in hysterics. This time even Lardner kind of chortled, then checked it with a scowl. Judge Conroy didn't find it funny in the least. He banged his gavel and looked at the clock.

Marilyn burst into tears. Ed saw Sara's eyes welling up too as she got up and made her way to Marilyn, who looked like she might faint.

Conroy banged his gavel and said to Marilyn, "Thirty-five kilos in Rightweigh!"

"That's seventy-seven pounds!" Sidney confided to Ed.

And so it went. At the end of the next case, Conroy banged his gavel and proclaimed "twenty-two kilos in Rightweigh!"

"Forty-eight pounds," Sidney reported.

Twenty more kilos here, fifteen there, then ten. Judge Conroy would clear his jurisdiction of this scourge if it killed him. And it would. Though Judge Conroy had six years left to retirement, absolutely everyone appearing before him this day would outlive him.

By the time Ed was standing before the diminutive judge and his sentence was handed down, there was no surprise: ten kilos on a first offence of disturbing the peace, which, according to his friend Sidney, was twenty-two pounds.

As they took him from the room and down a hall, he caught sight of Sara once more as she calmed others outside the courtroom. He admired her courage and persistence and wondered if he would ever see her again.

--

Lt. Lardner wasn't called to testify. He endured these hearings with mixed emotions. Lardner was a crime fighter. An honest cop. The kind of guy who keeps his promises even when it's not expected. There were better things to do than round up people because the tourist bureau didn't want them on the beach. "The overweight are sick," he would say to friends. "The way junkies are sick. The way people who don't use seat belts are sick."

Bill Lardner had been on the Toronto police force for seventeen years. He was a young constable when his brother-in-law died of an overdose of some crap he'd bought on the street. Lardner spent eleven years in Narcotics trying to take the stuff out of society, working his way up through the ranks. One afternoon he stumbled across a massive methamphetamine lab in the east end. He seized sixteen kilos of pure crystal and made eight arrests without even showing his firearm. His action resulted in a lot of good publicity for the force, and they promoted Lardner to detective. When the obesity problem came along, the brass decided that his compassionate, affable approach was perfect for the task. He took on the assignment reluctantly.

--

Lardner watched from a second-floor window of the courthouse as Rightweigh guards marched the large felons out and stuffed them into a convoy of white Rightweigh security vans in the courtyard. Lardner felt sorry for the big people. He watched as two guards tried to push on Marilyn Small, who was too slow to suit them. The two little men met with such inertia it actually threw *them* back. Angrily recruiting two more guards, they met with the same resistance. Lardner turned away from the window in disgust.

He went to the underground parking garage three levels below and sat behind the wheel of his unmarked police Ford. From this vantage point he could watch other, younger cops on their way to take part in the business of the courts.

And now here came his partner Bailey, who didn't look at all as tired as Lardner felt. He looked as if he still had important things to do. When Bailey opened the trunk of his car and wedged his brief-case in between two large Samsonite suitcases, Lardner wondered, 'What did Bailey need with suitcases? He wasn't due a vacation for at least four months.' Another odd thing: Bailey lived on the west side of town, so why did he turn east upon exiting the garage?

Strange.

--

The short procession of Rightweigh vans made its way from the courthouse east through morning traffic. A dozen detainees sat cheek-by-jowl jostled on simple benches in the back. Ed could see flashes of the outside world from a small barred window in the rear door.

Signs hastily added to the front of restaurants, like:

> NEW REDUCED PORTIONS
> SERVED DAILY

and

> NO SHIRT, NO SHOES, **220?** NO SERVICE!

and graffiti:

> FAT SUCKS BIG TIME

> LOSE IT OR LOSE IT

Slumping back against the greasy wall of the van, Ed looked at the others with sympathy. At the far end of the bench across from him, Alderman Adams squirmed, bound and gagged. Marilyn Small sobbed gently into a polka-dot hanky. The others, Ed didn't know, but he saw kinship in their blank stares and their shock at the injustice that they shared.

Ed still believed his sentence was a mistake, that he could straighten everything out as soon as he could hire a lawyer and appeal the conviction. But who would take his case? What would he use for money?

The sombre convoy drifted through the pastoral suburban landscape and pulled in through the majestic Rightweigh front gates, then up the winding path to the intake dock at the back of the barracks, out of sight of the welcome centre.

The soft heat of the afternoon sun played across Ed's cheek for thirty-three seconds as guards led the group inside.

A painfully thin admitting nurse carrying an iPad recited the drill to Ed's group as they rode the elevator down to a maze of sterile basement hallways. Right then, Ed had a strange thought. "why do we assume a woman wearing a white shirt, white pants and white shoes is a nurse while a man dressed exactly the same way is undoubtedly selling ice cream?" Doctors dress in green now. Dentists in the Dominican Republic worked out of their homes and didn't wear shirts at all. They also rarely used anesthetic of any kind. At his first and last visit to a Dominican dentist, the guy took up a grimy hand towel, stuck it and his whole hand into Ed's mouth, grasped the troublesome tooth firmly between thumb and forefinger and yanked it out. It cost three thousand six hundred pesos. Ed took great care of his teeth after that.

"You'll find that we run on a very strict schedule here at Rightweigh," the nurse said in a voice that suggested she was an avid smoker and scotch drinker.

"Visitors are permitted on Wednesdays and Fridays between 2 P.M. and 4 P.M." She had obviously rattled through this spiel thousands of times. "Everyone is up at 7:00. Breakfast is at 7:30."

Her heels clicked militarily on the terrazzo floor. Ed watched the stiffness of her bony back. He couldn't remember ever being turned off by visible panty-lines before, but this woman looked like she had three pairs of men's Y-fronts on under her slacks. He shuddered and didn't look there anymore.

"At 7:45 you have a six-kilometre walk in the woods, weather permitting," she growled. "And at ten you're in group therapy for an hour. After that there will be a full thirty minutes of free time to write letters, talk among yourselves or with any of the staff who may be available..."

"Fifteen minutes for breakfast?" Ed blurted.

"That's right," she said.

"When's lunch?"

"Lunch is after badminton and a session in the..." She cleared her throat. "um, the weight room."

She opened a door marked "ADMITTING" and everyone filed into a white-tiled room lined with weighing and measuring apparatus. A complicated eye chart and an intimidating diagram of the ideal human anatomy dominated one wall. A large heavy-duty weight scale took up almost a third of the space. It was a small version of one of those machines they use for weighing trucks along the highway. The admitting nurse handed her iPad to a pretty girl, also dressed in white. Ed wondered why she was wearing earplugs.

He spoke to the admitting nurse but looked out of the corner of his eye at the younger woman. "What about weekends?"

"What *about* weekends?" the older woman barked.

"I've been on a plane and in airports for sixteen hours," he explained, "and there are a few personal things I need to take care of, locate my mother and..."

"You can leave when you have lost..." She took the iPad from the younger woman and found Ed's mug shot. "... Mister Miller is it?"

"Yes'm." Ed smiled.

She swiped to judge Conroy's entry. "Twelve kilos," She said and handed the iPad back to the young attendant.

"TWELVE!?" Ed was outraged. "The Judge said ten!"

"Twenty-six-and-a-half pounds," Ed's Mars bar friend from court muttered from the back of the group.

"Well, it looks like twelve right here on your judgment," she said with a condescending grin. "I'm sure a strong boy like you can manage that, so I'd suggest you buckle down and get it done." She flashed a stiff officious smile to the young attendant. "I'll start down with the next group in fifteen minutes," then clicked smartly out of the room. Ed hoped he had seen the last of that one. He smiled at the young attendant.

"The sooner we start," she said patronizingly, "the sooner we can all go home." She indicated the large weigh scale. "Miss... uh, Small please."

Marilyn shuffled over to the machine and hefted her weight onto the big textured steel treadle. Suddenly a bright red light flashed on and off directly in Marilyn's face, a loud klaxon sounded and an electronically generated male voice boomed from the front of the machine loud enough to blow Marilyn's hair straight back on her head. **"YOU STILL WEIGH FOUR HUNDRED AND TWENTY-SEVEN POUNDS AND SEVEN AND A HALF OUNCES!!"**

Everyone covered their ears, except for the young attendant. She had earplugs.

The scales were from an American firm, so the readouts were in imperial measurements. This has caused considerable confusion as Canadians struggled for decades to adopt the more sensible metric system.

"That's one hundred and ninety-eight-point-five kilos," Sidney proclaimed.

Ed's brain immediately went into escape mode. He looked at the ventilation grates near the ceiling and the latch on the door. The place was clearly designed for security. Maybe he could hot-wire a car in the employee parking lot and just ram his way out.

Marilyn stumbled from the scale half deaf and the attendant waved the next person on. Ed and the others stuck their fingers in their ears.

--

Over a lunch of a tofu burger and a glass of soy milk, Dr. Eli Milrot, Head of Rightweigh Medical Research, decided he'd better tell Ruth Bracket about the strange new results of a covert experiment he was conducting. He gathered his courage and texted a request to meet at his lab.

Bracket received Milrot's message on her daily walk-through of the facility. She replied that she could be with him in fifteen minutes. She smiled and nodded to paying clients who were free to come and go at will. Each afforded her their respectful, though fearful, recognition.

It may be useful to point out that Ruth Bracket had as much of an eating disorder as Marilyn Small or Alderman Adams. She had become so obsessed with food and its effects, that the very idea of eating repulsed her. She avoided the activity as much as possible, and it showed.

Everyone in the lab stopped what they were doing to face her when she entered. Bracket knew that things were going on here that needn't be known of beyond these doors, perhaps not even by her. Plausible deniability. She didn't care as long as Milrot fulfilled his part of the bargain and didn't interfere with her plans.

There was Milrot and his assistant Gwen Djvani in the next room peering into a test chamber at a big man strapped into a modified cycling machine—his head restrained and his eyes held open with special clamps so he had no choice but to view a large video monitor mounted directly in front of him. He was pedalling steadily at a manageable rate while viewing a video of lithe sunbathers cavorting on a tropical beach. He was attached to computers and monitoring devices by wires that ran from spots on his body and scalp. The whole affair was mounted on a large scale that could measure and display microscopic weight variations as the experiment progressed.

While she waited, Bracket perused the framed diplomas on Milrot's wall from several prestigious universities. She knew all but one of them were fake, but then her own credentials wouldn't stand up to scrutiny either. Milrot made Bracket a little crazy, but he was the only accredited scientist she could trust to keep his mouth shut about certain things and still give what sounded like a scientifically accurate Power-Point presentation. Though she tolerated him, she thought Milrot was nuts. He would give batty advice like, "Always wipe your face in the middle of a bath towel because that's the least likely part to have come into contact with the toilet." But he dreamed up useful ideas, too. One of his best came after she told him she wanted to make everything associated with eating as unappealing as possible—especially for the paying customers. That very night he sprang from his bed with the sudden realization that 'Pommes de terre au gratin' in literal translation was 'Scorched Dirt apples under Rotten Cow Udder Drippings'. He immediately got to work on his laptop and, overnight, changed the tone of the entire Rightweigh menu. Bacon and eggs was now 'Pre-natal Flightless Bird with Carcinogenic Swine Slabs.' A simple cheese plate became 'Assorted Rotted Milk Products.' Mushroom soup was easy: 'Fungus Cultivated in Feces floating in Water of Boiled Bovine Skeletal remains.' He really wished that headcheese and haggis had been on the menu, but they weren't.

One extremely useful Milrot invention was the Socio-runner, an ordinary treadmill connected to a PC running Google Earth so exercisers could jog, walk, or bike in groups along scenic routes around the world.

Impatient at being kept waiting, Bracket began pacing the lab, looking at her watch. A worker must have pressed a button or something because suddenly Milrot and his assistant Gwen turned at once and saw her. Milrot came out. "Oh there you are," he said. Gwen even bowed. Milrot ushered Bracket into the inner chamber and closed the door quietly behind them. He held up a white-gloved hand and pointed to the subject. "Meet Mister Lou Kennedy," he said.

Bracket peered in at the glassy-eyed Lou, who was at the moment staring painfully at the video screen as he pedalled the cycling machine with a steady rhythm.

"As you may recall from our previous conversation, three things drive appetite in the obese." and he counted them out on his fingers. "The individual's lack of control over their automatic response to food cues, the abundant availability of food, and the ineffectiveness of the central nervous system in reporting to the brain that the stomach is full." He stopped and stared at Bracket as if to make sure she understood.

"Yes, yes," Bracket was eager to get going. "I also remember asking you to find out just how many calories, in fat and carbohydrates, we should include in their diet so the clients lose weight appropriately in a balanced way so they do not shed too much weight too quickly."

"Precisely," Milrot said with an enthusiastic finger in the air. "But to do that you must first understand appetite. Appetite drives them to want more. And so we've been looking into the so called 'orosensory self stimulation feedback mechanism' and how it connects with the chemical reward circuitry in the brain."

Bracket had no idea what the hell he was talking about.

"Now bear with me here," Milrot said. "This can

get technical and if you have questions please stop me and ask." He nodded to Gwen, and she went to work resetting the experiment. It was only when Gwen bent over and Bracket got to see the spread of her ass, that she recognized her as a former client of Rightweigh.

"We originally chose Mr. Kennedy here," Milrot went on, "because he exhibited the ideal Pavlovian response mechanisms."

Bracket resisted rolling her eyes at this. She hated the way Milrot talked. She even tried, at one point, using one of his lectures as a sleep aid. It helped. But what Milrot was saying was simple. Lou Kennedy was hungry all the time. He should have just said that, but because of his secret lack of education, he was compelled to speak in an overly pedantic way when it wasn't necessary.

"Let me show you something," he said and directed her attention to Lou Kennedy pedalling away inside the test chamber, staring idly at the video of beach frolickers. "There's a small but annoying charge being delivered to the subject's nervous system via the bike seat," he said. "It didn't take him long to learn that he could keep the charge at a manageable level by pedalling at this moderate rate. Now, depending on what he sees on the screen..." He scrubbed a mouse around the desktop and brought up an option menu then clicked on an icon marked 'ORANGE', "Watch this," he said. The picture on the monitor in front of Lou changed to a six-year-old girl peeling and eating an orange.

Immediately Lou's pedalling slowed. The cycle seat buzzed, the volt meter jumped and the hair on the top of Lou's head quivered.

"But how do you know whether it's the orange or the little girl that's causing the change?" Bracket wanted to know.

"Good point. I wondered about that too." Milrot clicked on another icon marked 'BBQ'. "Watch this." A group of people at a backyard barbecue appeared on the screen.

Lou's pedalling slowed down a little more and his mouth dropped open. The machine vibrated violently as more electrons flowed to Lou's seat, looking for a place to go. Lou's hair stood straight up on his head. A deep electronic hum vibrated through the air.

Milrot raised his voice over the din. "It's as though his concentration is taken from the pain by the sight of the food. It's as though the mere thought of food stimulates the release of dopamine into the brain and dopamine is a powerful natural painkiller. There is a growing belief that dopamine causes everything from the painlessness of trauma to the euphoria of the near-death experience." Milrot clicked the mouse, and the image returned to the sunbathers on the beach. Lou's pedalling sped up again, and everything quieted down.

"That's fascinating."

"That's not the interesting part." Milrot pointed to a particular number on one screen. "Notice this readout. It's the subject's current weight." The meter read 322.655 lbs.

"He's a big boy." Bracket said.

"Yes," said Milrot. "Now, see what happens when I hit him with a strong signal like this," and he clicked on a icon named "BIG MAC" the picture on the monitor changed abruptly to a solid close-up of a Big Mac fresh off the grill, steaming and dripping with melted cheese and special sauce.

Lou's jaw dropped into a full gape and he stopped pedalling altogether. His body pulsated at sixty cycles, and his scalp began to smoke.

Bracket was astounded. "Wow!" she said over the din.

Milrot let the effect run for about thirty seconds before switching back to the sunbathers. Lou's pedalling resumed and slowly rose back to normal.

"That's impressive, but what does it mean?"

"Look here." Milrot pointed to the weight readout.

Bracket peered at it. "And?"

"When we looked at it less than a minute ago, it read three-twenty-two-point-six-five-five." He tapped on the face of the dial. "Now it reads three-twenty-two-point-six-five-nine!"

Bracket gave him a blank look.

"Where did four one-thousandths of a kilo come from?" Milrot asked.

"What?"

"He ate nothing."

"I don't get it."

"Frankly, neither do I. You should see what happens when I show him the pie-eating contest."

"Weight gain without eating?"

"Yes. I'm at a loss to explain it but I'm working on it. If I can find out what it is and reverse it, we could cure the whole obesity condition once and for all."

Milrot's phone rang. "Excuse me." Milrot took out his phone and left the room.

Bracket looked at Lou dutifully pumping away on the cycling machine inside the chamber. Milrot's words buzzed in her ears. The last thing she wanted was a cure for obesity. It would put her out of business.

She looked at the computer screen, then at Lou, then took the mouse and idly swept the cursor over the icon marked "PIE-EATING CONTEST." She looked around. No one was looking. Curiosity got the better of her and she clicked on the "PIE-EATING CONTEST" icon.

Lou helplessly watched the screen as the master of ceremonies of a country fair pie-eating contest held a starting pistol aloft and fired. Eight enormous men, cheered on by an enthusiastic audience, plowed through dozens of cherry, apple, strawberry and rhubarb pies. At first Lou merely salivated. Then, caught up in the gross excitement of the event, he pedalled faster and, as the crowd cheered the contestants on, he pedalled even faster. The machine ran smoother and Lou's hair fell flat on his head. He leaned into it and clenched his teeth, and his rhythm picked up. It was as if he was all eight pie-eating contestants at once. The hum in the test chamber had become a crackling staccato buzz. As though an enormous buildup of electrons was about to leap into the room.

Bracket's own breathing was becoming heavy now as she watched Lou pedal faster and faster. The contestants on the screen literally dove into the pies one on top of another, fighting to win the obscene contest. The crowd cheered even louder. Lou was pedalling so fast now that a feedback loop made voltage flow in the opposite direction.

It was only because smoke emanated from two machines in the next room that Milrot noticed the emergency. He burst into the observation room in time to shut the whole thing down. Immediately the image disappeared from the screen in front of Lou, but his pedalling continued apace. The room was quickly filling up with smoke. It was like a nuclear chain reaction that, once started, cannot be stopped. But Milrot had ventured into this territory before and knew exactly what to do. Quickly he grabbed the mouse from Bracket and clicked on a big red "EMERGENCY RESET" button in the upper right of the screen. The image before Lou abruptly switched to a large man asleep in a barber's chair having his hair cut and receiving a manicure from two young women. Lou's pace slowly returned to the normal voltage flow. Milrot slumped back against the wall. Gwen went into the inner chamber and began unhooking Lou from the apparatus.

Bracket's breathing was so heavy she had fogged a large area of the test chamber window. Wiping a spot clear, she peered in at Lou. "Jesus, he's not even out of breath!"

"Yeah, I haven't been able to find out what that's all about yet either..." Milrot said. "Look here," and he pointed to Lou's weight readout dial. It now read three-twenty-two-point-six-eight-four lbs. "The man has gained almost a quarter ounce in..." he looked at his watch. "less than three minutes. I wish I could figure out where that increase is coming from. It's as if we're into some weird quantum effect or something."

"What's that?" Bracket gasped.

"Essentially, it's something popping into existence from nothing. It's dangerous work and I don't want another fire like the one we had last month."

Bracket looked back in at Lou, "*He* caused that fire?"

"Yes, we think so. He was in the rig when it happened. We all thought it was a random accident. Faulty wiring or something."

Bracket put a hand on Milrot's shoulder and produced the grimace she thought was a smile. "You're a fine man Eli, keep up the good work. But check your figures. Whatever is happening here, we don't want it getting out before we've tested it thoroughly ourselves."

"Of course," Milrot said.

"That means no writing about it. And I don't mean in scientific journals, I mean not even in emails to friends. Nothing. Are we clear?"

Milrot nodded yes.

Gwen led Lou out and held the door for him as he left the lab.

"You just let him go on his own like that?" Bracket asked.

"Sure." Milrot said and stabbed a key on the nearest keyboard. One of the computer displays showed a schematic of the Rightweigh grounds and a small blip drifting down the hall outside the lab to the stairs toward the barracks. "We equipped him with an ankle bracelet. It's interesting to see where he goes on his own after these sessions."

"Okay," Bracket said thoughtfully, "but let me be clear." She was already trying to cook up a way to exploit what she had seen. "All our work here has to move towards one goal." She nodded at the blip on the screen that was now moving through the tunnel to the next building. "We have to help rehabilitate these people so they can re-enter the world."

"Yes, the world."

"I'm glad to have you on my team," she said then turned and left without another word.

Milrot stared at the closing door and imagined his biography as it would appear in science textbooks of the future: Dr. Eli Milrot, dedicated, misunderstood, underpaid genius of the twenty-first century who gave his life for the common good. He imagined the scientific community coming to its senses, realizing—probably long after his death—that he had been right all along. He drifted out of the lab, visions of Copernicus and Darwin swirling in his head while Gwen went about dutifully shutting things down.

The Last Supper

They issued Ed standard extra-large boxer shorts, tee-shirt and socks, plain grey jogging pants and matching sweatshirt—both slightly undersized so weight loss could be easily observed. Just when he was wondering if the biodegradable plastic bag his underwear came in was edible, he got some good news: It was dinnertime. 'Hallelujah!' he thought. It was reasonable to assume the food would be dietary. So what? He was starved.

Attendants escorted the uniformed group down stairs to wide doors marked CAFETERIA, and again Ed thought of escape. Wondered if anyone had ever attempted it. Guards kept a close eye on things as they were shuffled into an obedient line at a self-serve counter where a waist-high, padded, chrome bar confined inmates into a single file. The counter was a high stainless steel affair that anyone under five-foot-eight had to stand on tiptoes to see over. That included the scrawny serving ladies behind it.

Ed's expectations were low until he got a look at the array of food on display: Roast beef and Yorkshire pudding, steaming mashed potatoes and... My God! There was a huge platter piled high with succulent fat barbecued baby back pork spareribs dripping in that shiny dark red sauce that looked so good you might even consider putting it on ice cream! 'I get it.' Ed thought 'They put you through the paces all morning, then reward you for work well done with a decent dinner at the end.' Maybe this place wasn't as bad as he thought.

Wrong again.

Sure, there were plain raw and boiled vegetables and something that looked like Melba toast but he hadn't had a thing to eat in what seemed like days and his mind went to work on how to stack things so he could get the most mouth-watering items on the tiny white porcelain plate provided. He picked up the serving tongs and was about to take the biggest meatiest rib from the top of the pile when an inmate grabbed his arm and nodded a stern warning. Ed took a step back.

"Are you kidding?" Ed said and wondered what sort of magic acted upon this poor guy. "I'll go on my diet tomorrow."

"No talking!" a guard barked.

By way of example and without a word, Ed's companion in line reached slowly up and carefully took three cold dry asparagus stalks then a tiny serving of a plain green salad and moved along ignoring the ribs and the buttered cobs of corn beside them, went straight past the mashed potatoes and didn't even look at the dessert section. Ed watched a cheerless woman carefully retrieve four dry green beans and place them reverently on her plate and decided they had brainwashed these sad souls. He made another move for the ribs. But before he could grasp the food, a bright spark leapt from the ribs to the tongs, then shot up his arm delivering serious voltage to his central nervous system, and he was catapulted off his feet and flung back against the padded railing where he dropped to a sitting position on the floor, the breath knocked out of him.

When he finally regained control of his respiration and could see between the purple spots, he looked up at the other inmates proceeding along the counter, choosing their meagre meals as if nothing had happened. Ed guessed correctly that there was also some rule about not helping someone in his situation. As he pulled himself to his feet, the only attention he got was from someone hidden on the other side of the counter who held up a small plate containing a raw carrot, eight blanched green beans and a small dry salad for his newly educated consideration. At first all he saw was the plate and a scrawny arm. As he stepped back up to the counter, he could see a white paper hat, then a female attendant's hawk-face, then her sadistic grin.

Ed's blood pressure rose, but he controlled himself and took the plate from her with a trembling hand.

Now Ed understood. They'd designed things to tear one away from the simple desires for a decent meal, a decent life.

What if there was no escape from this place? "How fast could you guys run if I got the front gates open?" Ed said to his companions, only half joking. One of them brought his finger to his lips, warning Ed not to speak, then looked around to see if any guards were watching.

They were.

In the eating room dozens of tables and wooden benches were arranged in rows. Everything was painted a dull grey—even the windows. 'God forbid we should see the sky,' Ed thought as he sat and looked around at the sea of dull faces, all methodically savouring each small morsel. He looked at the little plate of food before him and knew he'd have to eat it to stay alive. He picked up a green bean, and it flopped over like licorice on a hot day. A man was praying at the next table and Ed wondered if he was saying grace or asking to be struck down on the spot by the hand of a merciful God. Just then the inmate across from him noticed that a small flame, left over from Ed's weird encounter at the self-serve, had popped into existence on Ed's shirtsleeve and promptly blotted it out with his bare hand.

"Thanks man," Ed said, and the man shushed him. Save for the low clatter of several hundred people at the business of eating, it was eerily silent in the room.

Then Ed spotted something across the room. Only a glimpse and between the hulks, rows away, there sat a woman who looked startlingly familiar. She couldn't have weighed over one hundred and ten pounds, one fifteen tops and.... it was!

Ed stood. "Mom?" he cried and everything in the room came to a halt. "MOM!" Ed cried again as he fumbled to get out from between the two men inadvertently holding him in place. "It's me, Ed!" he shouted. So closely spaced were the tables that getting to her was like trying to cross a cornfield in a wheelchair.

Guards positioned around the room saw this and communicated via walkie-talkies, then slowly moved in.

As he came closer to her, Ed wasn't sure. Could this small woman in her sixties, hunched over a plate of dry green beans and a single boiled baby potato, really be the big woman he once knew? She didn't even look up as he came to her, knelt down beside her, turned her face to him. It *was* her! God, she looked like she was eighty! "Mom, what happened to you?"

She squinted at him. "What do *you* want?" she muttered like a tree creaking in the dry winter wind.

"It's me, Ed. Your son, Ed."

"You haven't changed," she looked him up and down, "a bit heavier maybe." She returned to her food.

"Mom, what are you doing in *here*?"

"What does it look like? I'm getting normal."

"They've brainwashed you! You don't even belong here."

"Don't be an idiot, I can do what I want." she said and looked to her neighbours. "The kid never was as smart as his father—and that's sayin' something."

Ed tried to pull her to her feet. "Come on, this isn't right. We'll find out who's in charge and get you the hell out of here." But as thin and frail as she was, the woman was immovable. "Mom, don't you remember the great times we had? What about the barbecues? The picnics. All-you-can-eat at Milo's Surf-n-...".

Without warning, two muscular guards extracted Ed from the unhappy reunion and ushered him back to his place at the table where there was nothing left of his dinner but the gleaming plate.

"Hey, where's my food?" Ed looked at his companions, but no one reacted.

After a silent, cow-eyed appeal to his guards, Ed stood once more before the behaviour-modifying electric cafeteria counter. The two guards kept a close watch as he bypassed the electrified spareribs and the high-voltage roasted potatoes to gingerly pick up a tiny plate of unadorned limp asparagus. The same skinny female attendant smiled him a crooked smile, and he smiled back.

"Could I have a little butter for this, please?" He asked politely. The woman's face dropped, and she looked away, ignoring him. Anger welled up inside Ed, but he tried once more to keep a civilized tone. "Uh, excuse me..." She ignored him. Ed snapped. "Hey chicken tits!" His shout shocked the solemnity of the dinner ritual. "How 'bout some fuckin' butter over here?" The women behind the counter glared at him.

He looked around. Everyone was frozen—even the guards. He looked at the heaping plate of ribs. Anticipating a situation, the guards tried to move to him but the padded rail blocked them. They could only watch as Ed put down his plate, gathered his resolve, flexed his arms and went for the entire plate of ribs.

Ed endured the initial surge of amperage to get a firm grasp on the platter. The attendants behind the counter heard the hum of electricity coursing up Ed's arms and smiled knowingly. He lifted the big plate a quarter of an inch off the counter and a shower of sparks flew out from the gap. It rocked Ed to his very soul. For long seconds his expression was steady. The current surging through him threatened to break his will, but he hung on. Finally, as the assault on his system was reaching a critical limit, he opened his mouth wide and let out a loud howl.

The guards and attendants all laughed.

Though shaking uncontrollably, Ed noticed that the women behind the counter were now all leaning on its metallic surface, doubled over with laughter. With what little strength he could muster, he slowly lowered the bare part of his arm into contact with the countertop, bringing the laughing women online. The electrified attendants let out loud simultaneous shrieks. Their hair stood on end and their hats were blown straight up in the air. This time, it was they who got thrown off their feet backwards against the wall.

During all this, someone had hit an alarm, and a supervisor came in from an office behind the kitchen. Before she could even assess the situation, there was a blinding flash and several circuit breakers blew all at once, plunging the scene into complete darkness.

Emergency lighting flickered on and off, giving the scene a strange disco effect.

Everyone fell away from the counter, gasping for breath. Ed managed a pained smile and clutched the ribs in both hands. It didn't take other inmates long to figure out that the goodies on the counter were now free for the taking, and they all lunged at the food. A man grabbed a piece of chocolate cake. A woman clutched three ice cream sundaes from the dessert section.

Two men got into a tussle over a roast turkey.

The supervisor clapped her hands together loudly, "Get back! Get back to your places!" she hollered. In this stroboscopic environment you could see her holding her hands apart in front of her and though they never came together, you could hear her loud claps in the intervals of darkness. "Move! Move! Move!" she barked.

Ed had won. He had the ribs. He picked one up in his un-paralysed hand. Not only was it cold, it was made of something solid... plaster.

When the woman with the sundae realized it was fake, she burst into tears. The men fighting over the turkey lost their grip, and it fell shattering to the floor.

"This isn't food," someone protested.

The illusion that had sustained the behaviour modification program of the electric cafeteria was gone. Soon the circuit breakers were reset, the lights came back on, and four guards surrounded Ed. In seconds they restrained him and brought him forcibly to the exit and out into the hall.

"Where are we going?" Ed's voice echoed down the empty corridor.

"To bed without our dinner," a guard growled.

Ed looked at a large clock as it swung past. "But it's only six-thirty."

"Shut up."

--

Soon Ed was standing just inside the double doors of one of the sleeping halls of the men's barracks. It was a big square room crowded with what looked to be two-tiered, heavy duty, steel warehouse shelves, each made up as a huge bed. They were large enough and sufficiently sturdy to provide enough room for a four-hundred-pound human to roll over without falling onto the floor. At first, there didn't seem to be anyone else around.

One of Ed's guards unlocked a supply closet door, took out a regulation bedding package and thrust it into Ed's arms. "Find yerself a bunk."

"What, I don't get my own room?"

"We can put you in solitary if you'd prefer, sir," one of them quipped and the other guards laughed. They left and Ed heard their loud jocular conversation echo away down the hall.

That's when he spotted Lou Kennedy, Milrot's experimental test subject, sitting forlornly on the end of a bunk staring, dispirited and exhausted, at the floor. Ed went to an available bunk nearby, threw his bedroll down, then extended a hand to Lou, trying to lighten the mood.

"Ed Miller, formerly of someplace civilized," he said.

Lou just stared at the hand and didn't move. Ed saw this as an opportunity to get some information. "What floor are the vending machines on in this place anyway?" he said as he spread his bedroll out on his bunk. "Even a small bag of Tostitos would go good right now."

No response.

Ed tucked his sheet and blanket into the three-inch-thick, plastic-covered futon mattress and decided that perhaps a serious approach was more appropriate. "I can tell you one thing." He lowered his voice. "I'm outta here first chance I get."

"They'll just bring you back." Lou mumbled, staring at the floor.

"Anybody ever try?"

"Yeah, twice. Never even got to the front gate."

"Is there a back way?"

"Twelve-foot fence all the way around."

Ed sat beside Lou and held out his hand again. "Ed Miller."

This time Lou shook Ed's hand. "Lou Kennedy," he said.

"What did *you* do that got you in here?"

"I signed myself up voluntarily?"

"What!?"

"Couldn't take the constant harassment. Besides, it was that or a divorce."

"At least you've got someone on the outside waiting for you."

"She took off with her trainer."

"If you volunteered, why can't you just check yourself back out?"

"No good. Once you sign the contract you're in till you lose the weight."

"I didn't sign any contract. They arrested me."

"What for?"

"Damned if I know. Far as I can tell, for not being able to count to twelve."

Lou buried his face in his two big hands and sank back into his funk. "I don't know if I even *want* to go back out there."

"Hey, hey, hey there. That's crazy talk." Ed waved his hand at the room. "This is hell in here."

"You don't know the half of it," said Lou. "Take my advice." Lou looked him in the eye for the first time. "Do as you're told, lose the weight and when you get outta here, don't jaywalk, spit on the sidewalk, or order pie with ice cream and they might leave you alone. That's the way it works."

"Lou," Ed put his hand on Lou's shoulder. Lou looked at him through glassy eyes. "That isn't the way it works. It isn't constitutional. We gotta stand up for our rights or they'll run over us."

"Look," Lou said and pulled up his pant leg to show Ed his electronic ankle bracelet.

"Jesus man, what's *that* all about?"

"You don't want to know," There was no way Lou could explain what had been happening to him in Milrot's lab. He pointed to a barren flower pot half full of earth on a nearby window ledge. "See that?"

"Yeah?"

"That guy planted three Grape-Nuts in there almost a month ago. Poor bastard still waters it twice a day."

'Finally.' Ed thought, 'someone with a sense of humour.' He didn't know that Lou didn't find this funny, only sad.

"Lou, these assholes won't give us any breaks, not even by mistake. I don't care how high the fences are. My mom's in here too, all brainwashed and suffering. I'm gonna get her and me and you outta here."

"It's not that simple."

Ed softened. "Okay, maybe what you say is right. Especially the part about the pie."

"Pie?"

"Yeah, you know the pie with ice cream?"

"Oh, yeah," Lou said, smiling weakly, "that just

slipped out."

Ed felt he was getting somewhere with this man, a possible companion, a kindred spirit who may be of some help in a crunch. Two heads are better than one. Just then there were voices and thunderous footsteps. The double doors banged open and a flood of obese male humanity poured in and took the entire place over like a mudflow in a shanty town.

Maybe Lou was right, maybe it was better to wait and watch how things unfolded, learn the lay of the land.

And that's what Ed did, he relaxed.

For now.

--

Traffic was heavy and Lt. Lardner was nodding off behind the wheel on his way home; not because he'd been working too hard or putting in long hours, he was bored stiff. He wanted to do real police work.

The light across the intersection turned green and almost immediately the guy behind him laid on one of those shrill European horns that cuts through like an ice pick. Lardner waved "sorry" and pulled away, looking for a place to grab a quick coffee. He pulled up at a convenience store, and that was when he spotted his partner, Ray Bailey, scurrying along the sidewalk. What the hell was he doing in this neighbourhood? Bailey lived on the other side of town. And where was his car? Had Bailey had an accident or something? He was staying close to the storefronts, looking furtively about. Had he parked his car blocks away where no one would notice it? When Bailey ducked into the convenience store. Lardner pulled his car ahead to a position from which he could observe the scene.

Bailey spoke with the man behind the counter. They seemed to know each other. Bailey paid the man what looked like eighty-to-a-hundred bucks and left with no groceries, walking back the way he had come. By the time Lardner could pull out, make an awkward U-turn and get to the end of the block, Bailey was gone.

"Damn!" Lardner cruised around the block looking for Bailey and wound up sitting once more across the street from the convenience store.

Ordinary looking situation. He went to investigate. As the clerk poured him a takeout coffee, Lardner looked around. "You open all night?"

"Twenty-four-seven."

Lardner dug in his pocket for some change. "I guess it's quiet late at night around here."

"Big condos on the next block," the man said and pointed his thumb over his shoulder. "Customers all night."

He wanted to ask him about Bailey but couldn't figure out how to do it without arousing suspicion, so he just took his coffee and left.

He tried to forget about the incident on the way home but couldn't. Bailey had been acting strangely lately. Did he have some secret life that Lardner knew nothing about? Couldn't be drugs; Bailey's too straight for that. Then what?

The Great Escape

Ed couldn't sleep.

The snoring in the barracks was deafening, but still, he could hear his stomach growling over the din. One guy had a nose whistle that sounded like a freight train approaching a distant country road crossing. Ed didn't know how many nights of this he could take. His time would be best put to use exploring the limits of the security system, trying the doors, maybe even locate his mom and have a good heart-to-heart.

Amazingly, the door to this roaring room was unlocked. The only illumination in the long hall outside was a few low-energy bulbs and a fire escape sign far at the end. The other way, the hall ended at a blank wall. Ed headed for the exit.

He didn't have to sneak at all. No sooner did he get away from the snoring in his room than the thunderous respiration of men in the next big room took over, drowning out any noise he might have made. Hundreds of human air pumps. He wondered what the carbon dioxide content of the air here was as he made it to the first intersection and peered around the corner. There, down another long hall at the centre of things, was a cluster of little guards lounging behind a circular security desk. He wouldn't get past them, but it was dark enough here to get across the open junction and continue toward the fire exit.

He found the fire door unlocked and quietly pushed

it open.

Good. No alarm bells. Nice moonless, starry night. Perfect for an escape. Iron fire escape stairs led to the second floor. He climbed them to see if the upstairs fire door was open. It was. Thank goodness for fire regulations.

The second floor was a whole different situation. There were wide carpeted, tastefully lit halls lined with private rooms. Each door displayed the name of the occupant on a small card inserted into a brass holder: A. Hemmings, J. Shein, C. Findlay, L. Kennedy, A. Coulter, M Hopkins.... "Wait a minute!" He went back. 'L. Kennedy?' he thought, 'this couldn't be Lou Kennedy, Lou's asleep downstairs next to me in that human engine room.'

Suddenly voices and footsteps, coming his way. Two guards in mid conversation.

"Yeah," one of them said, "I thought they were free."

"They weren't?" the other man said.

"Christ no, seven bucks each for those little bottles. If I'da known that I'da gone down to the bar in the lobby. Cheaper there, but not much."

As they came closer, Ed did his best to flatten himself into the recessed doorway. No good. He took a chance, pushed open L. Kennedy's door and slipped inside as the two rounded the corner and passed by. He could smell the excessive cologne many small men wear.

"Drinks are cheaper in the bar?" the guard asked. "Why would they do that?"

"I don't know, I guess they want you to get drunk and stick around casino and keep gambling."

"Shit!" said the guard, and they moved on.

Ed looked around the room: a small dresser, a tiny

table and chair in the corner, a nineteen-inch TV. The bed was empty. A framed photo on the bedside table was of Lou and a woman, probably his ex.

Ed realized something very unusual was going on with Lou. Why was he downstairs sleeping with the others? And why was he sitting alone in the barracks while everyone else was at dinner? What was the ankle bracelet on his leg all about? Surely that was an expensive item. No one else had them. Lou knew more about all this than he was letting on, that's for sure. Ed resolved to check back in with Lou the first chance he got. He left the room and continued down the hall, inspecting the name tags on the doors.

Ed was beginning to understand. These were the self-admitted paying clients. He came to a door marked L. Fischer, his mom's maiden name. He opened it and slipped silently inside.

This room was an exact copy of Lou's; small but comfortable. The TV was on: The original B&W *The Day The Earth Stood Still*. 'The old one,' Ed thought, 'the good one.' Mom was asleep, wearing small headphones, her TV-watching eyeglasses slightly askew on her head. She never could sleep without the TV on and Ed knew all he had to do was turn the volume down to wake her up. But for the moment he just sat on the foot of her bed and looked at her.

What caused this stupid situation? Okay, she'd come in here to lose some weight. That was understandable. But now she was a sad wisp of her former self. Her apartment was sitting downtown gathering dust, her cat almost starved to death. And then he thought of poor Lou again. Why was he sleeping downstairs on the rim of a rumbling phlegm volcano when he could be up here in his private room? What kind of power did this place have over people that they would behave in such irrational ways? And then he thought of Sara Allen. He yearned to be sitting with Sara and Lou in a nice outdoor pub sipping a flagon of beer and grazing on a bucket of fries—no, deep-fried beer-battered fish and chips.... no, why not one of those big hot pastrami sandwiches so full of fatty meat, it keeps falling over. And a big plate of fries and those crunchy new dills....

Wait a minute. What the hell was he doing? This was no time for useless daydreaming. It was a time for action. Ed picked up the TV remote from under his mom's hand and killed the volume.

"Hey, I was watching that!" It was as if she'd been wide awake the whole time. She tried to grab the remote. "Gimme that."

Ed held it away from her. Pretty soon she'd wake right up and be really pissed. "Mom," Ed said, "what were you doing, eating with the prisoners?" He waved his hand at the room. "You're first class here."

"No pain, no gain. Gimme the remote."

"Your cat Porky almost starved to death. I saved her just in time."

"Good. I hope you didn't eat her." she said. "Now go back to bed and get some sleep. You're gonna need it."

"Mom, you're wasting away. How much weight are you trying to lose, anyway?"

"All of it." Obviously her mind had snapped.

Ed gave up trying to reason with her. "At least loan me your card so *I* can go."

"Forget it, now gimme that remote."

Ed kept the remote from her. "Can you at least lend me the money for a private room?"

"You can't get a private room. You're a criminal, just like your old man. That fat clown. I'm not doing anything for either of you. Now get out of here and let me sleep."

"Mom, Dad's dead."

"Oh yeah, I forgot."

"And he wasn't a criminal."

"Who was it helped you when you got in trouble and needed money?" Mom said.

"You did, and I never forgot it. That's why I'm here, to save you." Ed knew this was a weak argument the instant he said it.

"Don't feed me that," Mom said, "you came back here, 'cause I cut off the cash. Now scram before I call for help."

"Okay, I'm sorry. You're right, it *was* the money. But look at the situation I find you in."

"What's wrong with it?" She held her arms out so Ed could see. "Look at me, I'm gorgeous."

Ed winced at her wrinkly upper arm flaps. "Mom, you're sixty-three."

"Sixty-two," she corrected him "and I'll tell you something else chubby..."

"Chubby!?"

"Your old man runs off with some floozie, so what do you do? You go traipsing after him to Goo Goo Land like his dog or something."

"I didn't traipse anywhere. I was helping Dad. I didn't see *you* at the funeral."

"That's because you had it down in that stupid banana republic you two love so much."

"Let me make it up to you. Take you back with me. They don't care what we look like down there. It's warm all year and..."

"I'm gonna count to three then I call for a guard."

"Mom, please..."

"One, two," Ed's mom took a big breath like she

was ready to scream. She wasn't kidding.

"Okay, okay." Ed placed the remote on her sunken chest, pulled himself to his feet and backed off. "But I'm not giving up on you. I'll be back."

"Yeah, sure, that's what you creeps always say. Get lost."

Ed felt crushed as he left the room, though she was right in a way. He hadn't really thought of her that often while he lazed about down south. He never really thought about much of anything. Didn't have to. His only responsibilities were to make sure his dad paced his morning drinking, and observe a few simple rules; don't talk to the police about the customers, and be careful how much credit you extend. Life was simple.

Ed walked, lost in thought, down the hall to the fire escape stairs and down, all the way back to his sleeping hall without thinking about being caught. Miraculously, he wasn't spotted once.

He lay back on his bunk in the roaring room, wondering what the spell was that had fallen over this city. Everyone incarcerated in this place had gone insane. Lou, his mom, everyone—even the guards. Slowly, as the injustice of it crowded his thoughts, he made his first important personal decision in years.

"No, this will not happen." He said it out loud, but it didn't matter, there was no one conscious to hear him. He leaned over to where Lou was deep asleep and gave him a shake.

"Lou, wake up." Lou schnarfled and snorted but didn't wake up "Come on Lou, wake up."

Lou rolled over and looked at Ed through lazy eyes and asked, "Who finished all the mayonnaise?"

"Lou, it's me Ed."

"What?"

"We can't stay here. We're breaking out. I need you

to show me the way."

"When?"

"Now."

"Now?" Lou woke up. "Are you crazy?"

"No, I'm the only sane one in here. Do you know the way or not?"

"There is no way. Go back to sleep."

"Lou, it's a fitness camp, that's all." Ed reached down, picked up Lou's shoes and placed them on the bed beside him. "Let's go."

Lou got up on one elbow and peered into Ed's moon face. "Ed, listen, there's a big fence, guards all over the place."

Ed grabbed and squeezed Lou's cheeks so he could hold his attention. "Lou, I've been out of town for a while but I bet the Chinese don't give a damn about any of this crap."

Lou tried to say "What do the Chinese have to do with it?" but with his face squeezed like it was it came out, "Vussh oo zuh shinies hash oo oo wish ihh?"

"The Chinese, my good son, are smart people who know that all things will pass. They have nice little restaurants with small dark back rooms where they will bring you a big steaming beef hotpot and you can get the deep-fried crispy lemon chicken with golden sweet and sour sauce and those big thick steaming noodles. We start with the big bowl of chicken and corn soup with those deep-fried doughnut things they make, you know, the ones you can have plain or with lots of powdered sugar on them?" He let go of Lou's face. Ed didn't know Lou had a penchant for good Chinese food. It was a lucky guess. "We'll have to get a car," Ed said. "You got a spare coat hangar?"

"I haven't got a coat," Lou said, then stuck his leg out from under the blanket to show Ed his ankle bracelet. "And what about this?"

"Gimme that." Ed looked quickly around then pulled Lou's regulation footlocker over from under his bunk, opened it, lifted Lou's leg and wedged the cheaply made ankle bracelet at the back of the footlocker lid near the hinge. "What the hell are you doing down here when you've got a nice room with a T.V. and everything upstairs?" Ed said. "And it stinks down here."

"Yeah, I know but sometimes ya get lonely, know what I mean?"

"I guess... Hold your breath."

"What?"

Ed brought the lid of the heavy metal box down on the ankle bracelet at its thinnest point. The device cracked open and fell to the floor in pieces. "Here's your shoes," Ed said and shoved Lou's shoes closer to him. Lou struggled to put them on. Ed helped. Good thing they had Velcro fasteners. Ed rummaged around in the footlocker and came up with a bent coat hanger. It would do.

As soon as Lou's ankle bracelet broke, an alarm sounded in Milrot's lab upstairs in the next building, but there wouldn't be anyone around to hear it until after 9:00 AM when the staff arrived. That wouldn't be for another seven hours.

Ed cursed Lou's shoes. One of them squeaked loudly with every step as the two men made their way out of the big room and down the hall towards the fire exit.

"Jesus Christ Ed, I don't know..." Lou muttered as the two peered around a corner at the guards gathered around the central desk.

"Is that all of them?" Ed whispered.

"All of what?"

"Come on Lou, you gotta follow the program here or we're gonna get caught. Is that all the guards there are?"

Lou squinted down the hall but couldn't make out the scene, "How many are there? My eyes ain't been so good since the experiments."

Experiments!? It amazed Ed how Lou could throw out a piece of information without realizing its import, but now was not the time to go into it. He counted the guards at the security desk. "Four," he said.

"Then there's one more makin' the rounds down here. They take turns."

Ed made a quick scan for the single guard and saw nothing. "Shit, five guards, that's nothing."

"And about every twenty minutes two of them go upstairs."

"Yeah, I know. Any outside?"

"I don't know."

"Okay," Ed was thinking fast now. "What would you say is the weakest point in the perimeter?"

"The what?"

Ed was wondering if bringing Lou along was such a good idea. "Where's the weakest point in the fence outside?"

"Ed, there's no weak point. If they don't let you out through the front gates, then you're not goin' anywhere."

"Okay then, the front gates it is." Ed checked that the guards weren't looking, then started across the open intersection of halls, but Lou grabbed him and pulled him back. "This is crazy, man."

"Deep-fried crispy lemon-chicken." Ed said.

"Yeah." Lou said and pointed. "But we better go this way."

"Good man. Go."

Lou led them back past their room and two other sleeping halls neatly skirting the security desk to arrive in a darker area and a corridor that led to another fire exit. Lou stopped and turned to Ed. "I don't know, man." Lou was losing his nerve again.

"Just keep thinking about the beef hotpot." Ed said.

"And the lemon chicken, right?"

"Yeah, trust me. We can do this. Come on."

Lou hurried after Ed, but something bothered him. He couldn't quite think of what it was. Then he remembered and was about to call out to Ed, but it was too late. Ed had no way of knowing that right at this point there was a steel treadle buried flush with the floor. The second he stepped onto it a bright amber light flashed on and off and a loud electronic voice echoed mercilessly up and down the empty halls: **'YOU STILL WEIGH TWO HUNDRED AND SIXTY-ONE POUNDS AND THREE OUNCES!!'**

"Holy shit!" Ed exclaimed, leapt from the device and flattened himself against the opposite wall. "What the fuck?"

The area fell once more into darkness and silence, but the experience was still ringing in Ed's ears and now his legs were rubbery and tingling strangely.

"Sorry," Lou said, "I forgot about that."

"Jesus, that scared me out of ten years' growth."

"Yeah, I think that's the whole idea."

Ed pulled Lou away. "Come on, let's get out of here before they come to see what's happening."

In seconds they huddled outside the fire door. There was the parking lot and about half a dozen cars straight ahead. The country silence would be both good and bad. Good, because they could hear guards in plenty of time to find cover, bad because any racket *they* made would carry well through the still night air. Ed hoped there wasn't some pencil neck standing outside keeping watch, someone actually doing their job.

Ed and Lou scurried across the open space to the night employees' parking lot. The cars were all locked. Ed deftly inserted the heavy wire coat hanger between the glass and the rubber seal of one of the older cars but, as soon as he released the manual door lock inside, the alarm went off.

"Aw shit!" Ed looked desperately around.

"Christ, Ed!" Lou said and stumbled back against the next car. Its alarm went off too.

A door banged open somewhere. Voices and footsteps. Luckily the car alarms were echoing all around the valley, making it hard to tell where any sound was coming from.

Ed swung a stunned Lou around and said, "Let's go!" then took off away from the buildings towards the woods. Lou followed, but he was too slow. Ed turned back, ran to Lou, grabbed him and hauled him toward cover. "We gotta run Lou."

"Where? There's no way."

Ed searched desperately around and saw the high fence hidden by the trees. "This way." Ed leapt toward the perimeter. Lou scrambled after him. It was farther than it looked. The ground was uneven.

Ed was less than ten feet from the fence when he heard a loud 'carrump' and turned back. Lou had gone down in a small thicket of brambles. The flashlights of the security men were angling all over the place now. Ed and Lou were only moments from being spotted.

"It's no use Ed, they got us," Lou mumbled into the dirt. "Go," he said breathlessly. "Save yourself, I'll be all right."

Ed couldn't leave his new friend to the merciless sadism of these bastards. Returning to Lou, he knelt down hoping, in their confusion, the guards wouldn't figure out which way they'd gone for a few more seconds.

"Lou," Ed said, "if they get rid of us, who will organize those big barbecues where there's always too much food?"

"Too much food?" Lou struggled to imagine *that* situation.

Ed pulled on Lou and got him up onto his knees.

"Yeah, and what about the all-night card parties, where everybody orders delivery and the loser pays?"

"How d'*you* know about those?"

"Everybody knows about those, but they won't anymore if these assholes have their way. Come on."

Lou got to his feet and made it to the fence. Ed grasped the wire mesh and quickly scrambled halfway up. "Pull yourself up, it's plastic coated, it's not that bad."

Lou grasped the mesh but couldn't get himself off the ground. Ed saw that several guards had arrived at the parking lot, found the coat hanger stuck in the car door and were now spraying the area with their lights. Soon they'd be on them, and it would be all over.

"What's the matter?" Ed said to Lou.

"I'll never make it," Lou wheezed. "It's too high."

Ed jumped back down and started pushing. He *was* heavy.

"Lou, I promise as soon as everything opens we'll go straight to the lemon chicken."

"What, what about money?" Lou was dizzy with fatigue.

"I got money," Ed lied. He didn't have money. They took all his belongings from him when they arrested him, but he figured his mom must have some cash stashed somewhere in her apartment. He forgot, however, that they had also taken his mom's keycard from him and it was now sitting with the rest of his stuff in a box in the basement of Rightweigh.

"Ed," Lou muttered, "what'll they do when they catch us,"

"What's the difference between that and what they're doing to us already? We gotta get outta here." Ed pushed on him. "Come on, you've got to concentrate. Give it all you've got." Lou looked up at the fence, "Think of the All You Can Eat Steak and Lobster Buffet," Ed said.

"Lobster?"

"Yeah, with plenty of butter."

"Butter?"

"Just think of that and GO!" Ed gave it everything he had and Lou huffed and puffed his way halfway up the fence. Ed looked back to see the guards now making their way toward them through the bramble thicket. He scrambled up the fence to Lou. Together, and with leverage, the two were heavy enough that the fence bent and waved back and forth. This gave Ed an important idea. Just in time too, because the guards had spotted them.

"You! Stop!" one of them shouted.

"Stop what you're doing and come down from there!" shouted another.

"I can't do it." Lou stopped climbing.

The guards were almost upon them. Ed climbed past Lou. Higher up he had a significant mechanical advantage on the fence and found that by shifting his weight he could make the fence sway more. He looked down at Lou. "Lou, look at me."

Lou mustered his strength, climbed another few inches, then looked painfully up at Ed.

"Good, now hang on and when I lean out like this,"

and he showed Lou how the fence swayed back towards the yard. "You do the same. And when I lean in like this," and he showed Lou how to make the fence bend back out towards freedom. "You do the same okay?"

Lou didn't answer.

"Just keep looking at me and follow what I do."

Ed didn't know if Lou got it, but there wasn't time to clarify the plan. The guards were almost on them. Ed leaned back. So did Lou, and the fence bent alarmingly back toward the guards. Ed quickly leaned into the fence and like a big spring it swung far back out the other way.

"Okay, just one more time like that," Ed said, and there was hope in his voice.

Both men leaned back again and the fence bent so far back into the compound that the guards stopped and took a step back for fear of being crushed.

"Now go!" Ed cried and when the two leaned into the fence, it groaned over and out like the miraculous impromptu machine Ed had hoped for and now lay almost flat on the ground. Ed and Lou could smell freedom.

"Now roll Lou, roll!" He yelled and the two men rolled over and over toward the top of the fence forcing it closer to the ground.

Realizing the real possibility of an escape, the guards clambered onto the fence and grabbed at Lou, trying to pull him back.

Ed was almost at the outer edge of the fence. "Come on Lou keep rolling," and he waited as Lou kicked and rolled away from his tormentors. Finally, the two were right at the top of the fence, now lying flat on the ground.

"Gotta roll off together," Ed said to Lou. "Not yet,

wait..." The guards scrambled up and were about to grasp both of them. "Okay, now!" and Lou and Ed rolled together off the fence onto the soft warm ground outside altering the dynamic so dramatically that when the fence sprang back to its original position, the tiny guards were flung all the way back into the bramble thicket.

A proud Ed leapt to his feet and peered with satisfaction through the fence at the fumbling fools and a job well done. The outcome amazed Lou.

One guard came up and banged his flashlight on the twisted but upright and impenetrable fence. "You come back in here right now!" he commanded.

"Sorry, that's not going to happen," Ed said, brushing himself off, helping Lou to his feet.

Another guard ran up to the fence, then another.

Ed laughed. "Sorry boys," he said, "but we just couldn't sleep a wink." He pointed towards the road. "We're going for a midnight snack. Don't wait up."

"Hey man," Lou said and pointed toward the main gate where lights had come on and two white vans were coming out.

"Whoops!" Ed said to the guards trapped behind the fence. "Gotta be running along now." Then he said loudly to Lou, "You know where the nearest bus stop is?"

"No." Lou said.

"Let's go." Ed shouted and pulled Lou away out of earshot. "Never mind, I just said that so that's where they'll look for us. We'll figure out something else."

When they got well out of sight, Lou and Ed made two hard left turns and doubled all the way back to the other side of the Rightweigh compound. It was tough going, and Lou wondered at the reasoning. Ed was using a common trick he learned from pickpockets back in Punta Cana: the police won't look for you at the scene of the crime.

"This is the way to the deep-fried lemon chicken," Ed said.

--

Bracket lived downtown. The drive out to Rightweigh to deal with the escape at two in the morning was annoying. There had been a few escape attempts, but they were halfhearted efforts that amounted to nothing more than good exercise for the runaway. But judging from what her assistant William had told her on the phone, this was a well-planned breakout.

William's BMW was parked in front of the administration building when Bracket pulled up. It always unnerved her that, though William lived almost twice as far away from Rightweigh as she did, he always got there before her when there was a "situation." The main reason was that she terrified her employees, so they always contacted William first in an emergency. He was so much better at breaking bad news to her. The other reason was that William was in a long-term relationship with a dancer who lived not fifteen minutes from Rightweigh, and he slept at his place six nights a week.

Randi Payne, a stage name, strip-danced for horny housewives, but he preferred well-to-do men. His real name was Andrew Parnell. A twenty-four-year-old perfect sculpture of toned muscle and bone, Randi loved the opera, played the stock market successfully, and looked good installing drywall. He drove a bright yellow Hummer. Randi could repair a broken-down car on the side of the road with pliers, a screwdriver and his considerable bare hands. William had seen him do this once, and it was love at first... repair.

William wasn't in the closet or anything, but wisely, he never let on to Bracket. What he did in his private life was none of her business and, besides, he felt it wouldn't sit well with her.

He was right.

"Shall I call the police?" William asked Bracket when he ran into her in the foyer.

"No. We'll find them. They couldn't have vanished into thin air."

William smiled. "Maybe they disappeared into fat air."

Bracket scowled at him. This was nothing to joke about. "Who got out?" she asked.

"We're not exactly sure yet," said William. "Two men, according to security." She pressed the elevator button fifteen times and the two of them stood in silence while Bracket looked William up and down. How the hell could he still look so good at... she looked at her watch, two in the damn morning?

--

It was nearly dawn by the time Ed and Lou emerged on foot into civilization and found a remote subway station. They were lucky enough to sneak in through a bus bay and made it down to the platform just as a train pulled in. It had been a long slog on foot. They slept past their station change and had to go back three stops. Finally, they were within a few blocks of Ed's mom's place.

The lock on the back door of her apartment building was the old-fashioned type that took a standard key. Ed had seen locks picked hundreds of times on television and thought he had a rough idea of how to do it. He was searching a row of nearby garbage bins for a tool when he heard a mighty crack and turned to see Lou standing proudly beside the door, which now gaped inward to a stairwell. "Jesus Lou." Ed was amazed. "That door doesn't even *open* in."

"Does now," Lou said with a grin.

"How much you weigh?" Ed wanted to know as they crept carefully into the dark basement stairwell.

"It goes up and down," Lou said. It was a mild understatement.

Ed struggled in the dark, trying to put the door back to some semblance of order, hoping a security guard wouldn't notice the damage. Then Ed started up the stairs.

"What floor's it on?" Lou wanted to know before he would take a single step.

"Third, come on."

"Isn't there an elevator?" Lou was exhausted.

"We better not take the chance. Let's go,"

Reluctantly Lou hefted his foot onto the first step. Ed leapt to the top of the first short flight, turned right and had almost sprinted to the top of the second before he realized that Lou wasn't with him.

"Lou?" No answer, Ed went back to see Lou at the bottom, leaning on the banister, his foot still rooted on the first step. "Can't do it Ed. It's all that walkin'." For Lou the journey had ended.

The elevator door squeaked and groaned, and Ed and Lou came out into the third-floor hallway.

Porky sensed their approach in that strange way that animals do and started yowling when they were still only halfway to the apartment. Lou commented on the anti-fat graffiti on the door. "Your mom's a big girl then, is she?"

"Uh, yeah. Used to be anyway. Now she's in that hellhole we just left."

"Why didn't we break *her* out too?"

"Didn't want to come."

"Oh, brainwashed." Lou said it as if he'd seen it many times.

Ed tried the door. Locked. His keys, wallet and his money were back at Rightweigh. He gave Lou a nod and said, "But this time go easy."

Lou laid his hip against the door and applied just enough force to spring it open with a small metallic pop. "Where's the kitchen," Lou asked.

Ed pointed down the hall and off Lou went in search of something to eat. Porky went after him, jumping and clawing at his leg. Ed was glad to see that the animal had regained some of its strength. He took another quick look up and down the hall before coming in and closing the door. He knew what was in the fridge. Soon Lou would be back complaining. He went to the window and looked out at the beginnings of a glorious sunrise.

Lou called from the kitchen. "Hey Ed, there's no food in here."

"I know, we gotta hang on a little longer while I go pick up a few things."

Ed took a large jar full of spare change from a shelf and poured it out on the coffee table. Good, his mom's car keys were here too. He sorted through the bigger coins and pocketed them. Lou came back in carrying a glass of water and two packets of Tender Vittles. Porky was now clinging to his pants, halfway up his leg. Lou sat on the sofa, and Porky nuzzled the hand that held the food. Lou ripped open one package and dumped a handful in his lap so Porky could get at it. Then he watched Lou pop three of the nuggets into his mouth like nuts and take a mouth full of water. "Jesus Lou, how can you eat that stuff?"

Lou sloshed the hard nuggets around in his mouth before answering. "Are you kidding? Locked up in Rightweigh for four months you learn how to prepare a roll of toilet paper on a heat vent so it's almost possible to imagine it's four-day-old pot roast." He held out a handful of the "food" to Ed, but Ed refused it with a nod. "Sure," Lou said, "I'd rather be lickin' a double malted rocky road hot fudge sundae too, but you take what you can get," and he popped three more Vittles. "Dry though."

Lou's head lolled back, and he imagined that he was chewing a nice big juicy.... wait a minute. Lou sat up, almost knocking Porky onto the floor. "What's that?"

Ed whirled around. "What's what?"

"Muffin!" Lou said and sniffed the air. "Muffin!" he said again and got up. Porky leapt to the floor.

"Calm down man, you're hallucinating. They've made you nuts in there. There's nothing here. I've checked." Ed said, but Lou ignored him and threw open the bedroom door.

"In here." Lou sniffed around the room quickly, zeroing in on an ornate bedside table and its ornate drawer. He opened it slowly as if it was a safe deposit box, took out a dark lump of something and brushed it off. "Must be a few months old, but still..."

"What is it?" Ed said from the doorway.

Lou sniffed the lump. "Maple walnut and raisin, I'd say." He carried the precious find back into the living room and sat down carefully on the sofa. "We'll split it. Got a knife and a plate?"

Ed figured there was no harm in humouring Lou at this point. He went into the kitchen, returning with a small saucer and a steak knife, sat down then looked closely at the find for himself. "It looks like a rolled up old crusty sock to me, man."

"I'll cut, you choose!" Lou said in a faltering voice. He took the plate and knife from Ed, gently placed the fossilized muffin on it and prepared to divide the delicacy in two.

Lou's hand shook. Ed worried he might cut himself. "Here," Ed said, "I'll cut, you choose."

But when he went to take the knife from his friend, his grasp slipped and Lou brought the knife down off-centre, cleaving the lump into one large piece and one small piece. Sweat popped out on Lou's brow and his face trembled but he stuck with his deal, "O... o... okay, you choose." He stammered.

Slowly, so Lou would see, Ed grasped the larger piece and lifted it off the saucer. Lou trembled. His pupils dilated and his mouth went dry. Then Ed took Lou's fist in his hand, carefully opened his fingers and gently placed the larger chunk of desiccated muffin in it. Lou stared at his portion in wonder. Ed picked up the T.V. remote, placed it on Lou's lap, then got up and headed for the front door. "You wait here, I'm going to do a bit of shopping. And eat that other piece for me, will ya?"

"Shopping!? Ed, you can't go shopping! Our pictures will be all over the T.V. This morning."

"No, they won't," Ed smiled at his friend, "Sit tight, I'll be right back with some real grub." He picked up the car keys and left.

It had been a long time since anyone genuinely cared for Lou, and a warmth rushed through his whole being. For about three-and-a-half seconds, Lou forgot completely about the muffin.

It was Lou's failed marriage that broke him. His ex-wife Fran met him as the nice simple guy he was.

Before he became Dr. Milrot's star experimental subject, Lou Kennedy was a city bus driver. If it hadn't been for Lou's testimony that the cyclist inexplicably turned out in front of Fran's red Mazda against a red light, the outcome of her trial surely would have been different, but because of Lou's simple nature and unshakable truth-telling, the judge ruled in Fran's favour. It was an emotionally charged situation for her and they awarded her ten weeks of psychiatric counselling. In one of her sessions, she confessed she had little success with men she met at her job at the bank, and the therapist dragged out the old but true axiom "It's better to be with a bus driver who makes you laugh than an executive who makes you cry."

It shocked Lou when Fran called one evening to ask what he was doing. Lou was always a big man, and she enjoyed having this big, strong man at her beck and call. It turned her on. They made a handsome couple back then. Fran was satisfied. Lou was in love.

The marriage worked for a time but Lou's thoughts strayed towards finding the best buffet in town while Fran concentrated on her physical appearance and the attentions of Marco, her personal trainer.

Eventually, when Lou hit two-hundred-and-eighty pounds, Fran persuaded him to join the Rightweigh program. Then Marco moved in with her. But at the very moment, as Lou savoured the muffin on Ed's mom's couch, Fran and Marco were occupying separate sleeping accommodations after a big fight they'd had the night before. She wanted him to drop his other clients, all female, and pay more attention to her. Fran should have stuck with Lou; her life would have been way more interesting, far beyond anything she could have imagined in her wildest dreams.

Life, Liberty, And
The Pursuit Of A Decent Burger

Ed went through the garage looking for his mother's car. He spotted a dusty maroon hulk and remembered that his mom's favourite colour was red. Luck was with him; there was plenty of gas in the tank.

Ed wheeled the car up the ramp to the street. It was still early. No one in sight. He felt secure in the comfort of his mom's car. For now, he'd settle for anything, ten takeout breakfast sandwiches. Did they serve desserts in the morning?

But signs on every restaurant warned of portion control and other restrictions. The usual coffee places no longer sold doughnuts. Besides, he was looking for real food here, not a snack.

Had they mounted a search for him and Lou yet? They had his wallet, credit cards and Dominican driver's license. No reference to his mom's address. She was using her maiden name. That was a big break. Lou would be safe at his mom's, at least for a while. He spotted a cop car at the curb, slumped down in his seat and turned early. If he got stopped, it would be all over.

Soon, he was in little Italy. Ed knew it was a tradition for the Italians to start early because the dishes they served for lunch demanded plenty of prep. In one good-sized trattoria, there was activity.

The front door was locked but a few loud tack, tack, tacks on the glass with his car key and in seconds here came a big woman wiping her hands on her apron. Ed explained that he'd just arrived overnight on a flight from the Dominican Republic and tried unsuccessfully to make a joke about airline food. All he wanted was anything she could manage quickly; two steaks; any kind of pasta at all... Jesus, a panini or four, he didn't care.

After looking up and down the street, she explained in broken English that maybe she could give him two salads in styrofoam containers and mix a quick vinaigrette but that would be it. Ed gaped at her as she told him she was afraid of losing her vendor's permit for serving an OP.

Ed speculated as to the meaning of "OP." It had to mean "opulent patron," or "overweight person", or perhaps it was even "potential over-eater" but then, that would be PO, and that already meant "pissed off," and PO'd was what Ed was quickly becoming.

Ed should have accepted the salads. Instead, he drove on, searching in vain for a friendly oasis. In a Pavlovian response to his previous experience, he avoided grocery stores, but now he realized he would have to deal with one of those if he was to bring home the bacon. Perhaps a smaller convenience store would give him an opportunity to make personal contact and perhaps find a kindred spirit. That's when he noticed a police cruiser that had fallen in behind him. Now what? He signalled and carefully pulled around a corner. Still there. Shit! He slowly and methodically made his way back to his mom's place and discreetly disappeared back into the darkness of Mom's garage. He needed time to think.

No one at Rightweigh got any more information on the identities of the escapees until Gwen Djvani, Milrot's assistant, arrived and noticed the alert from Lou's ankle bracelet.

"Lou Kennedy!?" Bracket remembered the man in the test chamber and Milrot's torturous experiment. The last thing she needed was the police interrogating Lou Kennedy. God knows what he'd tell them. "We have to get him back before the police or the press get hold of him," she told William. "Get his file, find out where he lives. We'll nip this in the bud."

William wasn't sure why she was so focused on Lou, but he followed orders. He got on the phone to Lou's ex-wife Fran under the pretext he was warning her of his escape.

"Don't worry," Fran said. "if he shows up here, you'll be the second person to know after Rolph."

"Would you have a number for Rolph?"

"One-six-three-three, that's his license number, he's a Rottweiler," and she hung up.

William went through the men's induction photos with two of the guards and it didn't take them long to identify Edward Miller as the other escapee. When Bracket learned that he was in their charge under a court order, she agreed with William that it would be prudent to call the police. "But don't make a federal case out of it," she said. "In fact, just call the local division out here so there will be a record in case we need to say so later. Tell them it's nothing urgent, we're still searching the outer grounds and nearby convenience stores. Say they've probably just gone on a picnic or something. You know, kind of make a joke out of it." She cast him a withering look. "You're good at joking, aren't you?"

William scurried off and Bracket stood at her office window. The morning sunlight was just hitting the tops of the trees across the parking lot. She wondered if poor dumb Lou had the wits to even think of talking to the press. She didn't give Ed a second thought.

--

Ed slipped back into his mom's apartment. Still asleep on the sofa, Lou didn't stir. Neither did Porky snoozing on his chest, one paw flopped across Lou's face. Ed was glad to see this picture of contentment, but anger was brewing inside him. He had become used to the general "live and let live" attitude In the islands. Okay, there was great poverty and suffering there, but anyone with their wits about them could always make their way. Ed realized he'd been stupid to let things go to where the bank had to foreclose on his dad's Cabana on the Beach. But there were other important things happening in the wider world. Now, in some odd way, he'd become energized. Adrenaline coursed through his veins for the first time in a long while as he went through the apartment looking for a tool, a prop, a weapon. Anything he could put to use. He wasn't sure just yet what he would do, he was making it up as he went along. At one point he searched for a balaclava and thought, 'What would Mom be doing with a balaclava?' Then again, in this environment, it wouldn't surprise him to come across a matching pair of AK-47s.

'The alderman was right,' he thought, 'it *is* a flagrant denial of human rights.' He thought of his mom. Rightweigh had no reason, no right to allow her to remain in their custody, willing or not. She should have at least received some sort of counselling. They just wanted her money.

--

The rural police duty sergeant who took William's call that morning wasn't sure what to make of it, so she dispatched two officers to Rightweigh to investigate. Before they could report back, she went home weary from the long night shift.

This was a small detachment, and the desk went unattended until her relief showed up and read the curious note she left:

> *Rightweigh*
> *<u>2</u> escaped unarmed*
> *<u>on foot</u>*
> *Unit dispatched*

Though the number "2" and the words "on foot" were underlined, the words "escaped" and the armed part of "unarmed" triggered the morning duty sergeant who immediately attempted to contact the unit sent to investigate. When he received no reply he called his superior, who tried to contact the officers again, this time by cell phone. But it was as though their radio and phones had been disabled. Inexperienced and slightly alarmed, he put in a call to police headquarters in the city.

The cops didn't receive the calls because they were inside the Rightweigh grounds where a jamming system was active. Nearby pizza delivery joints had been receiving late-night calls from the inmates of Rightweigh. Several times a week someone inside the compound placed a big phone order, prepaid with a credit card number, added a heavy tip and asked that the food be thrown over the fence at the back of the property.

--

Lt. Lardner was sitting in traffic on the Parkway when he received a call to report directly to Inspector Reznor as soon as he got in. The dispatcher told him that two escapees were missing from Rightweigh, and he heard laughter in the background. "If they're escapees," he growled into the phone, "then you don't have to say they're missing," then hung up. Minutes later he stormed into Reznor's office. "Why the hell can't people see that this is a public health issue?" he said.

"Good morning to you too," Reznor forced a smile.

"We don't have resources to spare on this crap."

Reznor pointed to mug shots of Ed and Lou on his computer screen.

Lardner's shoulders dropped. "This is gonna kill me, Jack." He nodded at the screen. "This isn't police work. No one escaped. It's a goddamn fitness clinic. Can't they handle their own mess?"

"I know, I know, but technically," and he pointed at Ed's picture, "when this one went home in defiance of a court order, it became our business."

"Then *technically* it's not much different from if the guy missed some community service. Let's just send some uniforms to knock on the door and take them back."

Reznor clicked his mouse and the printer produced mug shots of Ed and Lou. "Yeah, normally that's what I'd do but I want someone takin' care of this who can soft shoe it through, know what I mean?"

"No, what *do* you mean?"

Reznor grabbed the mug shots, and led Lardner to the door. "Bill, come on. We've known each other for a long time."

They headed together toward the main squad room. Lardner lowed his voice so no one else would hear. "At least rotate some other people through it. I'm taking it from all sides here."

"Bill, look at the facts. You're the only man I got with his head screwed on straight about this. I can't just assign the thing to *anyone*. I have to be careful. I hear what everybody around here is saying, and it's precisely because of that attitude that I can't have any of *them* handling this."

"I busted a gourmet restaurant the other night." Lardner said. "I got some flambés and a goddamn poached salmon as evidence. You know what the men here call what I do? The cupcake patrol. Today I gotta go out and apprehend some guys because they're fat. What's next, measuring doughnut holes to make sure they're not too small?"

Reznor laughed at this, then checked himself when he saw that Lardner was dead serious. "The place was illegal," Reznor said. "They should have shut it down long ago. It's a danger to the public. What if someone gets poisoned and winds up dead?" Reznor handed the mugshots to Lardner pointing to Ed's shot. "Just talk to this guy the way you do. Convince him to finish his sentence. Case closed."

Resigned, Lardner took the mug shots. "You got any addresses? Or do I just stake out Burger King?"

Reznor took a note from his shirt pocket and handed it to Lardner. "We haven't got a current address on this Edward Miller yet, maybe he's from out of town. But this is the last known address for Lou Kennedy. See the ex-wife and ask if..."

"Yeah, I know, ask her if there's anything missing from her fridge." He stuffed the paper into his pocket.

"See, that's what I like about having you handle all this; you got a sense of humour about it."

"Yeah, well, it's wearing pretty thin." Lardner warned him.

Reznor pointed at Lou's picture. "If they're still together, bring him in too if you can." He held up Ed's picture. "But get this guy and it's over." He clapped Lardner on the shoulder again. "Just take it one thing at a time."

Lardner cast Reznor a cheerless frown, then went into the squad room where several detectives were sitting around drinking coffee, preparing for the day's work. Lardner slumped at his desk and eyed Bailey across from him, pecking away on his computer. He didn't even afford Lardner a glance. When he was finished, he went to the washroom. Lardner took the opportunity to see what Bailey had been up to. One of the other men nearby called out, "Hey Bill, see me before you go, will ya? I got a lead on some hot sweet rolls on the east side."

The other cops in the room all burst out laughing like they were at some stand-up comedy club. As usual, Lardner tried to drive it out of his mind as he sat at Bailey's computer. All records of Bailey's online activity had been deliberately and meticulously wiped clean. He sat back at his desk as Bailey reappeared. Lardner told his partner about their assignment to interview Lou's ex wife. "We should call and see if she's home," Lardner said. Bailey picked up the phone and dialed Fran Kennedy's number, then hung up.

"What's the matter?" Lardner said.

"No point in alerting him so he can go out a back window."

"Ray," Lardner said. "It's a guy who left a weight-loss clinic without a permission slip, not some suicide bomber for Christ's sake."

"Why make our job harder?" Bailey muttered.

It *was* a good point. As they were leaving, the comedian detective of the division called out again "Hey guys, don't forget to take your canapé calipers." Everyone laughed.

On the way down the stairs to the parking garage Bailey said, "Those assholes should ride along with us when we have to do the tougher stuff. We're doing them and their families a big favour here. It's not our fault these people have recumbent DNA."

Lardner knew that obesity ran in families, but he was sure it wasn't due to relaxed genes. "You enjoy rousting the big folk, don't you?" he said.

"It's our job."

"Doesn't it bother you they've done nothing wrong?"

"Do you want your kids seeing *everybody* fat everywhere?" he asked.

"What kids?"

"Well, if you had hypothetical kids say."

Lardner had to think about this as Bailey pulled their car out of the garage then he said, "At one time they considered it fashionable to be fifty, sixty pounds overweight."

Bailey tried to imagine this. "Must'a been before my time."

"It was four hundred years ago."

"Well, there you go. What did they know back then?"

"People don't change much." Lardner said.

Bailey was curious. "Guys actually *liked* their women that way?"

"*Especially* the women. They considered it a sign of wealth and good health. Haven't you ever seen a painting by Rubens?"

As they stopped at a red light, Bailey cast Lardner a sardonic smile. "You read all those books and that's all you get, that the gals all used to be fat?" Lardner looked out the window. Everything about his partner was beginning to irritate him; his attitude towards the overweight; his strange off-duty activities; his secret computer use. "All I'm sayin'" Bailey continued, "is in no way shape or form are these people useful to society. They sit around all day watching TV and eating. Their sedimentary."

"Sedentary," Lardner corrected him.

"What?"

"They're sedentary, not sedimentary."

"See? That's what I mean. Too much education only confuses things with all kinds of big words all the time." Bailey muttered and went back to biting his nails.

Ironically, Bailey was right. People with an eating disorder in this environment *were* sedimentary; the pressures of bigotry and intolerance had driven them to the bottom of society.

Lardner watched Bailey twist his arm up to work on one particularly tough hangnail. He decided right then to make it his duty to find out all about this man's secret life. Now was as good a time as any to start. "Don't you ever feel like relaxing once in a while?"

"How do you mean?"

Lardner smiled at a sudden thought. "Ever wonder if people who bite their nails are cannibals?" Bailey gave him a strange look, then stopped biting and wiped his finger on the front of his shirt thoughtfully. "I mean, technically." Lardner added.

Bailey looked at his ravaged nails and thought about the question again. "No," he said finally then added, "not *technically*."

A horn blared behind them, and Lardner pointed ahead. "Green."

"What?"

"The light's green."

"Oh." Bailey pulled away through the intersection.

--

It worried Sara that her father might keep to his bed for God knows how long. Meanwhile, she would do her best to conduct the routine business of the church and congregation. Not that there really was a congregation anymore. Those who had managed to avoid the round-ups, no longer ventured out of their homes during the day.

Sara sat at the kitchen table and remembered the last time her father became lost in despair. He had always wanted to lead a television ministry, to see to the needs of many at one time. Father Allen despised the current crop of broadcast ministries, the phony healers and the greedy evangelists cluttering the airwaves with appeals for cash. There was a real need for the true word of Jesus. His dream was to remind everyone of the humble teachings, the simple meanings behind them, to show how they applied to modern life.

Father Allen's first and only telecast, in memory of his beloved wife Elspeth, was a valiant effort. A few wealthy members donated to the production of a live half-hour Sunday morning telecast on a local public access station. Everyone pitched in to get the word out. It was a real challenge getting the posters up, posting announcements on line and in newspapers, and distributing thousands of fliers. Some put in eighteen-hour days until Father Allen finally stood before the cameras.

It went pretty well, except for a small typo in the subtitles of a hymn; the misspelling of the word *friend*. Instead of friend, it was copied and pasted to appear repeatedly across the bottom of the screen as *fiend*. *Oh, what a fiend we have in Jesus* everyone sang as Father Allen held outstretched arms, and every time it came to that line in the hymn, the words they sang *Oh, what a fiend we have in Jesus* flashed across the screen again and again, *Oh, what a fiend we have in Jesus, Oh, what a fiend we have in Jesus*.

The phones didn't stop ringing for weeks. It was the first time Father Allen had ever received a death threat. He was at a loss to understand how a simple error could cause such a tremendous backlash. Fact is, it hadn't. What Father Allen didn't know—and what Sara made sure he never knew—was that a young volunteer worker, had made another fatal error: The Church's website had a URL that was almost identical to another, unrelated, service. The innocent visitor who clicked on the advertised link to the home page of the Church of the Safe Way expected to find angelic images and glorious music. Instead, they came upon something called Arigato Movie House featuring a Japanese video of a young futanari hooker delivering a variation of the Cleveland Steamer to an appreciative customer—a process involving the exchange of bodily excretions that would make any graphic depiction of a simple blowjob seem like a gentle and innocent kiss on the cheek. Larry Flynt would have been perplexed. Though several conversions were achieved, they were not the sort that Father Allen intended.

After the failure of the telecast and after Sara had

the website taken down, Father Allen slipped into a spiral of confusion and grief from which he never fully recovered.

Sara knew the project was ill-fated from the start. Once, while watching Joel Osteen's Easter show, she realized that her father's operation, working full time at peak efficiency would be hard pressed to organize the parking for such an extravaganza, never mind the complexities of an entire media empire. Not only the cameras and lights, the crew and staff, but the complex telephone infrastructure, social media campaigns, accountants, researchers, ushers and musicians. The lawyers!

Sara's doting parents made sure she received the best education possible, never once realizing that a well-rounded education is a deadly threat to religious training and faith. Sara knew a lot of what her father believed was not logical. However, in spite of the horrible things in his bible, Father Allen's morals, ideals and desires for a better world were rare virtues in this age. It didn't matter whether you believed in God, some of the ten commandments were still correct. Even the atheists didn't argue with that. Sara believed the universe had some purpose. It didn't matter whether you called it morality, conscience, love, reason, or God, some things were right and some things were wrong. She was intellectually grounded and theologically confused, as were many of her generation.

Sara came out of her reverie when the kettle screamed.

She slipped into her father's room ever so quietly with a tray of tea and toast points and set them on the side table, then cranked him to a more upright position. Father Allen had taken to sleeping in a hospital bed for reasons Sara could not comprehend. Perhaps some people needed to feel sicker than they actually were before they could get better.

She poured the tea.

Father Allen didn't touch the tea or the toast. Instead, he drifted in and out of sleep, and about twenty minutes after Sara left the room, Jesus appeared at the foot of Father Allen's bed. He stood floating serenely a foot or so off the floor and gazed tenderly down upon his cherished disciple.

Father Allen's sleeping face relaxed, and he smiled softly, revelling in the aura of his Lord.

--

Ed studied the hodgepodge of raw materials spread out on the kitchen table; a tube of crazy glue; several kinds of tape; two old-fashioned butane re-chargers; a spray can of green paint; various kitchen utensils; some party crackers; the rotten chocolate sauce and an assortment of discarded plastic screw-top containers. Porky came in, yawning.

"Hi there girl," he said to the cat, then leaned back into the living room to check on Lou still asleep on the sofa. "You looking for more grub?" he asked Porky. But she wasn't. All she wanted to do was purr and rub herself against his leg. She jumped up onto one of the kitchen chairs to watch him work.

Ed held his nose with one hand and squeezed what used to be chocolate sauce into one of the plastic containers, then screwed the lid on tight. The design evolved as he went. Whatever it was he was making didn't have to work, it just had to look scary, make a mess, maybe a few sparks or something. It was meant to intimidate.

He poked a hole in the container's bottom with a

turkey skewer, then inserted the butane re-charger firmly into it, pressing down hard charging the thing with enough pressure so it didn't all leak back out before he could slap a piece of the heavy tape over the hole. It didn't look dangerous enough. He added an ignition device with a party cracker that might create some sparks, then wrapped the whole thing together in foil and packing tape.

Finally, he had something that might produce the desired effect. He held in his hand an IED—an Inoperative Explosive Device.

Ed didn't have a plan of any kind, all he wanted was a decent burger and some fries. He made two more IEDs then set about figuring out how to hang them from his belt.

He needed dark clothing. The blouse from Mom's closet buttoned the wrong way, but it was big and covered everything nicely. In a drawer, he found a dainty but large pair of black silk dress gloves that fit.

Finally he stood before the bedroom mirror decked out in his makeshift commando outfit; dark brown woolly tea cozy on his head, the gloves and dark bulbous blouse, his darkest pair of Bermuda shorts and a pair of rubber boots he'd found in the front hall closet. The IED chocolate cocktails were slung around his waist on a string of kitchen ties.

He glared at the image in the mirror and flashed an *I'm not taking any shit from you* kind of look then turned away, then suddenly back to the mirror grabbing one of his chocolate cocktails from his belt. When he went to brandish it threateningly to see how that would look, he fumbled it and it fell rolling across the floor. He was retrieving it when Lou suddenly said, "What the hell are you doin' Ed?"

"Jesus Christ Lou, don't scare the shit outta me like

that!"

"I thought you were goin' out for some breakfast." Lou looked Ed up and down, then smiled for the first time. "What's with the getup?"

"Yeah well it didn't work out too well the first time, but just sit tight I'm going out to do some real shoppin' now.

"Ed, give it up, we're screwed here."

"No, we're not Lou. We got out, didn't we?"

"You want me to come with you?"

Ed could see that Lou didn't really have it in him. Besides, Lou would only slow him down. "No, you wait here and guard the fort. Like I said, I'll be right back with some grub," and he left.

--

It was mid-afternoon as Ed cruised the streets, scanning for opportunities. Everyone had settled back into their work for the rest of the day, that time when everyone's blood sugar rises after lunch and they feel more like taking a nap than looking after business. All thoughts would be of the long drive home in rush hour traffic, a sitcom on TV, what was for dinner?

What *was* for dinner?

It was all Ed could think about as he pulled in across the street from "The Char Pit" and watched the waiters taking their own late lunch. The sign on the front read:

FULL COURSE CHICKEN AND RIB DINNER
SALAD — POTATO — MEDIUM SOFT DRINK
ONLY $39.95

Management had crossed out the words "rib" and

"potato", added the word "diet" to "soft drink" and increased the price to $42.95 then to $49.95 and again to a straight sixty bucks.

Everyone was suffering from this oppression.

--

Kent Nason worked as a lowly camera operator at a local TV station, but he was young, and restless. He wanted to land one big story that swept the city. Recognizing his zeal, his boss finally put him in front of the camera as an on-air reporter and teamed him up with a crack young camera operator, Sally Bean. Together they ran around town in a cool black First News SUV grabbing interviews on everything from water main breaks and record-breaking potholes to long-after-the-fact robberies and traffic accidents. At Halloween they got a scoop on a pumpkin carving contest. For Valentines Day they delved into the manufacture of cinnamon hearts, and at Christmas they captured two drunk Santas fist fighting in a liquor store parking lot.

And they followed the growing controversy over the so-called obesity epidemic. They were at the burning of Wendy's Large Gals' Shop. So was Ed.

"I think it's a shame," one sweet elderly woman said. "Everyone should have the same rights and there should be peace on earth and good will toward men." though Christmas was still five months away.

A skinny guy with four teeth sitting at the wheel of a cement truck said "They should all BLEEPIN' be sent BLEEPIN'' back to where ever the BLEEP it was they BLEEPIN' came from."

People were beginning to have opinions. Kent and Sally's efforts were paying off. They wondered why they weren't allowed into Judge Conroy's court—not even as spectators. They looked into Rightweigh's operations, hoping to find an angle, a hint of scandal.

But the station manager wasn't happy with scraps. "I want more," he said.

"More!?" Nason lost it. "What more do you want than they're locking folks up because they're fat!"

"No, they're not," the boss argued. "They're putting law-breakers in a comfy fitness resort instead of jail. That's not a story. When you've got fat people hauled off the street and thrown in the fat farm because they belong to a visible minority, then you've got fat profiling and that's a story!"

Nason couldn't really argue. People wanted *bad* news—as long as it wasn't happening to them. He was just getting antsy. He had to hang in there and stick with the story. Perhaps think of ways to help it along.

--

Lardner and Bailey came away from their interview with Lou's ex-wife Fran thoroughly uninformed and no further ahead than they had been when they first knocked on her door. In no uncertain terms she'd told them that, as far as she knew, Lou was still trying to work things out at Rightweigh, that she felt sorry for him, but didn't want to see him again until he had confronted his "problems," meaning his weight. She had no idea who the heck Edward Miller was.

Lardner looked around while Bailey took Fran's statement. She sobbed, took out a hanky and dabbed at a perfectly dry eye as she told him of a marriage gone bad, and Lou's attempt to salvage the relationship by volunteering to enter the Rightweigh program. She left out the part about the affair with Marco, her trainer.

But Lardner and Bailey weren't looking for Lou, they were after Ed. Still, Lardner read the tiny facial expressions that gave away her contempt for Lou. And he saw the man's skimpy thong in the laundry hamper.

--

"Well, that explains why this Lou Kennedy isn't our priority," Bailey proclaimed as they came down the walk to their car. "Technically, he's allowed to walk out of there any time he pleases."

"Yeah." Lardner muttered, then wondered why Lou would risk it all by escaping.

Lardner and Bailey usually took turns driving the car whenever they went anywhere together, but lately Lardner enjoyed slumping in the passenger seat and letting his thoughts drift—off the case if possible.

Bailey enjoyed doing the driving. He was still a big kid at heart. He looked at pretty girls for too long and talked too soon and too loud in situations that called for reserved observation. Beneath his gruff exterior was a man seething with inner turmoil. Furiously gnawing at his fingernails every chance he got, he was quick to react to situations before they had revealed their true nature.

Now Lardner watched him work on that stubborn hangnail with his front teeth.

Bailey caught him staring. "What?"

Lardner looked away, out the window. "Nothing."

"You're lookin', what's with the lookin'?"

Lardner wished the case gave him something more interesting to think about than his partner's private life, but it would pass the time. "Look, no offence" he said, "but, do you think it's possible that cannibals get started by biting their nails?"

Bailey gaped at Lardner for long seconds without answering. Lardner returned to staring out the window at nothing.

Three blocks later Bailey asserted, "It's not the same thing."

"What's not?" Lardner had forgotten the question.

"When you bite your nails, you're only putting part of your own body back into your body. Cannibals eat other people."

"Oh... Yeah." It surprised Lardner that Bailey had thought about it. "Jesus," Lardner said to no one, "now they've got *me* thinkin' about nothing but eating."

"It's not just about eating," Bailey said, "It's about the public health, the well-being of the citizenry. We're enforcing the law on behalf of the little guy on the street."

"And the law is an ass." Lardner said. "Ever hear that saying?"

"Sure, but then, in the other event, conversely, you'd say shooting a drug dealer who sells smack to your daughter is murder."

"It's not the same," Lardner said.

"Sure it is. Somebody could be dying of cancer right now out west somewhere just because some fat tub of lard has to have a whole pack-of-bacon and six eggs every morning for breakfast... half a pound of butter on his toast..."

"How do you figure that?"

"Look," Bailey explained, "we got the public health. It's paid for by the taxpayer. That means there's a limited budget, and *that* means treatments have to get prioritized in some order. The sickest get treatment first, right?"

"Okay." Lardner struggled to figure out where this was going.

"Think about it. The guy out west gets diagnosed with stage four cancer, but if the fat pack-of-bacon guy has a heart attack first, the money gets used up rushin' him to the hospital and giving that fucker an eighty-thousand dollar bypass operation. The cancer guy gets his test put off till it's too late to do anything about it so he dies."

Bailey had made his point. Lardner conceded with a grimace then added, "You sure it's as simple as that?"

"Maybe not, but it only has to go like that once to be wrong. To serve and protect. That's what it says on the side of our car.... well not on the side of *our* car but you know what I mean. That's what I'm doin', serving," he waved an open hand. "And protecting. They put this Edward Miller in there on a court order."

"Yeah, I know all that," Lardner said "but there's gotta be other ways to work these situations out without invoking the death penalty."

"We don't have the death penalty," Bailey said, then added, "In no way shape or form do we have the death penalty."

"And why do you think that is?"

"Because with the death penalty you're just adding another killing without cognisizing why the crime happened in the first place."

"I rest my case."

"I don't get it."

"You know what?" Lardner said and looked out the window. "I don't get it either." After long moments of silence Lardner said, "If they would concentrate on the root causes of some of these things, study what made people get bad ideas in the first place, then maybe we'd be able to deal with real crime better when it happens."

That, apparently, was the last word. Bailey went back to work on his hangnail.

--

Bracket was on the phone with Kent Nason. Winning him over could generate free advertising. Besides, she had a real thing for handsome young men.

Kent proposed more than a simple interview with her. He wanted to present his boss with a full-length feature story that included a complete tour of the facility, interviews with her department heads and even some selected clients. He wanted to know her ideas, her philosophy, and plans for the future. The piece would be available to networks nation-wide as a feature human interest news special. Perhaps they could even get it aired in the U.S.

"Let me take it up with my staff and advisers, and I'll get back to you." she said.

It was a short, civil exchange that jacked the adrenaline in both of them. She mistakenly suspected Nason was naïve, exploitable. Kent knew Bracket was hooked. Nason *was* young and inexperienced, but he had a nose for news.

--

The person most inconvenienced by the escape was Milrot. He'd been studying Lou for almost a month now and, over the past few days, he'd devised ever more exotic tests to isolate where Lou's tiny weight gains were coming from.

At first he thought it to be errors in one of the computer algorithms. But this wasn't the problem. In Lou's absence, he tested the equipment on other subjects. The results came out as expected. They pedalled while viewing the videos, including the Pie-

Eating Contest, and they all lost a little weight, as expected. It was only Lou who emerged from the sessions with a weight gain.

Milrot considered the healing process. When the body heals itself cells divide and multiply to repair wounds. The process has to have fuel from the outside. This normally comes in the form of food. Lou couldn't be eating anything during the experiments, Milrot had Gwen strip Lou down to his boxers to make sure. He must be absorbing something from the apparatus. Milrot changed the seat and the handlebars and pedals three times but still got the same results.

Milrot was losing sleep. What was happening was outside his field. He decided to ask Harry Steckle, a particle physicist at MIT, working on the question of how matter originated in the big bang. Why there was something rather than nothing.

On Skype, Milrot told Harry about the test results and asked him if it was possible that Lou Kennedy could create matter from nothing. "Isn't there some violation of the law of conservation of mass or something going on here?" he asked.

Here's what Harry said after he laughed at Milrot's dilemma: "No." When there was only silence on the other end of the line Harry added "Matter gets converted into energy all the time. It's called sunlight. We create matter from energy in particle accelerators. How's the family?"

"I don't have a family. What about $E=mc^2$? Isn't that matter from energy?"

"Eli, here's the bottom line: Some believe that if you take two ping-pong balls and drive them up to a speed close to the speed of light, then collide them together, sometimes, maybe once in a hundred million years, the ping-pong balls and the energy used to accelerate them will combine and something like a bowling ball will appear standing still in the middle of your experiment."

"Have you ever seen that?"

"Are you kidding? If that ever happened it would blow our expensive machines to smithereens. Gotta go."

"Wait! Harry?" But Harry had hung up. Milrot put down the phone and stared at the wall for a long time.

He had to get Lou back.

--

Ed moved on. If he wanted to get in and get out and back to Lou with something fast, it would be smarter in this emergency to settle for something simple and familiar.

McDonald's!

He cased several Burger Kings, A&Ws and McDonald's before he found a place that had all the right elements: a good clear exit route in case he had to make a getaway and seating all on one side so he could see the whole place at once from a single vantage point at the counter.

He pulled into the parking lot and contemplated what he was about to do. He'd go in calmly. Staying cool was key. He'd approach the counter and keep his order simple. Four burgers, four large fries, two chocolate and two vanilla shakes, two more burgers for good luck. Would what he was about to do be considered a crime? Including the original offence of creating a public disturbance and his escape from custody in defiance of a court order, would this make him a three-time loser? It gave Ed pause.

He wondered about the scary-looking chocolate

cocktails he'd made. Was he biting off more than he could chew? Ed knew how things could get blown out of proportion. Right then, he made a wise decision. He left the chocolate cocktails lined up on the back seat of the car but took the spray paint can he'd used to paint them. He counted his money. Twenty-three dollars and forty-two cents. He wasn't actually going to *steal* anything. Was he losing his nerve? No. He left the car running, took a deep breath and ventured forth.

The walk across the parking lot seemed to take forever. When he finally got inside, Ed stopped and planted his feet apart in a kind of semi-combat mode.

No one noticed. Not even Sara Allen, who was sitting in a booth near the back corner quietly talking with a largish young couple. "What they sell here isn't nutritious food," she said. "It's loaded with fats, processed sugars, salt and who knows what chemicals. You can do better than this." The woman rested her head on her husband's shoulder. Sara pressed on. "Don't let this company ruin your lives."

The man looked down, embarrassed. "We don't want to be here, but it's the only place where we can have lunch in peace. When we go shopping everybody looks at what we have in our basket as if we're committing a crime or something."

"Ignore them. They probably also think that same sex couples shouldn't marry and dislike folks with a healthy expression of melanin in their skin. We should feel sorry for people who think that way."

The woman added, "And we don't want to attract attention and wind up in... that place." She was referring to Rightweigh.

"I know." Sara said with a sigh. The two were holding hands and she placed her hand on theirs. "Go, do your shopping. Buy sensible items, then go home and make a good nutritious meal." She reached into her bag and took out a wrinkled nutrition pamphlet. "Here take this. Use it when you shop. And come on Sunday. My father is preparing a beautiful sermon."

Both Sara Allen and her father knew Rightweigh and Ruth Bracket well. Bracket invited Sara to the Rightweigh opening for a red-carpet tour of the new facility and a long diatribe on her father's misguided efforts to keep the needy from the medical help they needed. Sara didn't buy it. She knew that a person's weight is no single measure of their health. It was a question of human rights. The people Sara was trying to help were victims, not perpetrators. If anyone was to blame for poor health and extreme obesity, it was capitalism and the fast food industry. Her father would say, "It's not a disease that is causing the trouble in our world, it is dis-ease. We have become foreigners in God's garden."

Determined to help people avoid Rightweigh, Sara mounted her own campaign. That's what she was doing that day when Ed came into the restaurant.

And still no one noticed Ed as he stood at the front of the store scowling at an official-looking regulation government sign above the counter:

NOTICE
SOME FAST FOODS CAN BE
DANGEROUS TO YOUR HEALTH

Another only slightly more friendly and much smaller sign:

ONE SINGLE PORTION ORDER
PER CUSTOMER RECOMMENDED

Ed stepped boldly up to the counter. The girl behind the cash couldn't have been more than seventeen. Ed's appearance—especially the tea cozy—gave her pause, but she managed a sweet smile. "Good afternoon, sir."

Ed tried smoothing things through first and smiled back. "Hi there. I'll be having two double double burgers, two large fries, four large shakes, two vanilla and two chocolate..."

He stopped short when the manager, a small brown-toothed man in his forties stepped in pushing the girl aside. He gave Ed a good once over, then said with a smirk, "Where did *you* come from?"

Ed recognized the type. His smile vanished. "A very large stork brought me" he said and continued addressing the now trembling girl. "And six turnovers, three apple and three cherry and..."

"How can you let yourself go like that?" the manager wanted to know.

"It grows on you." He smiled defiantly and continued his order. "That's three apple and three cherry turnovers and..."

The manager's smirk turned into a grimace. "We don't have all that stuff."

"Yes you do," Ed said. "You've got some of it stuck in your moustache, and you can super-size that for me."

"We don't super-size any more. Besides," and he pointed at Ed's paunch, "you could live on what you have there for a week." Then he looked past Ed's right shoulder and called out, "Next please," though there was no one there.

Now Ed wished he'd brought along the chocolate cocktails. So far things had been relatively civil. The growing disturbance hadn't reached Sara and the big couple at the back yet. But then Ed reached over, grabbed the man by his shirt collar and pulled him into a tight face-to-face. "Listen bud," he said, "I'm in no mood to fool around. Now snap to it. And I'll have a sundae with hot fudge sauce and peanuts while I'm waiting."

Unaccustomed to real confrontation, the man capitulated immediately. "Yes, sir, coming right up, sir. Yes sir," and he scurried off to the kitchen in the back.

Ed looked at the girl. She offered a trembling smile, but he thought she might burst into tears any second. A thought occurred, and he called out to the kitchen, "and make that to go." Now he had the attention of the few other people in the place. Ed took out his money and counted it. "How much do I owe you?" he said to the girl who had assumed they were being robbed.

"What?" she said.

Sara succeeded with the couple at the back and they were leaving when she heard Ed's commands and came up to him. "Sir, I want you to know that I can help you in this time of need and..."

Ed turned to her so abruptly that it set her back half a step. Then she recognized him. "I know you."

As soon as Ed laid eyes on Sara, he broke into his big charming, sincere grin. "Hi there."

"I thought they sentenced you to ten kilos in Rightweigh?"

"You remembered!"

"What are you doing *here*?"

"Picking up takeout. But if you know of a better place where we can be alone..."

"I believe it would be in your own best interests to..."

Right then Ed realized that he had lost track of his purpose and peered into the kitchen to see how his order was coming. Instead, he saw the staff huddled at the back and the manager talking on the phone.

"Aw shit!" he said.

Sara saw them too. "Are you committing a crime here?"

"If wanting three squares a day is a crime, then sue me," and he heard sirens in the distance.

"Hey," he called out to the back. "How about that order?"

No one moved.

Ed was now at the end of his good cheer. In one smooth motion and without thinking, he reached up inside his mother's blouse, took out the green spray-paint can and brandished it threateningly. It could have just as easily been a jar of peanut butter. It was Ed's performance more than anything that convinced everyone in the room that they were now in mortal danger.

One employee at the back of the kitchen screamed, "He's got a bomb!"

"Oh, for Christ's sake," Ed said and, in an amazingly athletic move mounted the counter, swung himself over and headed for the kitchen.

"What are you doing?" Sara asked.

"I'm getting it myself."

"You don't know how to work those machines. Besides, the police are coming."

She was right. He leapt back over the counter then went to a blank wall and sprayed the words "EAT THIS!" In foot-high letters across the bare expanse.

"Oh, that's clever." Sara's comment was cutting. "That's exactly the behaviour that caused all this trouble in the first place."

Ed was about to start a second message on an adjacent wall when Sara grabbed him by the arm and dragged him toward the door. "Come on, you'll get arrested, which won't do *anyone* any good. Where's your car?"

"Can we take yours?"

"I came on the subway."

"I hate these people," Ed said, stumbling along with her.

"Yes, yes, I know, let's go," and the two pushed through the front door into the parking lot.

The sirens were closer now. Maybe there was still time to get away.

Good, the car was still running. The two climbed in, and Sara immediately buckled her seat belt.

Ed squealed out of there.

Ed lurched the car into the street and caromed away from the scene of the crime. Sara braced herself against the door and eyed the abandoned chocolate cocktails rolling back and forth on the back seat. "You'd kill innocent people just to get something to eat?"

"Those wouldn't hurt anybody. Damn things don't even work, they were just for show."

Sara reached back, picked up one of the chocolate cocktails and inspected it.

Ed pulled on the wheel, trying to keep the big car under control. Sara scrutinized Ed carefully as he worked the vehicle through the narrow streets. He flashed her another smile. She stiffened with an indignation she suspected he already knew was false. She looked out the back for the police.

"You can slow down, there's nobody following us. They probably don't even have a description of the car."

Ed eased off on the gas. It was a good idea, find some traffic, blend in with it. "Want to come to my place?" he said.

"Isn't that where they will look first?"

"Good point, but I doubt it. It's, um, my mom's

place."

"You live with your mother?"

"No, I live in the Dominican Republic. I'm just visiting."

"Oh." That explained a lot. "How long have you been here?" she asked.

Ed had to think. "Jesus, that was only the day before yesterday... not even two days yet."

Now she understood the woman's blouse, unkempt hair and the two-day stubble. The tea cozy. "Walked right into it, did you?"

"Yeah, kinda."

"What are you going to do if you get caught?"

"Then I'll escape again."

"You *escaped*? From Rightweigh?"

"It was a piece of cake... so to speak." She looked again at the chocolate cocktail, rolled it over in her hand. "I haven't eaten in two days," Ed proclaimed, "I'm fighting for my right to go shopping." He slowed down and gave her a long look.

At that moment Sara made the snap decision to help him. "Turn left at the next light."

"Where are we going?"

"Someplace safe."

Ed liked her spunk.

--

By the time the police arrived in force, Ed and Sara were long gone. An explosive device had been reported, so the cops crouched behind their cruisers in the parking lot and waited for the bomb squad to show up.

The bomb squad robot couldn't figure out whether the door opened out or in so the police took a chance and went in, guns drawn. After interviewing the staff, they put descriptions of Ed, his "hostage" and Mom's car out in an all-points bulletin.

Lardner and Bailey heard the radio chatter. It wasn't until they broadcast Ed's description that Lardner realized, to his dismay, the fugitive terrorist was one of "his people". He knew it could turn into a circus.

Bailey was champing at the bit. "I'll bet he heads east," he said.

"Why?" Lardner wasn't really all that enthusiastic about joining in a high-speed fiasco, but he should probably make some effort.

"More escape routes that way."

Lardner said nothing as Bailey hit the siren, made an alarming 'U' turn and floored it.

Sara studied Ed as he did his best to keep their route erratic and impossible to follow. As he cut through narrow residential side streets and plunged down obscure lanes, she stared at the chocolate cocktail, then blurted "Civil disobedience!"

"What?"

"You know, Mohandas Karamchand Gandhi, Martin Luther King, civil disobedience. Why didn't *I* think of it? The non-violent refusal of co-operation with oppression and tyranny."

"Uh, okay," Ed said. "but what I need to figure out right now is where we're going."

"My place." Sara turned to look out the back again and saw a police cruiser following about a block and a half away, then another. She turned back to Ed with a strangely gleeful look. "If we have to get arrested fighting for our liberty, then so be it. Better speed up again."

"Why?"

"Because now they're back there."

"Shit!" Ed stepped on it.

"If we're doing this together," Sara held out her hand, "we might as well know each other. My name's Sara Allen."

Ed threw the car around a corner, then glanced at her hand. "Yeah, good, but I'm kinda busy here at the moment."

"Nice gloves." she flashed him an ambrosial smile that, for an instant, made him forget what they were doing.

He pulled the gloves off and threw them into the back seat, then awkwardly shook Sara's hand. "Ed Miller" he said, just making it between two parked cars.

She had a surprisingly firm grip. "Hello Eddie, it's nice to know you," and she looked out the back to see the police slow down to negotiate the narrow space between the cars.

Ed didn't let anyone call him Eddie. But this was no time to quibble. He would set her straight later, when they had a peaceful moment to get to know each other better, if there was to be such a time. He squealed the car around another corner onto a wider street and sped up, weaving in and out of traffic.

When the police cruisers were momentarily out of sight Ed suddenly turned the car down an alley towards a one-way street that would double them back the way they'd come. It was his reliable old trick.

"Where are you going?"

"Confound and confuse," was all he said, but Sara got it. It was risky but clever. She was becoming dangerously impressed with this man. "Jesus, all I did was order a takeout lunch for two!" he said.

"That was a lunch for five you ordered, not two." There was a reprimand in her voice, and she regretted it immediately. "If you'd just ordered a simple hamburger..."

"It's not just me, there's another guy."

"Oh." She looked again at the chocolate cocktail.

"Be careful with that. It would be just my luck that this one actually..." At that instant their eyes met. Ed was losing his resolve to avoid intelligent women. Sara never realized she had such a strong penchant for adventure.

"Let me help you," she breathed. Her offer was sincere, the effect seductive. Ed ripped his eyes away from her to the road. "Maybe we can discuss that when we get.... somewhere."

"Make a left at the next light, then the next left, after that." Sara glanced out the back. Still no cops following. "They've got our license number by now," she warned.

"It's not *our* license number, it's not even *my* license number, it's my mom's license number."

"Oh" and Sara fiddled idly with the cocktail. "Left here," she said and when he made the turn she dropped the cocktail, grabbed for it and pulled on the fuse. There was a pop and a spray of sparks.

"Uh oh," was all Sara could say.

"Toss it out," Ed yelled. "Toss it out!" He fumbled desperately with the power window buttons. Thinking fast, she closed her eyes and tossed the lively little handful over her shoulder, then scrunched as far down in her seat as she could. The cocktail landed on the rear window deck and spun and fizzled as expanding butane squeezed out through any hole it could find, creating a fine spray of putrid chocolate sauce. It was as if the car was being spray painted a stinking greenish brown from the inside. The windows, seats, windshield, dash, Ed and Sara took on the colour of spoiled confectioner's crude sludge.

Unable to see out, Ed frantically wiped a small area

of the windshield clear, only to have it covered again. They were flying blind. The loud boom they both expected never happened, but the sour shower didn't peter out for almost a full minute. Finally, Ed cleared a small spot in the windshield and pulled the car over to the curb as the spent cocktail burbled quietly on the back deck.

Silence.

No police sirens. A dog barked a block away.

"Where are we?" Sara said.

Ed peered out the small spot in front of him. "Toronto," he said.

Sara laughed.

Ed laughed. "You look like you've had a serious outhouse accident."

She wiped a small clear spot on the windshield for herself and peered out.

"It's not far now," she said and Ed took off his tea cozy and used it to wipe his spot on the windshield bigger and clearer. "Take the alley on the left," she said. "I think if we just go slow we'll be okay."

Ed pulled out and made the turn into the narrow alley. Then they saw a police roadblock up ahead.

"Whoops!" Ed exclaimed and quickly took a last chance right turn down a narrow alley straight into disaster. It wasn't exactly a route designed for vehicular traffic. Garbage bins and piles of crates everywhere. "Oh, perfect." Ed screeched the car to a stop, then slumped down in his seat. "The fuckers must have radios."

"*LANGUAGE!*" Sara said firmly.

"Sorry."

"Of course they have radios," Sara said. "They're the police. Get out. It's not far. I don't think they've seen us yet."

Sara and Ed piled from the car and were headed half-way down the alley toward an open street when Ed stopped. "Wait." They heard sirens all around. "They'll have this alley covered too." Ed tried a rear exit from a sporting goods store. Locked. He tried another. Locked. He spotted a fire escape that luckily came all the way down to the ground. He grabbed Sara and pulled her to the steel stairs and up to the second floor, then to the third and a small wooden roof deck.

From there they could see police cars pulling into the mouth of the alley, blocking Ed's mom's car. Ed threw open a door, and the two plunged down some stairs, into a small apartment and through the dark past five women folding pierogies—Ed could only grab and eat two—then on to another even darker room where men were playing cards and smoking, then out to a main front room crammed with South Asian women answering phones and a stairway that took them back down the front of the building to the street. Hardly anyone paid them any attention. It was as though chocolate covered fugitives barged through their workplace all the time.

Before venturing out, they fell against the wall to catch their breath.

"Maybe we should just talk to the police," Sara said. "You know, explain what happened."

"Obviously you've never tried that."

"What's the worst thing that can happen?"

When Ed truly felt trapped, he acted silly. It was how he released the tension and could think straight. "Hmm... Let's see, the worst thing that can happen?" He pressed his cheek against the dirty window glass and saw a small group of cops waiting in ambush for them at the end of the street. "The worst thing would be that the elastic in my underwear gives out at the Santa

Claus Parade. I hate that. It's cold and snowing. I've probably got kids..."

"I'm serious." Sara said, failing to suppress a laugh. "This is important."

"Ever actually *have* the elastic in your underwear give out on you when you're real busy?"

"Stop it."

He looked the other way down the street. Nothing. "I think we're okay." He pushed the door open, and they moved carefully away from the action. In a few seconds, they were gone.

--

By the time Lardner and Bailey showed up, the alley had filled with cops, guns drawn, and Ed's mom's car thoroughly surrounded. The cops couldn't see if there was anyone in the car.

"Okay, okay, hold up. Ease off fellas," Lardner took a bull horn away from one man as he pushed his way through and walked right up to Ed's mom's car. He looked into the empty car through Ed's clear spot on the windshield, then up and around. "Any sign of the hostage?" The blank-faced cops stood there. Some of them holstered their guns. Bailey waved one of the senior uniformed cops over and pointed to people hanging out of upper-story windows. "Get three or four of the guys to conversate with the community," he ordered. "Take statements from anyone who saw anything."

Lardner wanted to get into Ed's mom's car behind the wheel, look behind the visor for an I.D., check the glove box, but he saw that the chocolate mess was everywhere and thought better of it. He noticed the stressed driver's seat back with a sigh, then set about searching the car as best he could without touching the goo. He found the ownership and insurance in the name of Lydia Fischer in the glove box and noted the address. Good. All he had to do was go over there where he'd be sure to pick up the trail of Ed Miller if not the man himself.

Sanctuary

Sara was happy to find her father out of his bed, and at work in his study. "Daddy?" She stood reverently at the door.

"Yes, dear?" Father Allen didn't look up. He was preparing a new sermon inspired by the visitation the night before.

"Did *He* come?" Sara was referring to Jesus Christ. It was her way of checking into her father's state of mind. Sara never really believed that Jesus appeared before her father in any real sense, but if her father said he saw Jesus, then, he saw Jesus.

"Yes, He did dear," he said, and she relaxed a bit. His depression had eased considerably since she'd last checked on him. The good Father scowled, crumpled up the draft he was working on and started another.

"Sorry Daddy." Sara backed away. "I didn't mean to..."

"No, no, you're not interrupting." He smoothed his hair. "It's so difficult to be positive. What's the point of pretending we can help people if I can't even..."

"I've got someone here I think you'd like to meet." She pulled Ed forward. "This man seeks sanctuary."

"Sanctuary?" Father Allen was intrigued. Sara knew how to push her father's buttons.

Father Allen saw the guck in his daughter's hair, on

her face and clothing. "What the devil happened to you?" He looked at Ed.

Sara smiled. "This is Eddie Miller." The Father detected some pride in her introduction. Ed was uneasy in religious surroundings.

Ed flashed Father Allen an uncertain smile and advanced with his hand out. "Ed Sir, Ed Miller," he said in his most respectful tone.

The Father got halfway up and was about to shake Ed's hand when he noticed that Ed too was covered with slimy chocolate goo and pulled back. "You aren't in trouble with the police are you?"

"Hardly anybody ever gets in trouble *with* the police." Ed regretted the remark the moment he said it. He added a quick, respectful, "Sir."

Father Allen scrutinized Ed, then laughed. "And just where did you find this bright young smart Alec?"

"Daddy, Eddie escaped from Rightweigh."

"You don't say." Father Allen said, suddenly serious.

"Last night." Sara beamed.

"By all the saints above." The Father leaned across his desk and grasped Ed's hand in both of his, goo or no goo. "Congratulations my son."

"I think he can help us." Sara said. Father Allen indicated one of the big chairs facing his desk. "Sit down."

"Actually, I was kind of hoping that *you* could help *me*," Ed said hesitantly, reluctant to sit in the leather chair mucked up as he was.

But Father Allen came around his desk and all but pushed him into it. "We can help each other, I'm sure."

"Daddy, I think Eddie is the person we've been waiting for." Sara placed a careful hand on the high back of Ed's chair as her father sniffed his own hand, then pulled out a hanky and wiped off the guck. "I think perhaps the first order of business should be a good hot shower for both of you." Sara blushed a bright pink at this, but in the subdued light, no one noticed.

--

Kent Nason and Sally Bean arrived on the scene just in time to capture video of Ed's mom's car being towed away. Lardner was getting started on the incident report in his car half a block from the scene when their First News van zoomed past. He was glad they didn't notice him.

Bailey had taken two men and struck out on his own to look through the neighbourhood, following a hunch that led him to the nearby Church of the Safe Way. Bailey knew well of this notorious gathering place.

Father Allen had heard Ed's story—or at least as much of it as Ed thought wise to reveal—and decided that the young man's unexpected appearance was an act of God. He was fixing a celebratory lunch when he caught sight of activity in the main hall of the church across the way. Quickly, he threw on a vestment and waved to Sara and Ed as he went out the back door. "You two wait here, I'll see what's going on."

Ed and Sara sat at the kitchen table. The unspoken fear between them was that the police had tracked them after all.

--

From a vantage point behind the choir stall, Father Allen watched the three cops looking behind doors and under pews.

Churches are designed to intimidate, to carry and amplify the voice of a speaker at the altar. It is an effect that folks with a need to dominate others have used for thousands of years. It's why early religious rites were performed in large echoey caves painted in magical images—to mystify and frighten.

Father Allen moved to the sweet spot at the pulpit and summoned his best basso profundo. "Can I be of some aid to you men?"

There was a momentary confusion as the cops attempted to determine where the voice was coming from. Father Allen stepped down and they all turned at once to face him. "We're looking for someone," Bailey said lamely.

"The only one you'll find here, my son, is Jesus." The Father smiled.

Deciding he was no threat, the police continued their search.

Father Allen remained pleasant one more time around. "May I see your search warrant?"

"We don't need a search warrant," Bailey said as he got down on one knee to look under several rows of pews at once. "There is reasonable cause."

"Oh, really?" Now the Father's voice took on a distinct edge.

Bailey stood and confronted the Father. "We have reason to believe you are harbouring a fugitive."

"And I believe you'd better get the hell out of here before I inform your commanding officer that you have conducted an illegal search of private property *without* a warrant." Father Allen smiled again, but it was no longer friendly.

The cops stopped what they were doing and looked to Bailey for leadership.

Bailey deflated, realized the truth of the Father's

words and waved weakly to his men, "Let's go. He's not here, anyway." And they left without so much as another glance at the Father. Bailey didn't like being shot down this way in front of his men.

Through a clear section in the stained glass, Father Allen watched the cops retreat all the way down the front sidewalk. Only then did the Father's shoulders drop and he let out a deep sigh.

Father Allen opened the back door of the church and ran straight into Sara.

"That was close," Sara said.

"Those bereft of faith and weak of mind are easily swayed." Father Allen looked around. "Where's our friend?"

Sara looked around. "Eddie?" she called. There was no reply. "Eddie!"

She never saw Ed leave her side, scurry across the parking lot and vanish into the neighbourhood. The police would now have his mom's address from the car registration papers in the glove box.

He had to warn Lou.

The Man Who Fell To Earth

Bailey and Lardner pulled up in front of Ed's mom's building. Bailey had the strange compulsion many cops have to park on the sidewalk when it isn't necessary. Lardner looked up at the building, then watched Bailey work on his stubborn hangnail. "What about if you bite someone else's nail?" he asked.

"What?"

"I mean suppose, say, your girlfriend's asleep beside you and you see a nail sticking out and say you just bite it off. Does that make you a cannibal?"

Bailey thought about this for a second then said, "Do you swallow it?"

"Let's say you do, yeah."

"Oh, well, definitely. I mean that's officially eating somebody, isn't it?"

Lardner realized that if he'd taken the time to think about it, he wouldn't have asked. "Let's go," and they got out and went to the lobby.

Lardner ran his finger down the rows of apartment numbers, but Bailey stopped him before he could press number 304. "Hold it. Better we don't let him know we're comin'".

"Right." Lardner saw the sense of this and let his partner take the lead.

Bailey pressed one of the other intercom buttons at random. "Hello?" a man's voice crackled over the speaker.

"Collecting for the paper." Bailey said, trying unsuccessfully to simulate a teenager's voice.

"Up yours." Was the gruff reply followed by a loud click.

"Apparently not an obvious follower of concurrent affairs," Bailey said with a superior chuckle and pressed another button. Lardner idly tried the door to find it open. He was about to let Bailey in on this new information when a woman's voice wheezed through the broken grill work. "Yeah?"

"Telegram," Bailey announced.

"Telegram?"

"Yes, Ma'am."

"Read it" the woman said.

"Uh, well... uh... it's personal."

"Are you alone down there?"

"Uh, yeah."

"Well, I'm alone up here, so read it."

Only then did Bailey notice Lardner holding the door open. "Oh, sorry Ma'am, wrong address." He blurted, and the two headed for the elevators. When he noticed Bailey unsnap the catch on his holster, Lardner thought better of bringing him along. "Maybe one of us better stay down here, you know, cover the exits," he suggested.

"Huh?"

"In case he gives me the slip."

"Yeah, right. Good idea."

Lardner watched his partner cross back through the lobby and head for the car. A bad feeling was growing in him about all of this, but he couldn't quite put his finger on what it was.

Lardner knocked quietly on Ed's mom's door. There was no answer, but he thought he could hear a sound, snoring maybe. He noticed the popped door lock. It opened easily.

Enough light spilled in from the street that Lardner could make out the big man asleep on the sofa. He checked Lou against the two mug shots. "Jesus, they're right about one thing," he mumbled to himself, "they do all look the same." He thought he'd said this quietly enough, but Lou snorted and looked up at Lardner through swollen eyes then came awake with a start. "Edward Miller?" Lardner asked.

"I'm not going back there!" Lou gasped and grabbed at the sofa. Alarmed by the sudden action, Porky leapt from Lou's chest and ran across the room into the shadows.

Lardner pulled out his police ID and showed it to Lou. "Lieutenant. Bill Lard..."

"I'm not going back!" Lou hollered, then jumped up and wobbled backwards across the room. "No!"

"Mister Miller, if you cooperate I'll make sure no one harms you in any..."

But the situation was already out of control. Lou backed up again, stumbled over Porky and with nothing more than a slight gasp tumbled backwards through the open window, over the low railing, and disappeared silently out into the night.

Lardner froze in his tracks. "Holy shit!" He'd seen a lot of strange and violent things in his time, but this took him completely by surprise. His legs didn't want to work. It was like walking through knee-high liquid honey as he went to the window, dreading what he would see in the street below.

Bailey was finally prying the hangnail from his left thumb when the big man hit. There was a curious rush of air, then Lou landed on his back smack in the middle of the police car with such a force that the vehicle looked like it had been in a crusher. Inside, Bailey's world stopped.

Lardner leaned over the railing and looked down to see Lou sprawled on a flattened car below. He was so shaken that he could hardly manipulate his phone. He gave the dispatcher the address and added, "Poor bugger's probably dead, but you better get an ambulance out here ASAP." It had all been so sudden that, by the time Lardner made it down to the street, a crowd hadn't even gathered.

Lardner was shocked to see Lou's arm move, then his leg. Upon closer examination, he realized Lou wasn't even unconscious! Lou looked at Lardner and said in a clear voice, "I was sure there was some of that raisin bread left..."

Lardner peered up at the building and marvelled at the great height from which Lou had plummeted.

"Take it easy big fella, you've had quite a fall." He looked around for the ambulance. "Where the hell are those guys?" It hadn't been two minutes since the incident, but to Lardner it seemed like two hours. Some passers-by and neighbours were congealing across the street. Lardner heard distant sirens. "Finally," he muttered. Then the police radio inside the demolished car crackled, and Lardner realized that this was *his* car. He peered in, looking for Bailey.

Within the blackness of the police car, Bailey regained consciousness, and his mind searched for information. For the longest time he thought he'd been a ground victim in a plane crash and wondered why he hadn't heard jet engines before the impact. He listened for the moans and groans and outcries of the injured and dying, but all he could hear was a voice. A man's voice. "Ray?" It was Lardner. "You in there Ray, talk to me!"

"Aggbahh!" Bailey said. His throat was full of

saliva... no, wait, it was his tongue. It had somehow folded back and slid halfway down his throat. He coughed, but the compressed prison that used to be the police car pressed back. Another stifled cough, and he brought up his tongue. It hurt like hell. He managed a gurgling, "Bill! Hey, Bill!"

It relieved Lardner to hear his partner's voice. He tried to get a better view into the wreck. "Hang in there, Ray, we'll get you out."

It was difficult for Bailey to speak with his chin lodged in the middle of his chest. "What the fuck happened?"

Explaining what had happened to Bailey right now would not be productive, so all Lardner said was "Hang on. Help's on the way."

The paramedics arrived and Lou spoke as they rolled him from the car to a stretcher. "I... I'm alive!" he said and gave the ambulance attendant a stupid grin.

A glorious red and purple sunset born of industrial pollution was just wrapping up in the west when Ed emerged from an alley across the street to stand behind the group of onlookers. It was impossible to tell what was going on, but as he moved closer to the ambulance, he saw them wheel Lou toward him on the stretcher. Lou sat up and give an onlooker a goofy smile and again proclaimed, "I'm alive!"

The paramedic gently pushed him back down and explained, "Just relax now, we gotta see if you fit in our bus here." Ed wanted to go to Lou, but he knew the police would be all over him. Best to blend quietly back into the crowd.

As he moved away from the scene, he almost tripped over Porky who had made her way through open doors to the street, found his friendly scent in the gathering and was now rubbing against his leg meowing feebly. "Come on girl, we'd better get out of here." He picked her up and disappeared down an alley and away from his mom's apartment, a refuge to which he could never return.

A few minutes later a mechanic arrived at the scene of Detective Bailey's dilemma and Lardner filled him in on their problem.

"There's somebody *in* there?" The mechanic said, looking at the mangled car.

"Can ya just hurry up?" Lardner was becoming impatient.

"Yeah, yeah. It's gonna take a while." The mechanic said and went to his truck to retrieve the jaws of life. Lardner couldn't imagine the extent of Bailey's injuries. He thought the best thing would be to keep up a running dialogue with his partner, to keep him from falling unconscious. "Hey Ray, you still with me boy?"

"You think we could get some lights on in here?"

Lardner was glad to hear that his partner was alert. "Good man. Hang in there, we're working on it." No one got killed. Maybe everything would be all right.

With the help of uniformed cops, Lardner kept the crowd back while the mechanic cut Bailey from the car. A second ambulance arrived, and Lardner rode with Bailey to the hospital.

--

At one point, as they wheeled Bailey through the emergency ward of St Michael's Hospital, he passed right by Lou who looked at him and announced "I'm alive!". Bailey didn't pay any attention.

Lardner intended to confirm the prisoner's identity by checking the mug shots in a better light, but he forgot to do this when he learned that Lou was in perfect health. "It's not possible. This man couldn't have taken the fall you describe." The doctor, perturbed at Lardner for wasting his time, explained, "Aside from some bruises and a few scratches, an excess of greasy foods and a severe lack of exercise, the only thing wrong with this patient is that he has extremely bad breath. What would you like me to do with him now?" He waved his arm at the crowded hallway. "He's taking up valuable space."

Lardner recalled seeing four Rightweigh personnel gathered outside the hospital cafeteria on his way in. Maybe they could transport the prisoner back to Rightweigh, but before he could leave, Lou grabbed his arm and informed him, "I'm alive!"

"Yeah, good," a distracted Lardner said. "You have no idea how good that is," and he patted Lou on the shoulder.

As soon as they had loaded Lou into the back of a van, one of the Rightweigh men called ahead with the incorrect report that Edward Miller was in custody.

The doctor had been right. It was impossible that Lou could have fallen three stories and survived unscathed. Actually, Lou *wa*s fatally injured in the fall but his shattered bones, his punctured lung and deeply damaged spleen had regenerated so quickly that he never missed a heartbeat or a breath. It was all part of the mystery of Lou Kennedy that was to deepen in the hours to come.

Lardner found Bailey asleep under sedation on a gurney in a back hall of the maternity ward. He checked that he was being taken care of adequately, then told the nurse he was going for coffee. But he figured Bailey was in good hands, so he went home to bed instead.

--

It delighted Bracket to learn that her men had returned Lou Kennedy and not Edward Miller. She had him brought to her office on the second floor of the administration building just to make sure. As soon as she laid eyes on the poor soul, she knew her problems were over. Knowing nothing of the accident, she took his minor scratches and bruises to be signs of mistreatment by the police. This was an opportunity to learn what Lou Kennedy had to say about things. "Tell me something Mr. Kennedy." She was unusually calm given the hour. "Do you feel you're mistreated here at Rightweigh?"

Lou looked at her and smiled but said nothing.

She decided to dumb it down. "Yes, well..." She pointed to Ed's picture. "Do you know where Mister Miller is right now?"

"I'm alive!" Lou told her.

Good. He's an idiot. She waved a long finger at Lou's guards. "Take him to Dr. Milrot so he can check this man out. And be gentle." Then she spoke to Lou as if he were four-and-a-half. "Our main concern here at Rightweigh is always the welfare of the patient, isn't it Mr. Kennedy?" She afforded him a weak smile, then watched as the guards took him out.

--

Kent Nason's story went on the air later that day. It was less than two minutes long but it was the first piece featuring the disenfranchised overweight and a first tentative attempt to push back.

Nason had interviewed several witnesses at Ed's burger raid, but it was seventy-one-year-old Emma

Wheeler's summary of events that really got people's attention. Emma cracked a denture and got a swollen lip when she collided with the table she was trying to duck under so she slurred her words when she tried to say "That man, that man!" and it came out as "FATMAN! FATMAN!"

Everyone at City TV chuckled briefly and one of the staff artists did a quick sketch of a rotund man in a cape and tights with a large "F" on his chest. Canadian TV leaks over the border into the U.S., and minutes after Nason's piece aired, a buzz ran through the offices of The National Association to Advance Fat Acceptance in Detroit.

--

Ed heard none of this. He was preoccupied with his current dilemma of no place to go. Weakened by a serious lack of protein, tired and depressed by his failure to save his friend Lou, Ed debated returning to The Church of the Safe Way. Though he was wary of the whole religious thing, he couldn't get Sara out of his mind. He knew they wanted to help him, but *what* could he do in return?

He stuck mainly to the back streets where the lighting was poor, where the crack and heroin addicts congregated in hushed bunches in parks and on the littered street corners, doing their sad little deals with each other. Ed felt safe here. In a neighbourhood where *everybody* was assumed to be a criminal, he would attract less attention.

He slumped, exhausted, on a park bench. He'd gotten no sleep on the plane and in custody, and in a few minutes he fell over, unconscious with hunger and fatigue. Porky fell asleep on his chest.

It was a warm night and Ed dreamed that he was playing badminton with the two topless girls back on the beach in Punta Cana. In his dream he was younger and able to sip a Mai Tai while returning each volley with grace. And there was his dad's bar, now named *Ed's Fabulous Cabana on the Beach* and magically relocated to the head of the big dock instead of the rickety little one by the road where it really was. Porky was there too, her eyes constantly on the badminton shuttlecock.

--

News broadcasts of the notorious masked anti-hero, Fatman had made its way to Detective Bailey asleep on a gurney in a noisy hallway of St. Michael's Hospital. He was dreaming he was on foot in hot pursuit of Fatman. It frustrated him that someone this big could stay so well ahead, but every time he rounded a corner, Fatman seemed to be disappearing around the next.

Then luck was with him. Fatman had unwittingly run into a blind alley. Bailey stumbled into the middle of the tiny cul-de-sac, out of breath. Under the single streetlight, the fugitive was nowhere to be seen. How could someone so big be hiding here in an empty alley?

A sound echoed. Bailey looked wildly about, then up in time to see that Fatman, who had apparently tried to escape by climbing the sheer wall, had lost his grip and was now plummeting towards him.

Bailey threw up his hands to protect himself. But instead of being crushed, amazingly, he caught the huge suspect and was now holding the fugitive by the neck at arm's length. Bailey beamed proudly, then, holding his prey in one hand, he ripped the mask from his face and was about to see his secret identity when Fatman promptly changed into a giant oily Italian salami that slid from Bailey's grasp, sprouted legs and ran away back down the alley into the night. Bailey stumbled painfully back against the wall and slumped down. His eyes snapped open and he saw that he was awkwardly propped on the hospital gurney in the busy hospital hallway. "What the fuck am I doing here?" he said, and a soft female voice answered him from behind.

"We didn't have a room available when you came in but we can observe you just as well here as in a ward."

When Bailey turned his head to see the source of the voice, an excruciating pain shot down his neck and through his body. Thankfully, she got up and came to him.

"I gotta get back on duty," Bailey said struggling raise himself, but his chest hurt deeply and lightning bolts of pain exploded in his arms.

The nurse said, "You are a very lucky man. We get people flown in here who have hit a moose and they rarely fare well at all."

"Is that what happened?" Bailey tried to imagine a moose in the centre of town.

"I'm not sure exactly what happened, but..."

Bailey tried again to get up but only managed an agonizing sitting position on the edge of the gurney. Any of the Clint Eastwood or Bruce Willis or Vin Diesel characters he admired so much would have endured anything to do the job and so would he.

"You should rest," the nurse protested, but Bailey pushed her away.

"Can't," he said, and got himself to his throbbing feet, spotted his clothes on a chair and began painfully pulling them on. "It's a dirty city out there and it must be cleaned up." In minutes Bailey was out of there, angry and loaded for bear. Well, he wasn't loaded. Lardner had wisely taken custody of his weapon. It was impossible to know what Bailey might do with a firearm in his battered, sedated and irrational state.

And just as Bailey was hailing a cab in front of the hospital Lou Kennedy sat up on a cot in the back of Milrot's lab, opened his eyes, smiled, and said enthusiastically to the black air, "I'm alive!"

--

Lardner's wife Joan was already asleep, as she almost always was by the time he got in. He undressed in the bathroom so the clatter of belt buckles, keys and shoulder holster wouldn't wake her and he thought the same thing he always thought in this part of his day: that he hardly knew his wife anymore. Since he'd started on the cupcake patrol, all he saw of her was the back of her head. "Jesus," he thought, "now *I'm* even calling it the cupcake patrol."

He finally fell asleep to dream of real police work.

In the morning Joan would be gone and he would curse himself for becoming that unconscious man who lay beside her in the dark, week after week. He would get up, get dressed and go to work with no breakfast or even coffee.

Fat's

At about two in the morning, Ed awoke from his brief and fitful sleep on the park bench to a pair of undernourished hookers having an argument. One was screaming something about how the other was "probably not even gettin' five fuckin' bucks a throw" and the other one was yelling something about, "If you had five goddamn feckin' bucks you might get some feckin' teeth for yer feckin' head." And the first one declaired, "I don't need no fuckin' teeth, better for business."

While they shrieked at each other in front of the bleary-eyed Ed and a yawning Porky, Ed's stomach growled something fierce. He had to get something to eat soon.

That's when he spotted "Fat's".

First, he just saw the sign. Four big faded green letters painted on a bright yellow background half a block away lit by two flickering sodium vapour lamps.

Was this a safe harbour? The bar, or whatever it was, was attached to the sleazy Kingston Hotel, a strangely elegant Victorian building that could once have been a foreign embassy but now advertised ALL LIVE NUDES NGHTLY.

Ed picked up Porky and made his way toward the beacon. As he drew closer, he could see anti-fat graffiti covering the entire building:

     GET OUT OF MY TOWN
and
     THINK OF THE CHILDREN
and
       EAT DICK

and a meek and faded counter attack

    BRING BACK BUTTERSCOTCH

  The place appeared to be closed, the doors and windows boarded up. Even the boards were boarded up. Ed went around to the side and pulled on an inconspicuous fire door. It was open.
  It took several seconds for his eyes to adjust to the subdued lighting. At first he thought the place was empty. Then he saw that the four or five large clients were simply being silent, skulking about pool tables or sitting tucked into dark corners. Behind the bar, a terribly thin, one-eyed barkeep hunched over a week old tabloid paper. Ed stepped up to the bar. The barkeep "eyed" him and Porky. "Real cute, what can I get for you?"
  "What have you got to eat?" Ed said stating his primary concern.
  "Nuthin'." The barkeep nodded to a sign.

     "DON'T EAT IT HERE!"
Ed noticed other signage:
     "NO FOOD ALLOWED!"
and
   "LITTLE BROTHER IS WATCHING."

  "What about a bag of chips, anything?"
  "Sorry," the barman muttered tickling Porky under

her chin, "I can give you a light beer but that's about it,"

Ed dug in his pocket and fished out a handful of change. "How much?"

"Two bucks."

Ed slapped two dollars down.

The mono-eyed barkeep gave him the eye, then leaned over and said in a hush, "Look, I have one microwavable burger. I can let you have that, but you gotta eat it outside."

Ed's heart leapt, and he quickly checked his change. "I'll take it, how much?"

The barman saw that Porky seemed to wait for his answer too. "It's on me."

Ed swooned at the thought of real food!

The barman looked furtively around, then bent down behind the bar and pried a floorboard loose.

"What the fuck's going on here man?" said Ed. It was a rhetorical question. He knew exactly what was going on.

The barman popped back up and put a bony finger to his lips. "Shh. Keep yer voice down."

"Has everybody gone crazy?" Ed whispered.

"You from outta town?"

"I've been away."

The barkeep held out his hand and said, "They call me Tapeworm,"

"Ed Miller," Ed said and shook Tapeworm's hand.

Tapeworm nodded at Ed's scrawny companion. "Who's yer friend here?"

"Oh, uh, Porky."

Tapeworm laughed, "Funny," then returned to the secret compartment in the floor. But before he could retrieve anything, the side door banged open and Bailey and two uniformed cops burst in.

Ed recognized Bailey right away from court, but now his suit was seriously rumpled and torn and his hair looked strange. The uniformed cops silently flanked the door.

"Okay, Bailey's here!" he barked. "Everybody line up against the wall!"

Tapeworm grabbed Porky and hid her under the bar. He knew what was about to happen. All the men obligingly put down their pool cues and lined up against the side wall. Ed's first impulse was to protest, but he realized this probably wasn't smart. He moved into line with the others.

Bailey perused the group. "Okay, empty your pockets." Everyone but Ed dumped the contents of their pockets onto the floor. Bailey came to stand at Ed's shoulder. "Okay mister, let's see what you got!"

Ed turned from the wall to face Bailey. "Didn't I see this in a movie?"

"Turn em out!" Bailey ordered.

Ed took his change from his pocket and showed it to Bailey.

A big man at the end of the line coughed. Bailey turned on him. "What did you say?"

The man protested, "I didn't say nothin'."

"What's your name?" Bailey barked.

"Uh, Wilson."

When Bailey grabbed Wilson by his jacket lapel and tried to pull him out of the line, the lapel ripped off in Bailey's hand. Wilson laughed stupidly and Bailey slapped him across the face with the lapel then threw his whole weight against the big man several times, incrementally shoving him toward the men's room at the back.

"Everybody wait here while I have a little chat with chubby."

Ed turned to a large comrade in green coveralls with the name "TINY" emblazoned in yellow on his pocket and whispered, "Didn't he get this from a movie?" Tiny was the biggest man in Fat's, so they had to nickname him Tiny. Topping out at something close to four hundred pounds, this mountain of a man, caster of vast shadows and frightener of small children, was the gentlest and most kind-hearted of souls you would ever want to know. As Bailey and Wilson clattered through the door into the toilet, Tiny leaned over to Ed and warned, "Shhh."

In the men's room, Wilson and Bailey played out the scene to perfection for the benefit of no one because everyone knew what was going on.

Bailey slammed the toilet stall doors a few times, then took the mug shots of Lou and Ed from his pocket and handed them to Wilson. "Seen either of these guys?" he asked, then put his foot up on a wastebasket and re-tied his shoe laces several times though they didn't require it.

"No, I don't think so..." Wilson's mind was on another aspect of the investigation. "Listen, instead of, you know, sluggin' me this time couldn't we just...?"

Bailey spotted the remains of a crumpled up Mars Bar wrapper sticking out of Wilson's pocket and grabbed it. "What's this?"

"One of them offered it to me for five bucks. I had to go along."

"Gimme the bar."

"I, I, I had to uh, eat it."

Bailey's frustration was clear. "I didn't *want* to," Wilson lied. "I had no choice. They were all watchin'. Didn't want to blow my cover."

Bailey folded the wrapper and put it in his pocket as evidence, then stepped back, pulled up his right sleeve and made a fist. "Okay, where do you want it?"

"Well, that's what I was askin' you about. Suppose I just go out holdin' my chin? Or what about a hard kick on the leg?" Wilson bent down to show Bailey his leg and when he wasn't looking Bailey delivered a solid uppercut to the jaw.

Not even Ed was surprised when Wilson came crashing through the door and stumbled across the floor, sprawling on his stomach unconscious in front of them. Bailey emerged rubbing his fist and headed for the door.

"Tell everybody we'll be back in an hour." He said over his shoulder, then left.

"This guy's an undercover cop," Ed said to Tapeworm when he was sure they were gone. "I saw the same movie they did."

"Yeah, I know," Tapeworm said. "He's not a cop though, he's a security guy from Rightweigh. Been here for months."

The men silently put on their jackets and packed up pool cues preparing to leave. Ed called to them, "Where are you guys going?" Not one of them responded. "You gonna just let them push you around like that?"

"Let 'em go man," Tapeworm said. "Times are bad. They just wanna get left alone. How long you been gone, anyway?"

"Too long."

--

As Lardner drove down the Parkway that morning, he had no way of knowing that Bailey had checked himself out of the hospital, and in a fit of vengeful confusion, gone straight over and busted Fat's

Poolroom. He would never know that Bailey had called Bracket at all hours.

Bracket thought of Bailey as a potential ally within the police force, but it was the first time she'd experienced his radical anti-fat sentiments. Bailey ranted that no one in his division took the obesity problem seriously, that Lardner was soft on the fat felons, adding, "The police are just humouring you." Then he blurted his suspicions about the Church of the Safe Way. She had long suspected Father Allen was doing more than giving solace to some people with a weight problem, but actively going against a Church never really appealed to her.

She got right out of bed and stood in her rail thin nakedness before her window and listened intently as Bailey revealed that the Church of the Safe Way had something to hide and that he was gathering evidence to secure a search warrant.

When she hung up, she bypassed her morning exercise, showered quickly, forgot about her ritual granola bar, unplugged her car before it was fully charged, and headed for the office.

For once she was there before William.

--

Bracket allowed the confusion of the police to go on. Lardner and Bailey thought they had apprehended Edward Miller and returned him to Rightweigh. Lou was of no concern, he was in Rightweigh voluntarily. But if they knew their prisoner was Lou Kennedy, they would want to question him as to the whereabouts of the fugitive Ed Miller. Bracket couldn't have that. God knows what Lou would say. She left things as they were and moved on. It was time to talk to that young news guy with the good ass. What was his name? She flipped back a page in her day planner. Kent Nason. She rang his number. If any of it were to become news, she wanted to control it.

She told Nason that she had been considering his proposal to shoot a documentary but that she was booked up for the next little while. He pressed her and they finally agreed to a simple question-and-answer interview to start.

"My schedule is tight," she said "but perhaps I could..."

Nason seized the moment. "How about this morning?"

She considered this.

Bracket's voice squawked on William's intercom. "William, there will be a television interview this morning at eleven."

"A television interview!? But Ma'am, can we allow TV cameras in here without..."

"It will be out front, at the main entrance. Prepare a list of questions."

Bracket dug out the blue skirt and pantyhose she kept in her office closet and changed into it. She thought it made her look more... sympathetic than her usual pants.

William took a ten milligram Valium before noon for the first time.

--

When Lardner came into the office, he was surprised to find an agitated Bailey at his desk pecking on his computer. He looked frazzled. "What the hell are you doing out of bed?" Lardner asked.

"I added armed robbery, escaping and evading to

Edward Miller's charges," Bailey said. "What I want to know is why he got waltzed out to Rightweigh. We should have him locked up downstairs as we speak."

"The man fell three stories, Ray. They can take care of him better than we can. And *what* armed robbery? The girl told me he paid."

"He did?"

"Yeah. If we charge him for ordering and paying for a lunch, he didn't even get we'll never hear the end of it."

Bailey thought about this then said, "Just the same, that fat fucker could have killed somebody. He *was* armed."

"Yeah, maybe," Lardner knew the devices found in the getaway vehicle were messy, not deadly.

"I'm gonna call Judge Conroy," Bailey added. "He should be good for a quick warrant."

"What warrant?"

"I want to get into that god-damned Church and have a look around. I want to see for myself. No big deal."

Lardner watched Bailey bite his nails. A search warrant *is* a big deal—especially for a church. He didn't think Bailey could get one that easily, but he would have to keep an eye on him. He looked once more at the mug shots of Ed and Lou. Something was bugging him about the pictures. Did he have the two men mixed up? He couldn't quite remember which one was the man he'd seen fall from the window the night before.

--

Ed and Tapeworm sat at the bar all night talking. As fellow barkeeps, they had a lot in common. Tapeworm retrieved the burger from the secret compartment in the floor and Ed shared it with Porky as he brought Tapeworm up-to-date on everything that had happened since leaving the island.

Tapeworm was happy to have the companionship in his dreary world. When Ed told him about his feelings toward Sara Allen, Tapeworm said, "She sounds like a smart girl. Go with yer gut, man. If ya really like this gal, what's a little Sunday-go-to-meetin' bullshit matter?"

"Yeah, I suppose."

"She's not Catholic, is she?"

"No."

Tapeworm waved a ghostly hand at the air. "Ah, you'll be okay."

Tapeworm looked up The Church Of The Safe Way in a tattered yellow pages. Ed waited for a decent hour to call.

--

When the phone rang, Sara knew immediately who it was. "Hello?" She was a little out of breath and it turned Ed on.

"Uh, sorry it's so early, and look, I'm uh, sorry I just took off like that but I uh..."

"It's okay Eddie," she was happy to hear his voice, and it surprised her. After all, she hardly knew him. "You were in danger of being arrested, I... we don't blame you at all."

"Would you invite me over for dinner again if I apologized to your father?"

"Maybe I'd better come and meet you somewhere first. They might still be watching the Church."

"Good thinking. Know of a place where they'll

serve.... my kind?"

They both laughed, but Sara really had to think hard to answer the question. Ed's mug shot could be on display in every fast-food joint in town by now. Ed used the gap in the conversation to ask after her father. "I hope your father wasn't inconvenienced by what happened."

"Are you kidding?" she laughed. "He stands up to the police like that all the time. Do you know where Chinatown is?"

"Sure."

"There's a park just east of there. When can you meet me?"

"Two shakes of a leg of lamb."

He would be there faster than that. It was only eleven blocks from Fat's. Sara had to fix her hair, try on three summer dresses, apply makeup for the first time in years, then wash it all off and walk eighteen blocks.

Back In The Saddle Again

Milrot was up early and eager to get on with his experiments. During Lou Kennedy's absence he'd redesigned the experiment to include a biofeedback skullcap that would signal software to switch to a calming video if things got out of hand.

This would prove to be a big mistake, because it would also "teach" Lou's sub-conscious to focus his strange new matter-creating abilities *outside* his body and provide the circuit with which to do it. Instead of merely healing internal injuries or creating small amounts of matter in his stomach, Lou would learn to manifest mass in the outside world.

Milrot wondered if the solution to the mysterious phenomenon lay in the medial prefrontal cortex, which helps us to imagine new ideas and mediates our emotional state. Or could it be a sudden accelerated benign tumour growth? He was still very much in the dark.

Unfortunately, Milrot never learned of Lou's fall from the third floor. He didn't know Lou could repair and regenerate fatally broken and lacerated body parts instantaneously.

Guards brought Lou from his room. Milrot's assistant Gwen shaved his head and strapped him into the cycling machine. Milrot applied transmission gel to each of the contacts in the skullcap and Gwen switched on the EEG and ECG and booted three computers. Together she and Milrot carefully stretched the elastic skull cap over Lou's baby-bottom head and they were ready to go.

--

Bracket's interview with Kent Nason bothered William. He liked to plan all publicity carefully, especially free publicity. It could easily backfire. But Bracket insisted on going in front of the camera that morning and all William could do was try to minimize the risk. At least she had agreed to do it outside the grounds. He told the men at the front gate to hold Nason there and to call him when they arrived.

--

Dr. Eli Milrot believed he may have stumbled upon the answer to a question that had stumped science for eons: Could matter be created from nothing? He scribbled $E=mc^2$ on a piece of paper. Then he wrote $M=e/c^2$ and scratched his head furiously.

Lou wasn't producing matter from nothing. He was converting energy from his environment to mass inside his body. And his fall from Ed's mom's window had jolted his ability to the next level. When Lou hit the police cruiser, he broke his back, ruptured his spleen and crushed four ribs. But so intense was the experience, and so dynamically focused was his mind on what was happening, that even before Lardner had reached the window to look down, Lou's injuries were healing. New tissue fused a severely shattered vertebra; the soft tissue of his spleen reconstituted itself in seconds; cracks in his ribs were healed long before the paramedics hefted him from the wreckage. In the process, Lou drained the police car battery, the batteries in Bailey's cell phone, and dimmed the lights for a five-block radius.

Now Lou was pedalling leisurely and staring at the image of the little girl eating the orange on the screen.

This time Milrot was trying something different.

Below the video display was a pedestal. On the pedestal he'd placed a large butterscotch ice-cream sundae prepared from ingredients secretly purchased by Gwen and kept frozen in a cryo-chamber in the back of the lab. Milrot concealed the sundae from Lou by a small curtain that drew back with the click of a mouse.

Milrot wanted to see what would happen if they exposed Lou to a real stimulus instead of a video. He had no scientific reason for this; it was just a gut feeling.

--

Ed and Porky arrived at the park near Chinatown early. Sara had made a good choice. There was no one around except for three teenage girls playing hooky from school. They looked at Ed alone, holding his cat, commented in Cantonese, then giggled away out of the park.

Then, here came Sara.

Back-lit in the morning sun, her dress became semi-transparent and her whole being took on a kind of wondrous glow that caused Ed to stop breathing. How could he imagine that this intelligent, gorgeous, radiant creature could find *him* attractive? Doubts like this had never entered his mind before. Sara was the kind of person who read books for pleasure—probably even sometimes non-fiction. This scared him. The last book he'd read all the way to the end was... well, he couldn't think of one he'd read through to the end.

Sara spotted Ed holding Porky, and the sight made her heart melt. The image wasn't so much pathetic or sad, but it had an aura of melancholic desperation. Beneath his crude exterior here was a man of innate intelligence and compassion, a man who could find the positive, even in a crisis. And this was a time of crisis.

"I knew this would be a good place to meet," Sara said. "Not too many people around in the morning." She tickled Porky under her chin, then inadvertently fussed with Ed's rumpled shirt, caught herself, and tucked her arm in Ed's and lead him away. "We'll find a noodle house that's open early. You must be starving."

"Actually, I got a burger last night at Fat's..."

"Fat's!? There's a place called Fat's? Are you sure?"

"Yeah, you know, as in Minnesota Fats?"

She had no idea what he was talking about.

"You know pool, billiards, snooker?"

No clue.

"There's a famous old movie with Paul Newman and Jackie Gleason..." Ed's voice trailed off. He decided it wasn't important. The strange thing was, Ed wasn't actually hungry just then. Falling in love for real was something that had never happened to him before.

Ed was in a romantic dream. He observed some people doing Tai Chi while Sara talked to her father on the phone. She told him of Ed's reappearance and that they were looking for a good place to have an early lunch.

Sara pocketed her phone. "Daddy's glad you're back. He will prepare a nice lunch. He's a great cook. A chef, actually. Wait till you taste his asparagus and smoked ham soup and warm home made bread...."

Ed's hunger returned at the mention of food. "Can we talk about something else? If I think about food, I might faint."

Sara thought he was joking. He wasn't. She looked deeply into his eyes and said, "Eddie, aside from Daddy, you're the only person I know who wants to do the right thing."

This troubled Ed. Sara was showing a faith in him he could never fulfil. He wanted to level with her, tell her he was nothing but a slob who liked to lounge about snacking and watching female breasts bounce around on a tropical beach. He wanted to warn her off, but the sentences wouldn't form. The words that kept echoing around in there instead were 'asparagus and smoked ham soup' and 'warm homemade bread'. Still, he might never eat again if it meant being with her. It was all very confusing. Instead of 'fessing up and telling her the truth about himself, he heard himself say, "What do you think *I* can I do?"

Sara drew close. "You've already brought sanity to our lives." Sara's hair smelled like a fresh misty forest at dawn.

"Sanity?" he said. "I'm a rogue street gourmand wanted by the police for ordering two super-sized burger combos. What's sane about that?"

She smiled. "It's nice being with someone who has a sense of humour about all this for a change. Humour is the only thing that will get us through these insane times. If we could only stop thinking of it as *Us* and *Them* everything would be different. There are no sides in this."

"Yeah, tell that to the cops and the people who run that Rightweigh place..."

Sara absently gave him a small kiss on the cheek. It was a good thing they were standing still right then because it made Ed's mouth go dry. His vision blurred, and the park tilted bizarrely sideways for a second.

Ed had always been fast on his feet, never lost for a witty comeback, but now all he could do was smile stupidly.

Sara too was falling under the spell. It had been a long time since she'd laughed three times on the same day and enjoyed herself in such a simple way. She realized that she was falling and carefully backed away from the edge in that way that smart women do. "Maybe we'd better get going. Lunch will take a while so we have time to visit Mummy on the way," she took Porky from Ed, then pulled him along the path. "Come on."

--

William, accompanied by three uniformed Rightweigh guards, met Kent Nason and Sally Bean at the front gate of Rightweigh to tell them that Ruth Bracket would join them in a few minutes. "Our main concern is the welfare of our clients," he said. "They are understandably sensitive about being photographed, and their interests have to come first." He presented Nason with three pages of questions. The papers flapped wildly in a gusting wind. Nason scanned the list. He had no intention of sticking to them, though he had to be careful; he didn't want the interview cut short.

Nason saw the guards snap to attention, then noticed Bracket's smart black Mercedes heading toward them. He glanced impatiently at Sally who was standing on an up-ended camera case attempting to tape up a small gap between the Rightweigh sign and the wall that whistled loudly in the wind.

William ducked into the lee of the news crew's van and used their wing mirror to fix his hair. Though he was still young, William had a growing bald spot on the top of his head and he spent a lot of time making sure that his comb-over was always in place. But in this gale it kept standing straight up like a coal cellar door. Every time he ducked out of the wind to check himself in the mirror, his hair fell flat and seemed to require no further attention. William would do almost anything for an opportunity to appear on television. His plan was to insinuate himself into the scene at Bracket's shoulder and hope there would be a question he could help with.

Sally finally stifled the wind racket then jumped down, grabbed up her camera and panned it to the Mercedes as it pulled up. She zoomed in on Bracket as she emerged from the back seat.

Nason came to Bracket in a gesture of meeting her halfway. "Perhaps we could do the interview inside," he said nodding to the administration building.

Bracket responded with a smile, raised her voice over the gale and referred to the fluttering list of questions in Kent's hand. "Let me stress one thing," she said. "I've arranged the questions so one idea flows into the next. I want the viewers to understand the unique problems we're dealing with here."

"Yes, ma'am," was Nason's terse reply.

Bracket waved to William, who was checking his hair again in the van mirror. "William, I want you in this too." William was so pleased that he forgot about his hair, which became a coal cellar door as soon as he stepped into the open.

Sally gave Nason a tentative thumbs-up and a shrug.

"Okay," Kent directed, "let's get you over here..." He went to move Bracket into a position so the main building would be in her background, but found he couldn't actually touch her. Luckily, she obliged.

Kent signalled Sally.

"We're rolling," Sally hollered as she swung the camera onto Kent.

Nason hoped the wind would turn out to be a blessing. It might give the story action and a ruggedness that commanded attention. He looked into the camera and said, "I am at the main entrance to the most successful weight-loss rehabilitation facility in the country, Rightweigh Incorporated. I'm here with owner and CEO Ruth Bracket, the creator of a new weight-loss program she claims will sweep the nation, making obesity a thing of the past."

Sally swung the camera onto Bracket, who flashed her best fake smile.

Nason stepped to a position beside the camera so that Bracket would look tight to the lens as she answered. At that moment, emotion seized Kent and he abandoned his well-considered tactical approach, dumped Bracket's questions, and dove straight into the heavy stuff. "Ms. Bracket, could you comment on reports that describe some of your more successful techniques as being less than humane and the charges that the Rightweigh program may violate certain human rights?"

Bracket realized that any response to his surprise question could go on air so she just smiled at Kent as if waiting for him to ask a question.

Nason leap-frogged to the core of the issue with a semi-rhetorical question, "Two former inmates have told us about something they call the rack. What would that be?"

Bracket stood firm, still smiling as though no one had said anything. Nason's mind raced but before he could recover, there was a loud boom and a large cloud of smoke and dust erupted from two blown-out windows on the second floor of the administration building.

Everyone froze the way people do in sudden dramatic situations. All except Sally, who, good journalist that she was, panned and focused her camera onto the commotion. She zoomed in just in time to catch a large figure that had plummeted from the building and was now rolling on the ground.

She fine-tuned the focus to see that the man was topless and had electrodes attached to his head and torso. Severed wires flailed wildly about as he struggled to his feet, looked desperately about, then headed towards them.

It was Lou.

"Stop that man!" someone hollered as several guards emerged from the administration building.

Bracket moved to block Sally's camera, but Sally was good, and the action only made the shot more exciting. The guards near Bracket formed a phalanx to block Lou. The head of security left Bracket's side and dove into the back of the Mercedes, looking for something.

Bracket, William and Kent stepped aside in horror as Lou approached them like a freight train and it was all Sally could do to keep the camera safe while panning him through. Lou knocked aside the guards blocking his way like rag dolls and barrelled through the open gate. The head of security emerged from the back of Bracket's car holding a taser, raised it, aimed it at Lou's back and let him have it square between the shoulder blades. There was a loud crackling sound and Lou stumbled, jerked about for a second, then went down.

Nason and Sally exchanged knowing looks. Their pulses surged. It was that once-in-a-lifetime rush every journalist gets when they realize that their careers are about to take a grand leap forward. Sally kept rolling as the other guards arrived and gathered around Lou. It took all five of them to manhandle him to his feet and guide him wobbling back into the compound.

Nason directed Sally to get back onto Bracket, then he asked, "Could you comment on what we've just seen here today?"

William reached out and slapped the camera lens away with an open hand. The lens fell to the ground. The interview was over. Without another word, Sally grabbed up the lens, and she and Nason leapt for their van.

Sally immediately pulled out the mini-cam they kept as an emergency backup. Well before Kent had the keys in the ignition, she was at the rear window once more recording the scene.

Enraged, Bracket raised a bony fist at the departing news crew and screamed, "If I see one moment of this on the air, I'll sue you and your fucking television station right down to your goddamn Jockey shorts!"

"Did you get that too?" Kent asked over his shoulder.

"I don't know how good the sound is but yeah, I got it."

"Good man," Kent said, started the van and drove out. Sally liked this kind of compliment. She kept rolling until there was nothing left to shoot.

William could only think to suggest, "Maybe we had better call the police."

"Don't be funny!" Bracket barked at him then turned and marched past the car and up the road back toward the administration building in search of an explanation for what the hell had happened.

As William watched her depart, the wind caught

Bracket's skirt momentarily blowing it up almost over her head.

She was too furious to care.

William wondered why anyone would wear panties *outside* their pantyhose.

--

Here's what had happened: Milrot decided it was time to show Lou the butterscotch sundae while it was fresh. He and Gwen watched Lou closely as Milrot clicked the mouse button. The curtain slid back, revealing the sundae to Lou.

Nothing happened.

No change in the readouts and no apparent change in Lou. He just kept pedalling away, staring now at the huge sundae.

Then, suddenly, at Lou Kennedy's subconscious bidding, certain wavelengths of electromagnetic energy came under the influence of a strange and very strong new force: Proton, neutron and electron potentials appeared instantaneously and joined with more that had been part of the air, the walls and the lab equipment. These were abruptly sucked away and directed instantaneously to a point atop the ice cream sundae in a strong improbability at the focus of Lou's concentration.

Every room in the administration building went dark. A microsecond after that, a sonic boom flashed out in a loud explosion that blasted ice cream all over the place, blew out all the glass in the lab, threw everyone sprawling back across the floor, knocked a six-foot hole in the outside wall and sent Lou flying out and down onto the grass two floors below.

Here's why: The sundae had three scoops of ice

cream; chocolate, butterscotch ripple, and vanilla. Dripping down the sides and into the glass sundae flute was a generous helping of fudge sauce. The whole thing was topped with a perfect swirl of whipped cream. Lou gaped at the monstrous masterpiece and thought it still needed something, something to make it aesthetically complete.

The explosion of a bomb is an abrupt expansion of gases from a sudden compact chemical reaction. What Lou did was like that. The sudden appearance of a maraschino cherry from "nothing" was calamitous. In the same way high-frequency sound waves can break a wine glass, a highly destructive, high-speed shock wave went out from the maraschino appearance at many times the speed of sound. It was the largest mass Lou had produced so far, and it was the first time he had materialized anything outside his body. In fact, if he had created it inside his body it would have blown him to bits and that would have been the end of Lou.

Instead, in the centre of the chamber, atop a neat little pile of rubble, sat the perfect green candied cherry. Milrot saw it immediately and climbed over the debris to inspect it more closely. Gwen joined him, dabbing at her bleeding nose with a paper towel.

They both peered at the cherry, afraid to touch it.

--

Lou's captors didn't understand the awesome power they were dealing with as they wheel-chaired him away from the front gates back to the second floor of the barracks and locked him inside his prepaid private room. Now Lou lay exhausted on his bed while two guards stood on either side of the door outside. There was no way they would let Lou get out of this place again. Little did the guards, or Bracket, or even Milrot know that Lou could have willed a quarter-pounder with cheese to appear in the hall outside his room knocking everyone flat and blowing the fire exit door at the far end of the hall wide open. He could have eaten the burger on the way to the front gates. If anyone attempted to stop him, he could have summoned up an apple fritter or two and sent them flying.

Luckily for everyone, Lou didn't know he could do this either. Yet.

Strange Fruit

Milrot knew how evolution worked at the genetic level. Certain small changes could combine to produce sudden dramatic results, but nothing like this. Had Lou Kennedy, by some freak accident, become capable of altering the very fabric of reality with his mind?

And the horror of it was, if Lou Kennedy were to pass this monstrous trait on to future generations, it would spell the end of humankind as we know it. The atomic bomb, in comparison, would be like the invention of the cap pistol.

Milrot called Harry Steckle again. He stared at the strange fruit safely ensconced in double glass beakers as he told him how it came to be.

"What colour is it?" Harry asked, already becoming exasperated.

"Green," Milrot said.

"Green?"

"Yes, green. Why?"

"Well, don't you think it would more naturally be red?"

"Natural!" Milrot was frantic. "There's nothing natural about matter that's formed from... from... from nothingness! Aren't you listening to what I'm telling you?"

"Yes, I'm listening." He was only half listening. He had the Higgs boson and dark matter to worry about.

He resented Milrot's ridiculous intrusion. "You're telling me that a test subject somehow materialized a piece of fruit, a berry, from God knows where and now you have it in a beaker in your lab. Is that it?"

"That's it."

"Impossible."

"Why?"

"Why? You're talking about creating matter from virtually nothing."

"Yes, that's what I'm telling you!"

"And he's doing this with his mind."

"Yes."

"Eli, there's not enough juice in any of the apparatus you have out there to create any amount of mass."

"You haven't seen this guy."

"It doesn't matter how big *he* is, you can't create matter from nothing like that." Harry's mind was drifting back into the realm of tensor fields and negative energies. "Let me put it another way." Harry remembered Milrot's propensity for unnecessarily elaborate language and explained, "The probability distribution of such a phenomenon, especially at the organic level, makes anything like this so highly unlikely that it is safe to assume you are mistaken." That was about as complicated as he could make it. "Now I really must go."

"So it's impossible."

"I've never seen it."

"What about the big bang? Wasn't that something from nothing?"

"Okay, let me try to explain it as simply as I can." Harry was losing patience, but he was curious to see if he could explain the origin of the universe in less than a minute to a crazy man. "Normally, and under the right conditions, tiny quantum particle twins pop into existence from nowhere," he said, "Normally, they come back together destroying each other immediately. But once in a trillion, trillion eons, something very peculiar happens: A strangely unstable very high energy effect occurs where these pairs cannot annihilate and more appear. Then another strange thing happens: The whole kit and kaboodle suddenly snaps from something smaller than an atom to something half the size of a galaxy, and oddly, continues to expand. Before anything can stabilize and vanish, the baby universe cools down enough so everything freezes out and stuff starts shooting all over the damn place looking for a partner to disappear with again. Gravity takes over and things clump into gas and planets and stars until eventually you have the universe we live in, which, by the way, is still heaving explosively, trying to find the simple equilibrium it once knew." There was a silence on Milrot's end. "Hello?"

""That's a lot of strange unexplained events you have there, Harry," Milrot croaked.

"Granted, it's a very simplified version and so not completely accurate without going into quantum field statesand..."

"Are you sure about any of this?"

"No. But here's the thing: you're a biologist. You can't just step into particle physics like you're going up a department store escalator, from dress shirts to bedding."

"Didn't bicycle mechanics fly the first heavier than air...?"

Steckle was about to hang up on Milrot, "It doesn't fucking happen Eli. If it did, don't you think we'd know about it by now?"

"Well then, could it be that he's transporting matter

here somehow from some... some... somewhere else?"

"From where, a fruit salad factory in Florida?"

"I'm not joking with you, why are you joking with me? Weren't you the one who said that 'matter, the stuff we see and touch, is mostly empty space, a confluence of energy fields?'"

"Yes, as a way of keeping it simple for People Magazine, but there are many complex things going on down there at that level that we…"

"Okay, okay, look." Milrot was hyperventilating. "You agree that it's possible to disassemble an atom into its constituent quantum parts and then reassemble it again at another time or location don't you?"

"You've been reading too much science fiction, Eli."

"Do you agree or don't you?"

"It's possible on Star Trek. This is the real world. What's your point?"

"Let me send you the thing so you can examine it yourself," Milrot blurted, providing a nifty out for Harry.

"Okay, you win," Harry said. "Send me the... specimen, I'll have a look at it and get back to you. How's that?"

"You won't regret this, Harry. I promise."

"Okay" and Harry hung up. "Jesus Christ!" he muttered to himself, went downstairs, picked up a coffee and sat on a bench outside in the courtyard. He tried to forget the call and get back to his work, which was to ponder images from inside the Large Hadron Collider, pictures that looked more like pubic hair than anything else. It was up to people like Harry Steckle to solve the serious mysteries of existence, but he couldn't quite get the call from Milrot out of his mind.

Lardner got into headquarters in time to find Bailey recruiting a contingent of cops to return to the Church of the Safe Way and make a thorough search. Lardner grabbed him and pulled him aside. "Ray, what the hell are you doing?"

"I've had it with these fat fucks, Bill. In no way shape or form should they be wandering around free as the wind!"

One of the first things you learn in basic police psychology training is to never tell an agitated subject to calm down, but that's what most cops do all the time and that's what Lardner did.

"I don't have to calm down!" Bailey shouted and everyone in the squad room stopped what they were doing to watch. "I almost got fuckin' killed out there!"

"Yeah, I know." Lardner heard the suppressed laughter ripple through the room. He turned Bailey away from the other men, then said the *right* thing to him. "That was my fault, not the suspect's. The poor bastard fell three floors, for Christ's sake." Lardner could see the frustration in Bailey's eyes. He needed to defuse his partner's emotions, get him back to proper procedures. "Did you get a warrant?"

"I put in a call to Judge Conroy's office this morning."

"Good," Lardner said. "let's make sure we've got all the facts lined up so when he calls we know what we're talking about."

"Yeah, okay." Bailey was calming down.

Lardner surreptitiously waved the men back to work, then led Bailey down the hall away from the main office. "We got the main suspect back in custody so things aren't as bad as they were yesterday. Let's just take one thing at a time and see where it leads."

"Yeah, you're right." Bailey said. "Okay."

"We'll go talk to this Ed Miller guy out at Rightweigh, then figure out if we need to charge him."

Bailey thought this was a good idea.

But this was all wrong. Their suspect, Miller, was *not* in custody and things were actually about to become much worse.

--

On the way out to Rightweigh, Lardner thought if he engaged Bailey in idle conversation, anything not connected to the case, something about his strange nightly activities might slip out. He picked up on a topic they had already discussed.

"Suppose you got a hair in your soup, you know in a restaurant."

"What?" Bailey was lost in his own thoughts and still trying to ignore the pain wracking his body.

"You know, and say you swallow it by mistake, without seeing it."

"Yeah, so?"

"Well *then,* you're a cannibal aren't you?"

"No, no, no."

"Why not?"

"Don't you have to know you're eating somebody else before you're a cannibal?"

"I don't know, maybe."

Bailey thought for long moments, then said. "I had a guy once who was cutting hair off women in the subway, but we never found out *what* he was doin' with it. All we could do was get a minor assault conviction. For all I know he's back out there still doin' it today."

"I guess people have their secret lives all right." Lardner said, "I mean, for all you know I might wear women's underwear." He laughed, then noticed that Bailey was giving him a strange look and regretted the comment. Maybe it was better to stick to the subject at hand. "Why do you think the Church is involved?"

"He seemed to be headed there when we lost him. They're hidin' something, I can smell it. And I wouldn't mind havin' some clue as to the identity of the hostage, *if*, as I say, reiterating that she *was* actually a hostage."

Lardner had never considered the idea that the two could have been in it together. "Any of the witnesses say she was a *big* girl?"

"No. Normal."

It surprised Lardner that Bailey didn't have to look this up in his notes.

--

When Lardner asked after Ed Miller at the Rightweigh admitting desk, the head nurse said, "He's sedated." She was following William's precise instructions.

They left without learning a thing and drove back to town. Lardner didn't really care about Ed Miller. He had no intention of laying further charges. The whole purpose of this excursion was to get Bailey out for a drive in the country, get some fresh air, try to come back down to earth. Now, on the freeway back to the city, Bailey was sleeping like a baby, his face mashed against the sun-warmed car window.

--

The cemetery was small and tucked away in the back of the Church of the Safe Way tax-free property. Ed was sure he could detect cooking smells as he leaned over to read the inscription on one of the older, more weathered stones. It was that of a child who died of diphtheria in 1867, and it occurred to him that this cemetery and all cemeteries were death parks.

Sara called to him from a beautifully polished white marble stone in the centre of the cemetery. "This is Mummy over here."

In the top right, a plastic Ziploc bag protected a U.S. Congressional Medal Of Honor. A blue ribbon protruded from the plastic and fluttered in the breeze. Ed shifted Porky to his other arm and bent down to read the gold-inlaid inscription on the elegant little headstone.

ELSPETH ALLEN
Heroine d'aviation
1944 - 2012

Ed was surprised he understood the simple French epitaph. He inspected the small medal. "Amazing that this doesn't get stolen."

"It does. We find it at one of the pawnshops down the street and buy it back." She looked lovingly at the headstone, "Mummy passed away four years ago."

Ed didn't know what to say in these situations so he said, "I'm sorry... was she a French pilot or something?"

Sara swept dust from the top of the headstone. "No, her parents were from Belgium. Mummy died on a plane going to get her stomach stapled in Denver. She was in the washroom when some pipes burst in a cargo hold below her. Sudden decompression, they called it. They said it was a good thing she was sitting on that toilet and was as big as she was or it would have sucked her right out into space along with everyone else. They said they could have lost the whole plane."

Ed was speechless.

"It was a closed casket, obviously," Sara added, and the image of a woman's guts being sucked out into the sixty below temperature of the stratosphere, flash freezing, then falling to the fields and pastures of Colorado far below, blinked in Ed's mind, but he shoved it away. "Daddy said the Lord needed her urgently and seeing she was already that close, He took her then and there."

"Wow!" was the only comment Ed could think of.

Sara looked thoughtfully at the stone. "She was the one who was working hardest to get Daddy his television ministry. She was getting it all figured out." Sara's eyes welled up and for a moment Ed thought she might cry. But crying was something he couldn't quite imagine her doing. "If it hadn't been for Mummy," Sara said, "we never would have even had the Church. She never once thought of herself. When Daddy had his depressions—his episodes—she would take care of him no matter how long it took." She gazed at the headstone with a sigh, then pulled herself from her reverie. "But now we have you." She squeezed his arm in hers.

Again Ed thought he would eventually have to come clean even if it meant alienating Sara. She had to know he was nothing but an ex-beach bum, though beach bums are more traditionally thought of as young and buff, not thirty something, overweight and homeless. He wasn't the person Sara thought he was. Maybe now was the time for honesty. "Sara, don't take offence but... your father's idea to get those people out of that place is great, but it's uh, a little.... well, unrealistic." Ed held his breath. Sara looked away and for an instant Ed couldn't tell if he had offended her.

Still, it was more important to be truthful right now.

Sara looked back at him with tears of appreciation. "I know." She took his hand in hers. "That's why I feel better knowing you'll be with him."

She tucked his arm in hers once more and led him off toward the rectory. "I know you don't believe most of the things my father says," she said flatly. "He thinks God brings all things but... I must confess, sometimes I don't think God is really there at all." Her gaze drifted toward the rectory. "But he doesn't need my doubts, not at a time like this." Sara sighed. "You must believe in something. Even the atheists believe in entropy."

"Entropy?"

"You know, where everything eventually turns into everything else?"

He had no idea what she was talking about, but he knew it was time to lighten things up. He handed Porky to her, stepped back, threw up his arms, and flashed his best smile. "Here's what I believe: I'm a fat guy and I'm lookin' good." He did an awkwardly graceful twirl.

Sara was glad they were standing under a big shade tree because she was now blushing furiously. Could he know she found him attractive and wasn't afraid to flaunt it? He knew nothing of the kind. He was just clowning around. But Sara saw the real man beneath the bluster. "You're not really fat," she said. "Not all people have the self confidence you do." She looked back toward her mother's grave. "My mon had confidence like that, too."

Ed placed his arm around her shoulder. It was a spontaneous gesture intended to be comforting. To his surprise, she didn't retreat from his touch.

Sara was becoming hooked on this unlikely character, flaws and all.

Ed struggled to keep from swooning as her sweet

breath swept across his face. He should say something, but words would not come. Why did he keep feeling like a little boy when she drew near? As he gazed into her hazel eyes, he wanted to lock lips with her. His brain went for it, but his body was frozen.

Suddenly, Porky yowled with hunger and Sara said, "Lunch must be ready," and the spell was suspended—for now.

The three of them drifted dreamily out of the cemetery and down the well-worn path towards the rectory.

Sara slipped her arm around Ed's waist. It made him feel fat.

The Wrong Man

When the TV station manager saw the footage Kent Nason and Sally Bean got at Rightweigh, he agreed that they may be onto something. "But let's hold off on it for now."

"Why!?" Kent protested. "It tells the story."

"Not quite," the boss said, "If we don't release it, we have something to bargain with so we can get in there and take a good look around."

Kent saw the sense of this.

--

Father Allen took to the scrawny Porky right away and opened a can of sardines. As Ed watched the cat tuck into the feast, he felt dizzy. "You wouldn't happen to have an extra can of those would you?" he asked with a slight gasp.

"Oh, are you hungry?" Father Allen asked.

"Hungry's not the word."

"I'm sorry, I didn't realize the urgency. Sit down, I'll prepare something to tide you over."

As he sat at the dining room table, Ed saw Sara and her father exchange odd glances and realized that they were probably in the same no-food predicament as everyone else.

Father Allen went to the kitchen, then returned right

away with a bundle of warmed bread sticks wrapped in a heavy linen napkin and placed them on the table. Ed quickly took a bread stick with as much reserve as he could manage and took a polite bite.

"I've thought about what you were saying earlier," Father Allen said sitting across from him, "and by God son, you're right!"

Ed didn't know what the Father was referring to. He couldn't remember saying much of anything.

Father Allen leaned across to him and quoted in a conspiratorial hush, "Those who profess to favour freedom, yet deprecate agitation, are men who want crops without plowing up the ground. Rain without thunder and lightning."

Sara filled in the details as she did whenever her father produced these august quotes. "That's Frederick Douglass," she said.

All Ed wanted to do was get his hands on whatever was cooking in the next room. He was dying here.

"You've convinced me," Father Allen said. "What we've been doing is all wrong." Father Allen stuck a fat finger into the air and quoted, "If you do what you've always done, you'll get what you've always gotten."

"Daddy," Sara said, "that's Tony Robbins. You hate Tony Robbins."

"Darling Sara, I *hate* no one." Then he wrinkled up his nose. "Was that Tony Robbins? What were *you* doing reading Tony Robbins?"

"I don't know, it came up in some Web search I think."

"Oh..." Father Allen said thoughtfully.

"Do you think something might be burning?" Ed interjected, trying to get things back to the important subject at hand.

"I'll accept your challenge!" Father Allen declared

and slapped a hand on the table.

"*My* challenge?" Ed hadn't said more than a dozen words since he sat down.

Father Allen stood and held his finger in the air. "This struggle may be both moral and physical," he proclaimed, "but it must be a struggle. Power concedes nothing without a demand!" With that, he headed back into the kitchen,

Sara flashed Ed a big smile. "We like Frederick Douglass a lot."

Ed heard the oven door open and close with a loud squeak. Father Allen came back in carrying a huge covered bowl of something. "Just a few more minutes," he said placing the bowl on the table dangerously close to Ed.

"You, you made a whole roast?" Ed asked.

"It's a special occasion," Father Allen smiled.

Ed swooned. He was doing a lot of swooning lately. He wanted to peek under the cover of the bowl. Instead, he discretely slid out another bread stick, took a bite and said, "You know, these are the best darned bread sticks I've had in my life."

Sara threw out a quote of her own. "An empty stomach is not a good political adviser."

Her father laughed and said, "I believe that was Albert Einstein." He looked at his watch. "Everything will be ready soon." Then he leaned across to Ed once more and asked in his most serious tone, "How can we get our people out of that abominable hellhole?"

The directness of the question surprised Ed. "Uh, well I suppose we could figure out how to get one or two out but more than that... The people who run things are not nice."

"Do you think Rosa Parks worried about the consequences of her actions before she sat at the front of that bus?" the Father said, then thought about it. "Well, probably yes, but did that stop her from taking her rightful place? No. Why? Because she had courage."

Ed couldn't stand it anymore and decided it would be okay to peek inside the covered bowl. He'd only opened it a crack before the Father grabbed Ed's hand. The steam from the mashed potatoes fogged the Father's glasses. "What do you think of this?" and he waved his free hand in the air. "A big demonstration, a mass gathering. We could stage it right out in front of Rightweigh. We'll carry placards, chant our slogans. The press would have to cover it!"

Then Sara said something that Ed would have taken to be a joke if he hadn't known better: "What about a mass escape?"

Father Allen gaped at his daughter then turned to Ed. "Do you really think that could be possible?" he asked.

"Is what possible?" Ed wasn't thinking straight.

Father Allen fixed his gaze on Ed. "Do you really think we could do such a thing? Can we get *all* our people out at once?"

The question took Ed aback. "Uh, well, I don't know. There's a twelve foot fence all around, dozens of guards and..."

"*You* did it," Sara pointed out.

"Sure, me and one other guy, and *he* was a handful. Now they've got him back in there, anyway." Ed saw their hopeful looks. He sniffed the air. "You *sure* there's nothing burning?"

"No." Father Allen glanced at his watch. "Soon."

Ed struggled to keep the conversation on the topic of food. "How could you feed that many people?"

Sara and Father Allen exchanged looks, then the

Father put a hand on Ed's shoulder. "Come with me, we have something we'd like to share with you."

'Oh Christ,' Ed thought as the two got up and led him away from the food, out the kitchen door, across the yard and into the main hall of the church. "Hope I don't have to sit through a whole sermon before I get my crust of bread." Ed resigned himself as he followed them up the three steps to the altar and wondered why they were now wading into the choir stalls.

Father Allen wedged himself behind the last row of benches, pulled back a curtain and opened a small trapdoor near the back wall. "This way." Father Allen flicked on a single light bulb that dangled over a steep flight of stairs leading down into darkness beneath the altar.

Sara gave Ed a reassuring look as Father Allen disappeared below.

"Watch your step right at the top." Father Allen's voice echoed from the underworld. Ed stepped through and carefully picked his way down.

They descended into a long, narrow room lined with gardening tools, folded tables and chairs. There was a clatter from the dark and again the good Father's voice "What do you think should be on the menu for tomorrow?"

"Tomorrow?" Ed said, "I was more concerned with today..."

"Well, it's good to think ahead. What would you say to a nice juicy steak with mashed potatoes and gravy?" Father Allen said from the back of the room. "Then again, a few Cornish Pasties might be faster."

"Don't joke about that stuff." The quiver in Ed's voice was self-explanatory.

"I don't joke about the Lord's blessings."

As Ed's eyes became accustomed to the dimness, he

saw the Father move an old lawnmower from in front of a heavy wooden door.

"This is where we keep certain things out of sight," Father Allen said as he pulled open the door.

The first thing Ed saw was his own breath. "Cold in here."

Father Allen led the way into the large room. "Yes, it has to be."

Sara flicked a hidden switch, and the lights came on. The sight awed Ed. It was a very large cold storage chamber lined with shelves loaded with large bags of rice, potatoes, beans, various pastas, canned fruits and vegetables. Everything needed to feed the multitudes.

"Holy shi... uh cow!" Ed exclaimed.

"Yes." Father Allen said and pulled open another, heavier door. A blast of frosty air billowed out. Ed stepped in and looked into a large freezer locker. Here were plastic wrapped briskets of beef, racks of pork and lamb ribs and a lot of other boxed and wrapped provisions, enough to stock a sizable restaurant for weeks... months.

"When all this trouble started," Father Allen explained, "members of our flock were worried their stores were in danger and, instead of having them confiscated, they brought it all here. One of our people is a refrigeration contractor and, well, getting all this put in took quite some doing."

Father Allen picked up a binder and flipped through the many pages of inventory. "All of those who donated are now in hiding, or in that blasted Rightweigh place." He ran his finger down a page. "Let's see, tomorrow we could have a nice roast duck with a creamed cherry sauce and roasted potatoes and...?"

The Father's words stabbed at Ed's brain like cruel

slam poetry. The subterranean stronghold spun, slowly at first, then Ed's knees became weak and when he steadied himself against the door frame, his hand immediately stuck to the cold steel. As he struggled to pull it painfully away, everything—the cold, the hunger, the exhaustion, the accumulation of bad experiences he'd suffered—conspired against him and the world went black. Ed stumbled forward, then slid down a shelf, taking a large plastic bag of frozen cauliflower with him.

It was all Sara and her father could do to get him out of there before he succumbed to hypothermia. It took them almost an hour to negotiate his dead weight up the stairs, through the Church and back to the rectory. Good thing wheelchairs are standard accessories in all churches.

--

Lardner had taken a minute to compare the mug shots he had of Lou and Ed and realized they had the wrong man. The fugitive in violation of a court order was still out there, so he and Bailey were back at Rightweigh to clear things up with Bracket. She acknowledged that the man she had in custody was Lou Kennedy, not Edward Miller, and insisted there was confusion on both sides. Lardner wanted to talk with Lou regarding the whereabouts of Ed Miller. Bracket asked why he wasn't questioned when taken into custody, and Lardner explained that he was incoherent.

"Unfortunately, he doesn't seem to have improved much since then," she lied. "We're taking good care of him, and we will let you know as soon as he's alert and able to answer your questions." She smiled her crooked smile.

Lardner really disliked this woman, but he had to come to some arrangement with her. He took out his card and placed it on her desk. "If he says anything about this Ed Miller, I'd appreciate it if you'd call us."

She picked up the card without looking at it. "I will certainly do that," she said and slid the card into her blazer pocket.

"I think he's hiding in the Church of the Safe Way," Bailey said. "We're waiting for a search warrant."

Bracket wanted nothing more than to dispose of this entire matter. If these two could put their hands on Edward Miller, her problem would just go away. She clicked on the intercom. "William?"

"Yes, Ma'am?"

"Get me Judge Conroy on the phone, please. Even if he's at home." She smiled at the two cops. "Judge Conroy is a friend. You'll get your warrant."

--

On the way back downtown, Lardner lamented the fact that a private citizen could secure a search warrant faster than a cop could. As they waited in traffic, Bailey took out his wallet and counted his money. Out of the corner of his eye, Lardner estimated it to be about two-hundred-and-fifty bucks. The most Lardner ever had on him was usually about forty dollars. Was Bailey deliberately trying to avoid leaving a trail of credit card transactions?

Lardner dropped him off at headquarters, then drove up the street and pulled over. Soon Bailey drove from the lot and past without spotting him. He wasn't the most observant man on the force.

Lardner followed him across town, then south and onto Richmond Street until he parked on the sidewalk in front of a small diner. Apparently he never went to the same place twice to do whatever it was he was up to.

Lardner stopped and watched Bailey go into the diner and have words with a waitress. Before he could see more, impatient traffic honked him through the intersection and into a gas station up the block.

Soon Bailey drove past and Lardner followed carefully to a short, heavily treed Howard Street. Bailey pulled over and stopped. Did he know he was being followed? Lardner didn't want to confront Bailey, so he turned up a side street and drove off. Howard Street. What the hell was on Howard Street?

--

It was only yesterday that Harry Steckle spoke to Milrot about the magic maraschino cherry, and here it was already—the so-called specimen from Milrot's crazy experiment. It arrived by Critical Care Courier, tightly enclosed in a special vacuum-sealed security thermos normally used to transport live organs for transplant. When he noticed the armed courier's wildly unkempt hair, he realized he had arrived by helicopter. All this so Harry could examine a candied cherry. As he signed for the package, he worried again for Milrot's sanity.

Harry went to his office, sat at his desk and stared at the canister. He unscrewed the lid of the vessel, opened the inner container and unceremoniously rolled the green cherry out into the palm of his hand, then placed it on a fresh piece of photocopy paper on his desk.

Looked like an ordinary maraschino cherry to him. He smelled it. Smelled like an ordinary maraschino cherry. He picked it up and held it up to the light.

Strangely, there appeared to be no pit. He took a Swiss army knife from his desk drawer and sliced it in two. Sure enough, no pit.

He sniffed it again, then gently touched his tongue to the fleshy interior. Tasted like an ordinary maraschino cherry. Then he performed the first unscientific procedure on the strange specimen. He picked up one of the half cherries, popped it into his mouth, then got up and walked out of the room.

Harry Steckle wouldn't have thought of Milrot's cherry again if it hadn't been for two things. The first was a casual inquiry he made of a biology professor in the employee's cafeteria line at lunch: "Is it possible to grow a seedless cherry?"

The significant part of this conversation was not the question but her straightforward and surprising answer, which was, "No."

--

For a while during the night, Sara sat at Ed's side on the sofa, wondering if she should be falling for this rascal.

When he awoke, it wasn't because she was gently stroking his head; it was the nightmare he was having. Something to do with hang gliding and a debate about weight-to-drag ratios.

"Here," Sara said, reaching for a mug of steaming liquid. "This will do you good."

Ed raised himself to a more upright position and sniffed the contents of the cup. It was soup, chicken soup. Never in his life had he ever welcomed something so simple as plain chicken broth.

"Careful, it's hot," Sara said.

He sipped the steaming liquid. "Oh boy, is this good. What happened? How long have I been out?"

Sara smiled. "You slept through the night. We didn't realize how serious your condition was and thought it best not to wake you." Ed could hear cooking sounds coming from the kitchen. "Daddy's making breakfast," she said, and Ed got right up to sit on the edge of the sofa. Sara steadied him as they went to the dining room.

This time Father Allen and Sara hurried about preparing the sustenance Ed so desperately needed. Ed watched Porky attack another bowl of sardines until Sara placed a vision of scrambled eggs, ham with toast and home fries before him. Ed gaped at the grand fulfilment of promise.

Sara and her father sat opposite him and watched.

Despite everything, Ed felt self-conscious. "Aren't you having anything?"

"Wait a minute," Father Allen said and got up. "I forgot the gravy left over from last night, it'll go well with the potatoes."

He returned with a steaming gravy boat and put it down, then sat and folded his hands in prayer. "Thank you, dear Lord for giving us this day our daily bread and for bringing us Ed Miller in our time of need to help us in our mission of righteousness for our brothers and sisters unjustly detained in the name of evil, and against the tyranny of those who would imprison and degrade and humiliate and unjustifiably impose their will..."

Sara was sneaking a peek at Ed when she spotted, over his shoulder and out the window, a small motorcade comprising Ruth Bracket's Mercedes, a white Rightweigh van, two police cruisers and a paddy wagon making its way up the street toward the Church.

Sara decided it was appropriate to interrupt the prayer. "Father."

Father Allen looked to his daughter, then followed her gaze to the vehicles now circling in the parking lot beside the church.

"Here we go again." Father Allen scraped his chair back abruptly. "You two make yourselves scarce while I handle it."

Father Allen went to the front hall closet and quickly pulled on a full Sunday Vestment. Ed didn't really know what was going on, but he saw that they were deadly serious and grabbed up three thick wedges of home fries and two pieces of toast before Sara took his hand and pulled him away. Porky tried to go with them, but Ed thought it best that she remain safely behind. "You stay here girl." he said and held her back with his foot as he closed the door.

As they hurried across the small yard between the rectory and the church, Ed caught glimpses of the force disembarking the vehicles. He knew he was responsible for what was happening and he saw no need for Sara and her father to become more involved. "Look, it's me they're after. Why don't I just duck out for a while?"

"No." Sara pulled on him. "We'll protect you." Ed dropped his precious toast.

Father Allen marched ahead into the fray, his robe blowing wildly behind him in the morning breeze.

Father Allen held the back door for them as they slipped inside and headed for the choir stalls, then down the stairs to hide in the basement.

Father Allen took up a position just to the right of the pulpit and stood stock still. He knew that any object, even a large colourful one, was invisible against the ornate trappings of the Church as long as it remained perfectly still. He watched the little troupe come up the front walk: Lardner, Bailey, Bracket, two Rightweigh security people and four uniformed cops.

Bailey directed his men to split up and cover the side exits. Lardner stuck close to Bracket as they entered the main hall.

They slowed in the natural hush of a holy place.

Father Allen gave them time to get halfway into the big room, then drew breath and filled the cavern with his omnidirectional voice. "Can I be of some assistance?"

Everyone but Bracket gaped about. She knew exactly where the voice was coming from. Her gaze swept onto the Father like a death ray.

Lardner stepped forward and called out in the wrong direction. "Is there an Edward Miller here?" Lardner only spotted the Father when he moved towards them. Father Allen could see that they were deadly serious. They probably had a search warrant. Indignation would not work this time.

Bailey locked onto the Father, then noticed the curtain fluttering at the back of the choir stalls. He wondered if this is where the Father had come from or was someone hiding back there? He quietly headed down a side aisle to investigate.

Father Allen smiled warmly to Lardner and held both his hands out in a welcoming gesture. "Come, 'eat of my bread and drink of the wine which I have mingled...' For those who may not know, that's from Proverbs nine, verse five." He waved his arm towards the rectory away from the Church. "We'll sit down and discuss your needs."

Ruth Bracket knew the police were no match for his intellect. She stepped in. "Look Father, this needn't be unpleasant. A man has committed a crime, and the police are here to bring him to justice. I'm here to see that he receives fair treatment."

Father Allen put on a good front, as though he was

genuinely happy to see her. "It's nice to see *you* again," and he waved them further into his territory. "Please, come in, come in. All are welcome in the house of..."

"Father..." Bracket cut in holding her ground, "though I don't know why you call yourself that." She was already struggling to maintain patience. "I doubt you're even an ordained minister."

Father Allen's smile tightened. "And we are assured that you are a licensed nutritionist."

Lardner attempted to defuse the situation in the only way he knew how. Slumping his shoulders in an expression of reconciliation and placing a gentle hand on the Father's sleeve, he stepped between them. Father Allen knew Lardner to be a compassionate man and in a clever expression of surrender, Father Allen moved to a pew, gathered his gown and sat. He wanted Bracket to be seen as the aggressor.

Lardner sat in the next pew back and leaned in close to the Father, attempting to create an intimacy. "Father..." He took the photo of Ed Miller from his pocket and showed it to Father Allen. "You may not know that there is an outstanding warrant on this man. He's defying a court order," he said calmly. "We're here to return him to custody. He'll get a fair and just hearing."

Father Allen studied the picture of Ed Miller as though he were seeing the face for the first time. "I'm sorry Detective, this man is not one of my flock..." he said without lying.

"So he *is* here!" Bracket said bluntly.

Father Allen maintained a passive strategy but got to his feet in a move like a cloud rising in the hot summer air. He looked Bracket in the eye and softened, bringing his hand to hover a sixteenth of an inch above her shoulder. "But come," he quoted the Bible again, "eat of my bread and drink of the wine which I have..."

Bracket brushed his hand away. "Yes, yes, we know all that," then she threw out her own biblical quote and moved into a face-to-face with the Father. "Neither will I eat bread nor drink water in this place!" She smiled. "I believe that is one Kings 13:8. Where's Edward Miller?"

Lardner, still seated and at a distinct disadvantage, sighed and leaned on one elbow.

Father Allen gave Bracket his best smile. "I *am* impressed."

"A childhood in convent will do wonders." Bracket said coldly. "So, how about it, where is he?"

Father Allen's eyes widened. He waved an open hand at the empty church. "See for yourself," He spotted Bailey snooping around the back of the choir. Again, like a cloud nudged by a gentle breeze, he drifted off that way.

Lardner realized that he had lost control of the situation as Bracket went after Father Allen.

Just beneath Bailey's silent footfalls, Sara and Ed stood in the gloom at the bottom of the basement stairs. Ed placed gentle hands on her shoulders. "I'm serious," he said. "Why should you and your father want to get into this trouble when I'm already.... let's see, how can I say it politely... *screwed*?"

"Don't even think like that. We have to help each other."

"Sara, you don't even know me. I could be anybody. How do you know that the things I've told aren't lies?"

"Because a liar wouldn't ask me that." Somehow, the peril and excitement evoked that same dangerous feeling Sara had felt in the car escaping from the police. Only this time there wasn't a careening car to deal with and they drew slowly together until their lips met in a long, passionate kiss—a mutual gentle embrace that stopped time—made them both forget, if only for a moment, what was happening.

A few feet above them Bracket caught up with Father Allen and grabbed him by the arm, turned him to her so they were now almost nose-to-nose. Her voice cracked. "Cut the crap, *Father*." She held up a piece of official looking paper that Father Allen assumed was a search warrant. "We're here to take Edward Miller back into custody. And while we're at it, investigate anything else that is against the law."

"Against the law?" The Father managed a genuine laugh. "We have nothing to hide here. As it says in John 6:35, 'I am the bread of life; he that cometh to me shall not hunger.' What in heaven's name could ever be illegal about that?"

"Oh, really?" Bracket barked. "Then 'They *did* eat, and were filled and became FAT.' Nehemiah 9:25."

Bailey ignored all this and kept snooping about the choir stalls, coming dangerously close to discovering the secret door to the basement cache. Father Allen realized he needed a diversionary tactic, but what? He pulled away from Bracket's grasp in a motion that bent back one of her nails and sent a jab of pain up her arm. He was at maximum decibel level as he threw out another quote, trying to stall things so he could think. "Eat ye that which is good and let your soul delight itself in fatness. Isaiah 4:2!" and he moved closer to Bailey's position.

Again Bracket stopped him, turning him to her, sticking a bony finger in his face. "Oh yeah? Well, Exodus 11:15."

It took Father Allen a second to retrieve and play that one back in his mind. It took him less than that to produce a suitable comeback. "Really? Well, Matthew, seven verse nine!" he bellowed. "And ten too, for that matter!" His jowls fluttered. He was desperate. There was only one thing to do.

Bracket turned, expecting to see Lardner at her back. Instead, she saw him still seated in the pew halfway to the exit. "Put this fellow in prison," she hollered at him, "and feed him with the bread of affliction." She turned back to the Father. "That's one Kings, 22:27 in case you don't know..." But Father Allen was already hurrying for the side doors. "STOP HIM!" She screamed.

Father Allen yanked the heavy doors open wide then turned to her back-lit in the afternoon sun and yelled, "Thy carcass shall be meat unto the fowls and beasts of the earth and no man shall fray them away!" And with that he ran out into the dazzling daylight.

It was a desperate tactic, but it worked.

Bracket screamed at Lardner, "get after him you fool, arrest him!"

Lardner took out his walkie-talkie and calmly ordered his men outside to detain the Father, then got up and followed Father Allen out to make sure no harm came to him. He would deal with the question of Ed Miller as soon as he had regained control.

Bracket wisely kept her men out of the chase. She wasn't interested in Father Allen and the attendant negative media coverage. All she wanted to do was get this whole issue of Ed Miller off her agenda and get the police out of her life.

Sara and Ed were still locked in their little infinity when the shrill squeak of the trapdoor behind the choir cut through and a shaft of light fell across them.

Ed saw Bailey.

Bailey saw Ed.

Ed stepped away from Sara and raised his hands. "Okay, there won't be any trouble, I'm the one you're looking for."

"Eddie, what are you doing?" Sara grabbed at him but he pulled away. There was nothing she could do.

"These people are innocent." Ed said and started up the stairs. "I forced them to hide me here."

"You're under arrest." Bailey said finally.

"Yeah, I know," Ed said and climbed the stairs into Bailey's clutches.

Bracket was delighted to see Bailey escorting the fugitive towards her.

"Well, well, Mister Miller, I presume."

But before Ed could conjure a snappy response, Sara appeared behind him and called out, "Why don't you just leave these people the hell alone?" Sara felt like striking Bracket. The instinct for violence was new for Sara, but she held back, fixed herself to the floor, put her hands on her hips and said "Did it ever occur to you that some of us might just like big men?"

"Big men, yes." Bracket replied then looked Ed up and down as Bailey cuffed his hands behind his back. "But big FAT men?"

"I'll have you know they're stronger, smarter.. a lot more fun to be with and..."

Bracket turned on Sara. Her patronizing smile was like a slap in the face. "Really. And do you also enjoy tying their shoe laces for them?" She came close to Sara, tempting her to strike.

Ed tried to come to Sara's defence but Bailey turned him around and gave him a shove towards the exit. Bracket followed.

"Where's my father?" Sara wanted to know.

"He managed to draw those fools off," Bracket said and Bailey shot her a look. She ignored it. "No doubt he's conversant with all the seamy back alleys of *this* grimy little neighbourhood. When they catch him, they'll charge him with obstruction of justice," and she waved her men out of the Church then followed Bailey and Ed out to the parking lot.

"This isn't over," Sara called after Bracket.

"No doubt." Bracket muttered.

Though impressed by Ed's sacrifice, Sara felt defeated by the sudden change in circumstances. She had confidence in Ed's abilities and believed his intention was to withdraw to fight another day. She assumed that the police would apprehend her father and take him to the local police precinct to decide what charges they could lay, if any. At that point Sara could retrieve him. She was confident that, since he was a man of the cloth and known well to police as a neighbourhood goodwill activist, she could get him off with a stern reprimand—even in Judge Conroy's court.

Bracket went to her car. Ed Miller's hearing would be the next day. Her job was to see that his escape and arrest evasion brought criminal charges and a prison sentence. She didn't want this troublemaker back in Rightweigh.

Ed banged his head on the car frame when Bailey shoved him into the back seat of his cruiser. "Hey, aren't you supposed to protect me from that?"

Bailey didn't answer him. He was listening to chatter on the radio, something about a "subject on foot" and the relevant street intersection coordinates. Bailey turned on his siren and roared out of the Church lot.

Sara looked everywhere for her father's car keys and eventually decided he had them in his pocket. It wasn't far to the police precinct. She'd walk.

Two cops taking one of their many coffee breaks were sitting in their cruiser when Father Allen stumbled around a corner and headed their way, his robes flowing wildly behind him. Whenever these loafers spotted something unusual, they enjoyed speculating as to its nature. It helped pass the boring hours on routine patrol.

"The collection plate got robbed, and he took a wrong turn chasin' the thief," one of them suggested.

"No, no, no, he's been foolin' with little boys and one of the dads found out." The other one offered.

"No, they're shootin' a movie near here and he didn't hear them yell 'cut'." Both men laughed, then saw the other police pursuing the Father. They poured their coffee out onto the road and joined the chase.

Bailey called Lardner on his cell phone to find out what was going on. Ed only heard Bailey's end of the brief conversation. "Hey Bill, what's up?" Bailey made a sharp right turn. "Yeah, okay, I'll head down by the market and look for him there."

Coming Out

Three-and-a-half blocks away, three-hundred-and- forty pound Russell Kelly was putting the finishing touches on a costume. Russell was a sensitive man who couldn't take the constant harassment anymore. Every time he ventured out of his penthouse, he was met with rude comments. Sometimes crews of teens would follow him, pelting him with nasty epithets, if not rocks. So, he confined himself to his home. But Russell was a social animal with a real need for human contact. With online access to local grocery delivery services, he'd had brief contacts with the delivery people, but he needed more. He needed to feel he was part of the real world. He needed to get out and move among people.

Now, in one delirious and insanely creative act, he had figured out how to do all this without attracting unwanted attention, or so he thought. Russell had disguised himself as two people. He had built a prosthetic rig that made him look like a man and a woman in love. He believed this would not attract attention. People didn't like to stare at lovers, especially fat ones—Russell would never look like two *thin* people. For that he would have to be a threesome.

Now, after weeks of hard work, he was ready. *"She"* was dressed in a full-length skirt in tie-died pastel shades and a billowing blouse crudely sewn from two flowered shirts. A large floppy hat covered the ridiculously inadequate papier mâché head and face—Russell didn't know that Cher Halloween masks were available on eBay.

The man wore a grey suit cut down the right side to accommodate his "mate." The man's head was Russell himself.

Finally "they" were ready. He checked himself one more time in the mirror beside his front door. In this light he *did* actually look like two people. In his delusion, his intention to only venture out at night was long forgotten.

Russell stepped out and looked up and down the dark hallway. The elevator arrived quickly, swallowed the "two" up, and Russell was on his way.

He paused in the lobby at the big front doors and looked out into the sea of surging humanity, steadied himself, pushed the door open, and set forth.

It was at that moment that Russell, and Father Allen met. The good Father had gained his second wind and, as he ran from an alley onto a busy street, he peered back over his shoulder for his pursuers. Just then Russell emerged from the front door of his building.

It was like the combination of relative motions of billiard balls. The massive slow moving Russell was stopped dead still and the lighter, faster, Father Allen was propelled at right angles toward the traffic. The Father spun twice, first on one foot then the other, trying to regain his balance. Suddenly he slipped from the curb, plunged between two parked cars, a horn blared and a speeding florist's truck slammed him broadside throwing him several metres to land back on the sidewalk in front of a trendy tavern two doors up the way.

The collision rattled Russell's already fragmented consciousness, and he wobbled around for a few seconds before being surrounded by cops and arrested. Then he passed out.

Bailey saw the commotion in front of Russell's place and pulled his cruiser onto the sidewalk across the street, got out and waded into the melee of gawkers. Slumped in the back seat, Ed recognized an opportunity to escape. It wasn't easy. The back doors were locked, and the cuffs were already seriously digging into his wrists, but he huffed and puffed and lifted and rolled himself into the front seat, opened the passenger door and tumbled out into the street. Quickly gaining his feet, he stumbled back away from the action, down an alley and out of the area while Bailey was busy calling an ambulance for the Father.

Ed resorted to his favourite tactic. He circled back and headed for the Church of the Safe Way. They would never look for him there.

--

"Hospital?!" Sara's reaction startled everyone in the immediate vicinity of the information desk at the police precinct. "What's he doing at the hospital? What happened?"

"I don't know Ma'am," the duty sergeant lied, "you'll have to ask someone down there."

Sara bolted from the place, flinging the big glass door open so fiercely that the sergeant thought it had broken.

On the way across the small plaza in front of the precinct, Sara thought she heard something, no, felt something. Something, a wisp of presence that swept past her consciousness the way an invisible stray hair troubles a cheek. And somehow it made her feel more strongly for her father than she already did. It was as though her father was trying to communicate with her. But no. Sara didn't believe in such things. She pushed it from her mind.

--

Lardner's priority was to find out how Father Allen was doing. He and Bailey went straight to Emergency Admitting at St. Michael's Hospital.

After a short computer search, the receptionist told them they had taken Father Allen to a basement holding area for troublesome or unruly patients.

Bailey and Lardner headed to the basement. "All we had to do was bring him back home," Lardner said. "What was so hard about that?"

"I don't know," Bailey said weakly, "I wasn't even there."

"Where the hell were you, stopping off at Howard Street again?"

It shocked Bailey to learn that Lardner knew about his secret excursions to Howard Street, but he couldn't explain what *had really* happened without mentioning Ed Miller's escape.

They spotted three cops gathered at the far end of the basement hallway and figured that must be where they were holding Father Allen.

Lardner pulled on the holding cell door. Locked. Bailey peered in through the small wired glass window and said, "How come nobody's in there with him?" Lardner pushed Bailey aside and looked into the room to see Father Allen laying motionless on a gurney. "Shit!" Lardner said and added, "He better not be dead." One of the cops mumbled that a doctor was on the way.

A door slam echoed down the corridor and the two

men wheeled around hoping it would be someone with keys to the room.

It wasn't.

It was Sara Allen, and she didn't look happy.

"Oh, shit, this won't be good," Lardner said.

"What have you done to my father?" Sara was still some distance away, but the acoustics in the bare hallway brought the question to the men as if she'd used a bullhorn. Lardner nodded to the cops, and two of them moved to cut her off.

When she shoved past them, Lardner went to meet her. "That's what we're trying to find out, miss..."

"Allen, Sara Allen. That's my father. Get out of my way."

She pushed Lardner, but he held on to her. "We're not sure *who* that is in there. We just got here ourselves," and he pulled on the door to the room to show her it was locked, "but we're told he will be okay." Lardner hated lying about things like this. The Father's situation didn't look at all good, but right now Sara could only complicate things. "How did you get down here? This is a secure area."

"I've been here before," she said looking him in the eye. "Where's my father?"

Lardner had to put himself with her on the same side of the situation. "Ms. Allen, I promise you, my main concern right now is the same as yours." This was true. "I'm told that an attending physician is on the way here right now." This was also true. "We must be patient."

She tried to get a look into the room. "If you've done anything to harm him, there will be trouble!" Lardner decided he might as well let her look into the room. All she could make out was a large indistinct shape on a gurney. "Is that him?" she said.

"I don't know. All we know is there was an accident, our people weren't there, so we don't know exactly what happened. We're trying to find out." He put a hand on her shoulder. "I know this is difficult for you, but your cooperation will help us sort this out faster." He moved her to a heavily vandalized wooden bench nearby and nodded to the cops who took up positions near her. Sara reluctantly sat, fuming and worried.

"She's right." Lardner said to Bailey when they were out of earshot. "If that is him and he's badly injured, we're screwed." He looked around. "Where the hell *is* everybody?"

"I think he's kicked it," Bailey said as he peered once more into the room. "Something's rotten in Copenhagen here, Bill."

"Denmark," Lardner corrected him.

"What?"

"Something's rotten in the state of Denmark."

"Yeah, well, there too." Lardner said nothing. "Point of fact," Bailey went on, "there's something rotten no matter where you go."

It was the most accurate statement Lardner had ever heard his partner make.

Somewhere Over The Rainbow

Father Allen opened his eyes to a grey brick wall. There was no pain. Not that he had been in much pain before, not physical pain. It had been more like an extreme discomfort at being broken in some way. Not broken from being slammed by the florist's truck, but the constant distress of just being alive. He'd felt pain all his life. Life *was* pain.

Now, staring at this wonderful grey wall, he was no longer confined in that dark tunnel of doubt, anguish and a constant feeling of not belonging, never being in the right place at the right time. It was hard for him to put his finger on it, but whatever it was, it was gone.

Consciousness returned bit by bit as Father Allen forced himself awake. He turned his head slowly, tried to see where he was. It was a featureless room.

No, there *was* something. A door, a small window, men's faces looking in. He tried to determine what his next move should be. He remembered the police, the chase. There should be pain. Hoisting himself onto an elbow, he rolled easily to a sitting position on the edge of the gurney and thought perhaps he could even stand up. He did. Looking down, the damage to his clothing was vanishing before his eyes. He felt his side and his leg where a long deep gash had rent his flesh to the bone. The injury had disappeared. Maybe he could walk out of here and return to his Church, his daughter... His lovely daughter, the one person left in his life. And suddenly he was somewhere else, outside, and there was Sara coming out of a building. A police station. She looked angry. His instinct was to reach out and touch her on the cheek as she passed. And he did.

Then he was back in the dark cell in the hospital's basement. Was this a dream?

Strange. The floor beneath his feet felt spongy with an undulating texture that suggested a living thing. He rested a hand back on the gurney but came into contact with flesh. He looked. It was his body lying inert on the bed. There was the torn clothing, the rent flesh and battered skull. What the hell?

Father Allen looked back to the door and wondered if he could push his way through the thick damp air to it, push it open and go out. Then a bright white light shone from nowhere and his Lord, the magnificently rotund Jesus walked, no, glided a foot off the floor, right through the cement wall as though it were nothing more than a grey fog.

It was easily the clearest and most substantial vision he had ever had of his Lord. His beard perfectly trimmed, His skin reflecting a light Mediterranean copper, His white three piece suit shimmering with a divine brilliance.

There was something else about Jesus that Father Allen wasn't able to discern. The Lord's previous visitations had been more dreamlike, indistinct. This time Jesus appeared sharp and real and when He emerged from the wall, it wasn't like some Hollywood special effect. Father Allen could easily see that both Jesus and the wall continued to exist at once, and yet neither was in any way displaced or transparent. And another thing: this time Jesus looked more familiar than He ever had. It was as though Father Allen had known Him all along. He was magnificent. The Father's being resonated in the glorious presence of his Lord. He glanced back at his body on the gurney, stained with blood, the face ashen. Was that what he really looked like? The inanimate morbidity of death made his face a hardened mask, as though cast from the same material as the cement walls around him.

He was dead.

Father Allen tore his fascinated gaze away from his own corpse and looked to his Lord, then uttered his first postmortem words. "Is, is this it?" he asked. "Am I... Have I, uh, passed on?"

"Yes." Jesus said softly. "Though it would not be correct to state it that way exactly."

"Oh," Father Allen was confused. Jesus unfolded an ornately carved twelfth century chair out of the seventh, eighth and ninth dimensions, turned it to face the Father and sat. The chair too hovered above the floor. Jesus nodded to Lardner and Bailey, frozen, peering through the wired glass door. "It would be more correct to say that *they* have passed on. And just about everyone else. They have gone on, in a way. You are staying here."

"Where, where is here?"

"Not where is here, when is here? The question you mean to ask is '*when* is now?' This is *your* moment," and He nodded at Lardner and Bailey in the window again. "To them, your last moment is past. It is a very tiny instant in that old world, but over here... well, it's complicated. Time doesn't work the way you think it does. Each single moment has immense dimensions that are not observable back there in that small, old place."

"I see." Father Allen understood none of it.

Jesus smiled a smile that set every atom in the good Father's body aquiver.

A notebook computer appeared in the air in front of

Jesus. The machine automatically logged on to some great celestial network and began compiling the elements of Father Allen's life.

"You use computers?" Father Allen said.

"What, you expect me to do all this with stone tablets or something?"

"No, of course not, but..."

"Anyway, it's more conducive to your adjustment if I use the accoutrements of *your* life experience."

"Oh."

"I'd offer you a chair but the last thing any of you ever want to do is sit down." Jesus explained softly, His words gliding buoyant in the air. Father Allen looked down to see that he too was floating a foot off the ground. Father Allen felt he could do whatever he wanted. If he had wanted to float up through the ceiling, he could have. If he'd wanted to turn into a pool of water and drain out under the door, he could have done that, too. The last thing he wanted to do was sit down.

Father Allen tested the notion by slowly rotating his whole body in a three hundred and sixty degree head-over-heels spin that brought him back to his original orientation facing his Lord.

Jesus smiled. "Your work here is done." These five words enveloped the Father in something like heat, but not temperature. The words were not only here in the room with them, but at once, everywhere in creation.

Then Father Allen realized that another peculiar thing was happening to him. Not only was he here in the room with Jesus, but in a way, at once everywhere and "everywhen" in his entire life on Earth. He *was* himself as a child singing in his father's choir. At the same time he was himself on his first date with and, at once, married to, and attending the funeral of his good wife Elspeth. At the same time as he was here with his Lord, he was being born in the living room of his parents' house in Saskatoon.

Father Allen's life had flashed before him before. Once, when he was a child, while helping his father at a community barn raising, he had lost his footing and plummeted eighteen feet to the ground. And there he was tumbling from that roof and there went his short young life flashing before him again.

He smiled. How brief and silly it all seemed now. He remembered something Sara said once during the time she became fascinated with eastern religions: "Life is like a Tibetan sand painting. It's a lot of hard work that goes into the wind in the end."

Father Allen pulled himself back, back to the task at hand. "I can't leave now," he heard himself say. "There's still so much work to do." It was a genuine concern for the fate of humankind. "What of the people in my care?" he said.

"They'll be fine," Jesus reassured.

"But they need all the help they can get, especially in these times."

"Trust me." Jesus smiled.

"Oh, yes." He had to remember to Whom it was he was talking. The Lord waited patiently for the computer to do its work. "I'm afraid it doesn't matter what you do, these things will always be insufferably slow." Jesus said.

"Surely You have better ways of doing it." Father Allen said, nodding at the computer.

"Well, sort of. But with aliens from other planets, reincarnation, vampires and all that, I have to stay abreast of current technology."

He looked around the featureless room. "Let's see if we can't find a more accommodating setting." And before Father Allen could draw his next breath, they were sitting at a small table in the window of an intimate cafe. Brilliant sunlight filtered through thin curtains. Father Allen could see a street outside buzzing with cars, trucks, motorbikes and pedestrians hurrying about in what appeared to be a golden-hued European afternoon rush hour. Father Allen was agog. "This is incredible!" He looked around at the restaurant and dared to inquire, "Is, is this.... are we in heaven now?"

Light reflected off a car outside and flashed across Jesus' face as He made another entry on the computer. "Um, technically, there is no such place."

"Oh." Father Allen had a lot to learn. Another thought occurred to him. "*Are* there aliens from other planets?"

"Around here? Heck no," Jesus said. "Too far to come."

It was a stupid question, anyway. Father Allen knew by now that all he had to do was look. There they were, myriad life of all kinds sprinkled randomly throughout the vast universe—and not alien either! It wasn't so much that they were like humans; they weren't. It was that there was nothing strange about *anything* anymore. Not any more strange than the undiscovered fifteen-foot slug-like creatures scattered about the deep Pacific Ocean floors or the foot-long scorpions in Africa.

Finally, the computer gave up what Jesus had been looking for. "Ah. Here we go." Father Allen returned to the matter at hand. He didn't know why he hadn't noticed before, but there was a beautifully groomed purebred collie sitting quietly at Jesus's feet.

"What a beautiful dog." Father Allen was getting used to making these stupidly obvious observations. "Is she yours?"

"Oh no, that's Lassie." Jesus scrolled down a

column of entries in Father Allen's file.

Father Allen patted the dog. "Hello girl, hello Lassie..."

"She follows me almost everywhere, but I don't mind," Jesus added.

Father Allen laughed. "You know I learned there were four or five different Lassies."

"Yes, in the movies. This is the real Lassie."

Father Allen had never liked dogs, but this was the first one he'd met that he somehow knew didn't slobber.

"Holy Smoke!" Jesus exclaimed.

"What?"

"I see here that you had one hundred and three down front at the end of your Easter service last year."

Father Allen blushed. "Thanks... but it's really the number of souls really saved that's important, not the number who come down front."

Jesus consulted the database again. "Only seven. Still nothing to sneeze at."

Father Allen was flattered. Later—though there was no longer any such thing as later—he would realize that Jesus knew what he was thinking all the time and "later" still, Father Allen would understand that he knew what Jesus was thinking, and everyone else too for that matter.

Jesus looked around impatiently. "What the heck do you have to do to get some service around here?" He took a plain-looking watch that hadn't existed before from a pocket that hadn't existed before and looked at it. Then Father Allen noticed that Jesus' suit had slowly transformed from shimmering white to a soft creamy avocado to match the decor of the restaurant.

"Oh heavens! I'm due at the Vatican in ten minutes." Jesus said.

"You'll never make it." Father Allen had forgotten the dynamics of the situation for the moment.

"Sure I will, it's just down the street."

Father Allen blushed.

Jesus snapped His computer shut, and it vanished. Then He pulled what seemed to be a single piece of paper out of the air. "I wanted to spend a little more time with you on this, we have so much to talk about." He handed the paper to Father Allen.

"What's this?"

"Oh, nothing. I just need your signature on it at some point."

Father Allen looked at the paper and saw that, though it was gossamer thin, it was really many, many pages of closely printed text.

"It's a contract?"

"No, no, no. It's everything you've ever done. You just need to sign off on it. It's a silly formality that We sometimes find handy."

As Father Allen leafed through the pages, he found the document to be thousands of delicate pages and every event in his life was there. He turned to page two thousand three hundred and fifteen and read a moment-by-moment account of his third birthday. He flipped through to page one hundred and twelve thousand and thirty-one and read of his first visit to a particular highway hamburger stand at the age of six.

"I *am* impressed. *Everything's* here."

"Yes, all sixty-eight years, one hundred and twelve days, fourteen hours, six minutes and thirty-three and two-thirds seconds, more or less. Take your time. You don't have to sign it now, read it over. It's quite a lot, but you'll enjoy the task. Now I really have to run."

Jesus got up, but Father Allen stopped him. "No, I'll sign it now." He went for his pocket but found that he was no longer wearing his vestment robe. Instead, he had on a gown of pure white unidentifiable material, something akin to satin. The garment was without pockets.

Jesus produced a beautiful glowing, jewel-encrusted quill pen and handed it to him.

"I mean if I can't trust You," Father Allen laughed as he signed at the bottom of the last page numbered somewhere up around three hundred million, "then who can I trust?"

Jesus laughed too, "Good point."

Father Allen held the document out to Jesus but He waved it away, "You keep it, I already have a copy."

"Shouldn't I sign that too?"

"We copy everything right away."

Father Allen was desperate to ask just who the "Us" and the "We" were that He referred to but couldn't before Jesus got up to leave.

Father Allen got up too, but Jesus stopped him with an ever-so-warm hand on his shoulder. "Don't get up. And don't be a stranger. Keep in touch," and with that Jesus and Lassie swept magically toward the door and out like a rush of sweet summer air into the bustling Roman street beyond.

"I'm sorry you had to wait Sir." It was a woman's voice. "What would you like to have?" Father Allen, his heart racing, tore his eyes away from the front door to see a pretty dark-haired teenage waitress standing at his table. Though she spoke in Italian, he understood every word perfectly. And he realized too that she was changing. Slowly, her hair was becoming red, and she seemed to get shorter or something. And the room was changing too, not out of control but slowly and steadily like mid-ocean water. Everything was the same but different. Not exactly the sort of thing you'd want to have happen back in the old physical world, but here it seemed logical, even soothing. Father Allen smiled blankly at the waitress who had already turned into a beautiful woman in her forties.

Still, Father Allen could not speak. 'God's works are most great and wondrous,' he thought. "God!" he said aloud remembering Jesus' words: "... a formality that *We* sometimes find handy." Did "*We*" refer to the Holy Trinity? Father Allen pondered the question. He'd always thought the Father, Son and Holy Ghost were to be one in heaven. But Jesus had told him this was not technically heaven. The Father knew exactly which book he would consult in his study if he could.

But wait! Couldn't he just will the entire Bible into being and read it right here? As soon as he thought of it, there it was invisibly before him, the entire enormous King James version. This was okay, but he preferred the New American Standard Edition; it was the same thing, but zippier. And his consciousness filled with the New American Standard and he read it faster than a hungry man reads a fast-food menu.

It surprised Father Allen that nowhere in the Biblical text was there any clear mention of a three part God, a Trinity. There was Matthew 28:19 stating, "Therefore go and make disciples of all nations, baptizing them in the name of the Father and of the Son and of the Holy Spirit." That was pretty explicit, wasn't it? And here was Second Corinthians 13:14 that implied rather vaguely "May the grace of the Lord Jesus Christ, and the love of God, and the fellowship of the Holy Spirit be with you all".

This was fascinating to the good Father. He searched further afield, and while he was perusing ever more esoteric versions of the Good Book and wondering still about the Trinity, his consciousness expanded and he found he could simultaneously peek back inside the holding cell in the hospital's basement where his lifeless body remained. Then he was at the Great Wall of China, strolling on the far side of the moon and suddenly on all the other inhabited and uninhabited planets in the universe. Father Allen was no longer constrained by the singular and linear dimension of time. He experienced time and space "now" as the single thing they were.

Was this all real or was it happening in his mind? Does each of us create our own reality? Does the entire universe live only in thoughts, coming and going as each of us pass in and out of existence? Is a cockroach's universe just as real as that of the pope? He would have to remember to ask his Lord all this next time they met.

He could have asked Augustine, the very first Archbishop of Canterbury because right then the great holy man was enjoying a fine lunch of Pappardelle al Sugo di Lepre and a generous glass of Tuscan Rosso di Montalcino, not six metres away at a table on the other side of the restaurant.

Instead, Father Allen noticed that there were now many "directions" to what he had once thought of as time's single direction into the future. There was Neil Armstrong, taking his first step on the moon. It was a bleak, lonely little affair. Buzz Aldrin's diarrhea, churning away aboard the Lunar Module, was a significantly more important situation at that moment. Father Allen laughed heartily for the first time in this bizarre afterlife.

Years back, he found his wife, Elspeth, waiting breathlessly with the congregation just before he was to take the pulpit for his 1979 Christmas day sermon. She rocked infant Sara in her arms. And he could feel how intensely Elspeth loved him. His chest flooded with emotion, and a warm tear rolled down his cheek. Father Allen knew she enjoyed being with the congregation at moments like this to share the hope and inspiration they experienced in his words. He saw the anticipation and love in her eyes and those gathered there that day. He so wanted to go there and be with them, but he was torn; there was so much hurt in the world he had left and again he felt he was abandoning everyone in their time of need.

But then again, if Father Allen could have roused himself up from his death on the gurney in the security observation room in the hospital basement, how could he make that useless old hulk, bereft of the true nature of creation, understand *this* wonder. Besides, any return to that small world seemed an absurd notion to him now. Though he inhabited nothing more than the fleeting instant of his death, that instant was of immense scope. Existence for Father Allen was expanding in so many new and strange ways that his former appearance on Earth was lost in its simplistic irrelevance.

This would take some getting used to.

"Sir?" The waitress leaned closer to peer into his face. She was now a middle-aged Arabic woman whose hijab did little to hide her beauty.

"Oh, sorry, I was thinking about something else."

"Would you like to order now?"

"Yes, yes." He took the menu in tingling hands.

Just then the front door of the restaurant swung open, Jesus came back in and swooped over to him.

The sudden encore startled Father Allen. "What, what, what, what," he kept saying.

"My pen." Jesus held out His hand. Father Allen got to his feet, "What?" he muttered again.

"My pen, I forgot my pen."

"Oh." Father Allen opened his hand to see that he still clutched the Lord's pen which, upon closer examination, appeared to be a priceless collector's piece along the lines of one of the most fabulous of Faberge Eggs. "Oh, sorry." He sheepishly handed the bauble back to his Lord.

"Forget it. Happens all the time. I got it from Pope Gregory, you know the one who futzed so much with the calendar, did it with this very pen in fact." Jesus pocketed the pen. "He'd kill me if I ever lost it." Then He reached out and turned the page of the menu. "I recommend their antipasti to start, particularly the carciofi alla giudia, moscardini e spuma all'aglio e prezzemolo," He said in a perfectly accented Italian. "Then, whether or not you like fish, the sogliola alle mandorle, topinambur e aria di carote to follow is *very* special."

"Uh, thank you...." Father Allen wondered why Jesus didn't simply zap the pen to Him when He realized He'd forgotten it. Perhaps there were many standards of decorum in this realm he had yet to learn. But it gave him a chance to make his inquiry. Jesus was about to turn away and head for the door when Father Allen took his cue. "Uh, excuse me." he said.

"Hmmm?" Jesus turned back to him with a gentle smile.

"If I may ask one other thing..."

"Shoot."

"Is my wife Elspeth here too?"

"Oh, well, sort of. It's hard to explain. She can't come to you, you will have to go to her. He noticed the Father's confusion and added, "It's not as though we can just fly her in."

"Fly?"

"It's a figure of speech. Be patient, you'll figure it out. As I said, time is way more peculiar than any of us ever imagined." Jesus turned to leave.

A calm feeling came over the Father. It emboldened him and he called out after his Lord, "Um, and what about God?"

Jesus muttered, "Such a nudzh," and turned back to the Father. "God?"

"Well, yes, God."

"What about Him?"

"Will, will, will I... *see* God?" he asked hesitantly.

Jesus' drew closer. His answer was matter-of-fact. "No, uh, not really."

"He, He *is* here isn't he?" Father Allen waved at the cosmos.

Jesus leaned close to the good Father. "Uh, well you see that's a question we've always had some trouble with." Jesus scratched the back of His head. "Especially with people of faith." Jesus was choosing His words carefully.

Father Allen pressed the point. "I'm just curious. He *is* here, isn't He?"

"Well," Jesus thought hard about this as He peered at Father Allen's childlike expression, then said finally, "Let me be frank with you on this".

"By all means. Absolutely."

"The simple answer is... We don't know."

"I beg your pardon?"

"At least we haven't been able to find him."

"Has he... uh, forsaken us?"

Jesus laughed. "Funny." He shrugged. "Beats me." "As far as we know, it's just us. Listen, I really must go."

Father Allen was shocked. "You, You, You mean there's, there's just _us_?" Father Allen stuttered.

"Some factions believe He has chosen, for some reason, not to reveal Himself to us and..."

"Wait a minute." Father Allen held up his hand, halting his Lord in mid-sentence. "You mean to tell me that despite all this..." he indicated the marvellous transformations and small miracles that were taking place around him every instant.

"Yes, I know," Jesus said. "I have to admit it is embarrassing."

"Embarrassing?!"

"Even *I* had a little trouble with it at first, but you get used to the idea."

"Let me ask you one thing then..."

Jesus held up His hand, stopping him. "Look, you're going to ask me about certain scriptures, then I will tell you that you have to stop thinking in terms of what *men* have written or translated or opined, then you will question my use of the word opined and ask me something about Abraham, and we'll be right back where we started. So look, it's better for you to be alone with your thoughts for the time being. It's really not as bad as it may seem right now. It'll make a lot more sense as you get used to the way things work. Now, I really must run. We'll talk more about it later." And with that He breezed out of the restaurant.

Father Allen was flabbergasted. No God? As he sat back down, the chair rose to meet him as the universe continued to unfold and enfold itself in its fluid state.

"Your order, Sir?" The waiter, now a handsome young South East Asian man, was "still" waiting to take his order.

"Oh, I'm sorry," Father Allen said, only he said it in Tai Dehong, a language spoken only in the northwestern part of Yunnan province. He looked back at the menu but could not concentrate on it. "Uh, I'll have the uh...."

"The carciofi alla giudia?" the waiter reiterated Jesus' suggestion.

"Yes, yes." Father Allen waved his hand in the air. "All of that."

The waiter bowed and left. In this infinity of a single moment, Father Allen stared out the window, past the street, past the city of Rome, beyond Italy itself, through the new and the endless expanse of the cosmic void. He wondered at the protestations, gesticulations, rantings and great harangues of humankind that made not a whit of difference in the end. Why, there were countless thousands of civilizations that had accomplished far more than his tiny tribe adrift on the mote of unimaginable insignificance that was Earth, and yet even most of *them* had come and gone like the trembling leaves of an autumn sapling.

The good Father was a quick study. He knocked about in this crazy afterlife until everything melded smoothly, and as he joined with the eternal oneness, he almost casually looked at the beginning and end of all things.

And he saw that it was good.

The Revolutionary

For Ed, moving about in the city handcuffed without being noticed was quite a chore. Finding no one at the Church of the Safe Way, Ed picked up Porky and headed for Fat's.

Tapeworm didn't have a hacksaw, but he was an adept lock pick and Ed was free of his cuffs in seconds. Undercover officer Wilson was in his usual corner, head down, sleeping off his dust-up with Bailey. Others lurked about unseen in the gloom.

Tapeworm held Porky in one hand as he poured Ed a Coors Triple Light and offered barman-to-barman advice. "You're not thinking straight, man," he said, checked Wilson to see that he was safely asleep, then produced a bag of dried pork rinds from the secret panel beneath the bar. "The hunger has made you mental in the head or something," he added making a circle around his left temple accompanied by a cross-eyed grimace—which didn't work because you need two eyes to do that effectively. He squeezed the bag, and it split with a loud pop sending a few of the rinds bouncing across the bar to Ed.

Ed picked up one of the pork rinds and looked at it, oddly disinterested. "I gave Lou my word," Ed said and gave Porky the rind to nibble. "I told him I'd be back with grub and look what happened. I set him up to take a fall. Literally. I don't even know if he's still alive or what, but I owe him."

Tiny emerged from the dark beyond the nearest

pool table. "Who's this Lou you keep mentioning?" he asked.

"Lou Kennedy." Ed said.

"Lou Kennedy?" Tiny seemed to recognize the name. So did Tapeworm. Rivets complained loudly as Tiny sat on the wobbly stool beside Ed. "I was in there for sixteen weeks. They forced me to lose forty-five pounds. Just getting my strength back now."

"You know Lou Kennedy?" Ed asked.

"Big guy?" Tiny ran his hand across the top of his head. "Peach fuzz on top. Talks about his divorce all the time??"

"That's him," Ed said. "I'm going to break him out."

A second man stepped into the light, followed by the rest of the group. Wilson snorted in his sleep.

Tapeworm nudged Ed and rolled his eye in Wilson's direction—another gesture that works better when you have two eyes. "Careful Ed," Tapeworm said. "He might be fakin' it there asleep like that."

Ed let seconds of silence settle in then said loudly, "Medium rare roast beef with baked potatoes and Yorkshire pudding smothered in piping hot gravy."

When Wilson didn't react to this in any way Ed said, "He's asleep," and went on. "But I can't do it alone. Who wants to help?"

Each man had the same blank expression as visions of medium rare roast beef with baked potatoes and Yorkshire pudding hung in the air.

Tapeworm looked Ed in the eye and whispered, "Face it Ed, they're out to get rid of you people." He picked up one of the tabloid papers from the bar, opened it randomly then turned it to Ed. "Look, 'Five-hundred pound man eats own mother's leg.'"

Ed laughed. "Come on, they just make that stuff

up."

"So what? People believe it." Tapeworm flipped pages and pointed out another article. "Look at this."

Ed looked at the headline: 'Fat not allowed in Heaven!' Somehow the quote was attributed to God.

Ed pushed the paper away in disgust. "This shit doesn't have anything to do with us, or the people in that Rightweigh place! It's just wrong."

"That's not the point." Tapeworm poked at the paper. "This is the way normal.... I mean, uh, thin people think. Okay, not all thin people. I don't for instance, but listen, when many people all think the same way about something you got a situation, that's all I'm sayin'."

Ed saw that the men were waiting for his next word. If he did something dramatic, he'd keep their attention. He crossed the room, leaned close to undercover Officer Wilson and spoke loudly.

"How about you?" The men all froze.

Wilson stirred and looked up at him. "Whaa?"

"You," Ed said. "Are you with us or them?"

"What, what do you mean?" Wilson stuttered.

"There's half a dozen of us here and one of you. Are you with us or them?"

Wilson's cover was blown. He stood up and became a parody of Bailey. "Everybody against the wall!" He barked.

No one moved.

"Move!" he commanded again. "Everyone against the wall!"

Still no one moved.

Wilson called to Tapeworm. "Tape, call 911 and tell them an officer needs assistance."

Ed gave Tapeworm a nod and a wink; universal barman's code for 'fake it.' Tapeworm said, "You got it." He picked up the phone. Wilson moved confidently to Ed. He failed to notice that Tapeworm had put the phone back down, produced a large black jack from under the bar and was now silently creeping up behind him. Ed laughed. "Come on man, you're not a cop. You don't even have a gun." Ed kept Wilson's attention on him. "How can you do this to your own people?"

"It's my job. I got kids, I need the work."

Ed notched it up. "What will happen to all those women out there who like big guys like us?"

Wilson looked over his shoulder to Tapeworm. "How's that call coming?"

In a stroke of inspired improvisation, Tapeworm quickly put the black jack to his ear and reported, "I'm on hold."

"Ask for Detective Bailey then hand it to me."

"Yes sir," he said and shot Wilson a fake wink that didn't work.

Tiny whispered to Ed, "Uh Ed?"

"Yeah?"

"Uh, what women were those?"

"Women?"

"You know, those women that like us big fellas."

"Oh, them. I've met plenty. I'll tell you all about it later." Ed held Wilson's attention. "You realize as soon as you turn all of us in, they're gonna lock you up with us."

Tapeworm was almost within striking distance.

"No, they won't," Wilson said. "I did this to help *you* people. You think I enjoy being this way? Putting on this weight was part of my job." This wasn't true and everyone knew it. "You think I like keeping three spare toilet seats in the hall closet? I can only see my dick in a mirror and now when I make love with my wife I have to be on the bottom and last week I..."

Ed was through. He gave the nod. Tapeworm raised the blackjack and said, "Here's your call."

Wilson held out his hand for what he thought was a phone. He never heard the dull thud that was Tapeworm's precise blow to the back of his skull before slumping silently to the floor.

"Thanks Tape." Ed bent down and checked Wilson's breathing.

"He's gonna be okay." Tapeworm slapped the blackjack in the palm of his hand. "That was a twenty-minute dose I gave him."

"Good." Ed reached inside Wilson's jacket, took out his wallet, several candy wrappers and, to his surprise, a nine millimetre handgun. A murmur went through the group of men at the sight of the weapon.

Ed's heart went out to the big man lying inert on the dirty floor. He realized that Wilson could have pulled the gun on them any time but didn't. Ed decided not to give up on Wilson.

Tiny knelt down close to Ed's side. "Hey, Ed?"

"Yeah?"

"Where did you meet those women you were talkin' about, you know, before? Was it in some other country or something?"

"Yes," Ed said frustrated, "but they're here too." He wanted to get back to the matter at hand.

It wouldn't have mattered what Tiny's weight was or how he looked; though he was compassionate and intelligent, he was a shy, introverted man, frightened of women. His love life would have been just the same if he weighed one-sixty and played in a rock band.

Ed got up and faced the men. "Listen guys. We can do something about this but we need to do it together."

An imposing aboriginal man, nicknamed Billy Eats Five Times by his friends, stepped from the shadows.

"Ed, you haven't been here long. You don't know how bad it is. There's nothing we can do, believe me."

"No, not alone. One at a time, they've got us. But together we can beat them."

The men balked. Several, wary of Ed's powers of persuasion, drifted away, towards the exit.

"Come on guys," Ed said, "it will only get worse." Three of the biggest men were almost out the door. "Come on, you don't even know what my plan is!" But these guys were only interested in one thing and Ed knew what it was. "There's a lot of food involved," he blurted at the last moment.

Everyone froze.

"Food?" they whispered collectively.

"Aren't you even hungry?" The group coalesced again.

Someone asked, "Where is all this food you keep mentioning?"

"Sorry man, can't say. I gave my word to someone important that I wouldn't tell and, for now, it has to be that way until they tell me I can say. But trust me, I've seen it."

No one seemed to object.

"Tape, break out some beers." Ed dug in his pocket and put the rest of his money on the bar. "I don't have an exact plan yet," he said, "but here's something I do know. I'm hungry."

"At least tell us what this food is," Billy Eats Five Times said. "Is it, say, burgers or like big meals, or what?"

"Believe me," Ed made a grand gesture. "there's more than you can look at."

A new camaraderie of mutual benefit was forming. Tapeworm broke out some harder stuff—on the house. The men loosened up and Ed got to know them better as each told his story.

Some of their ambitions were beyond the realm of possibility for people in their situation. The Boston Marathon and spelunking in central Africa were out of the question. One big man told him he wanted to take flying lessons so he could become an airline pilot. At three hundred and twenty plus, this guy would hardly qualify as an airline *passenger*, never mind a pilot.

And so it went. The alcohol kicked in, spirits lifted enough that Ed could get on with the 'plan'. "Tiny, you work at an auto wrecker, right?"

Tiny showed him the big insignia on the back of his coveralls: 'MAX AUTO WRECKERS Free Estimates.' "Yay, Max!" he yelled proudly.

"Good, think you can get us a van painted up to look like one of those Rightweigh vans?"

"I suppose, why?"

"We're getting some people out of that place."

"Outta Rightweigh?"

"Yeah, outta Rightweigh. Who works in the garment industry, you know, clothes, uniforms, stuff like that?"

Little Tony, a big guy in his thirties, put up his hand. "My wife works at a shirt factory across town."

"Think she'd be willing to help?"

"Ask her yourself," and a woman appeared from the darkness. She too had a name flash on her blue cotton uniform dress: "Louise." Ed hadn't noticed her before.

"I'll help if I can," Louise said shyly.

"Okay..." Ed was making it up as he went along, but a vague plan was forming. "Which one of you is the best cook?"

On this there was an immediate and unanimous response. All eyes turned to one man who looked like he was about to go to work at a lumber camp.

"Pete's the best." Tapeworm said, and all agreed.

"Good. Pete, you're the head chef. Who's the next best?"

Louise put up her hand and waited for Ed to give her permission to speak.

"Louise, we're not in grade five here," Ed said smiling, and she smiled back. "Just say what you want to say."

"Slim's a real good cook." She looked around at the others. "Remember the steaks in the park last fall?"

An enthusiastic wave of excitement ran through the group and Ed pointed to Slim, a man fifty pounds Pete's junior. "You're Pete's second, the sous chef."

The sudden prestigious appointment intimidated Slim. "Hey guys, I'm no chef. I only drive a forklift at the food terminal."

"You work at the food terminal?" Ed asked.

"Yeah, but don't start thinkin' we can get any grub outta that place, it's like Fort Knox out there."

"We don't need food, but a powered forklift is a good idea, think you can get one of those out?"

"Jeez, I don't know, maybe."

"Good."

Tiny put a large sincere hand on Ed's shoulder. "Ed, I just got one question."

"What's that?"

"Where'd you meet those women that like us big guys?"

Ed smiled at Tiny, then at the others. The men were going along with Ed's impromptu scheme, but for the moment they were with Tiny on this.

"Yeah man, where *are* these women?" someone asked emphatically.

"Look guys, there are plenty of people who want to have big uh... partners..."

"In bed?" one of the Bills asked.

"Yes. Trust me, I know." He pointed to the front door. "They're all right outside that door." The men all looked blankly at the door, then back at Ed. "You guys have been hidin' in here too long," he said. "You just gotta have the right attitude..." Wilson moaned. Ed grabbed Tiny's hand and turned it to look at his watch, then whistled. "Jesus Tape, twenty minutes exactly. I'm impressed."

Tapeworm patted the pocket that held the blackjack. "Want me to give him another twenty?"

"No, I gotta talk to him more. We need him." While the woozy Wilson slowly recovered, Ed laid out more of the plan for the men—or as much of it as he could come up with on the fly.

"Okay, who here has been in Rightweigh?" Every hand in the place went up and one older man said, "Never make a grilled cheese sandwich with cinnamon raisin bread."

Tony leaned in close to Ed and said, "That's Goofy Stan, he talks like that all the time."

Ed looked at Goofy Stan and softened. "How long were you in Stan?"

"Nothing keeps on happening until something does." Goofy Stan replied.

"Did Rightweigh make you this way?" Ed asked him.

"Never try riding yer bike with yer arms crossed." Goofy Stan declared. "You'll kill yerself," he added.

"He's always been like this," Tony said, "but they only kept him for a few days each time. He probably scares them."

"Some times he says good stuff," someone said.

"Word is he holds four patents," someone else said.

Ed turned to Stan. "That true about the patents,

Stan?"

"If you want people to use only one little square at a time," Stan explained, "the paper's gotta be *six*-ply."

Ed looked at Stan with a new respect. "How many times did they put you in there?"

"If yer afraid of dyin', ya haven't lived." Stan told him.

"Three times," said Tony, "He's all right."

"Yeah, he *is* all right," Ed said and peered into the darkness. "There any more women here?"

Nothing.

Ed shook his head and looked at the group of round faces. "Jesus you guys, you gotta get out more."

Louise put up her hand, then put it right back down and said aloud, "There's Nasty Jeannine."

"Yeah, yeah, Nasty Jeannine," Burrito Bill said, someone else added, "Yeah, Jeannine will go along."

Tapeworm was worried. "Hey man, I don't think you can just drive into that place and take people out. You'll get arrested, or worse."

Dread struck everyone in the room.

"If Rightweigh *wants* us in there so bad, we'll go," Ed said. "As soon as we have a solid plan."

Louise said, "And there's Sylvie."

"Oh yeah, Sylvie," said Burrito Bill. "She's a tranny, though."

"A tranny?" Ed asked.

"She's a man who dresses like a woman." Louise explained.

"Oh, she's transsexual?" asked Ed. "Will she pass as a woman?"

Louise grimaced. "She looks like Raquel Welch when she was twenty-seven,"

"Think she'll join us?"

"I'll ask her," Bob said, "she's a dancer at the

Kingston next door."

While Tapeworm poured more drinks, everyone busied themselves devising wild schemes, Ed wanted to deal with Wilson still shaking out the cobwebs at his table. Ed would need his help as much as any of the others. He got two lite beers from Tapeworm and sat down with him.

--

Lardner and Bailey located an intern with a key to the holding cell and were now inside peering into the face of the late Father Allen.

"Is he...?" Bailey asked the intern. He had heard the question asked this way on TV.

"He's not meditating." The Intern had heard this on TV, too. "They get all puffed up like that sometimes," he said. "Big fellow like this probably shouldn't have been runnin' in the first place." and with that he left the room.

Lardner had plenty of experience breaking bad news to the relatives of victims, but how was he going to explain Father Allen's death to Sara—and to his superiors? The incident report he would write must remove all blame from his men. They were doing their job. It was a freak accident.

The intern was the first to learn Sara's reaction to the bad news when he ran into her in the hall.

"Uh doctor?" She stood and moved away from the men guarding her.

The intern pretended not to hear. She followed him. Her guards attempted to stop her, but she remained convincingly calm. "I just want to ask him a question." She explained, then reached out and touched the intern's arm. "How is Father Allen?" she asked softly.

"You mean the prisoner in the security room?"

"Yes." Sara said.

"He's dead," the man said flatly, then turned away.

The frank statement was more than a shock to Sara. Before her heart could sink, it froze solid. A large part of her world had just ended, but something new now surged inside. She didn't feel the adrenaline, the hurt, the loss or anything else as she moved forward after the intern.

"Oh, Doctor."

"I'm a very busy man." He kept walking.

"Just one more thing."

"What is it?" he said, turning back with a sneer.

It was one, two, three steps to him. Then Sara performed a perfect deception. She dropped her head, and, without warning, rose up delivering a stunning uppercut to his jaw just under his left ear. Instantly, from years of experience, the intern knew, before he felt the pain and hit the floor, that the lower part of his face would need surgery.

The guards jumped to the fore, but before they could get a firm grip on Sara, she decked them too.

Lardner and Bailey emerged from the examining room to see the intern and the cops sprawled on the floor. Sara was gone.

Sara, stricken by the disaster, didn't go into the holding room where her father lay. She knew only that she had to get out of there before she exploded. Her emotions roared in such rage she knew she could lose all control. Stunned, cold, shocked and empty. Her senseless feet and legs took her to a door, out through the parking lot and across the street where she sat in suspended animation at a sheltered bus stop, too stunned to cry.

A short while later she sat at the back of a city bus

gazing blankly out the window; no idea where she was going. In her brain, jumbles of disconnected thoughts echoed, zigzagging in a low-voltage blur. Father Allen had given his life, spent everything in the service of others, and what did he get for it? Nothing. No respect. No gratitude. Not a shred of dignity. She thought of her mother and took comfort in the faint hope that her father was now with her, the one person who respected, loved and glorified him the most.

Storefronts and houses appeared and disappeared outside. She felt sorry for the multitude of faces that swept by in these troubled streets. They would never know the goodness of her father, never experience the reassurance that one felt in the glow of his innocent benevolence.

She still didn't know where she was going or what she was even doing on a bus. It was only a fifteen-minute walk from the hospital to the Church of the Safe Way, but that no longer seemed a place for her to go. The thought of it felt empty and alien.

After riding the transit system for over three hours, Sara returned to the hospital. She found the room where her father's body was being kept and remained there, at his side, for hours, ritualistically, guarding his remains until they removed him to the morgue. She sat on a bench in the hall. She could stay there all night if she wanted.

Then she cried.

--

Ed and Wilson sat together at Wilson's usual table at Fat's. When a cop regains consciousness to find that his captors are in possession of his firearm, have not harmed him, and are still trying to convince him of their cause, he is inclined to cooperate.

Ed told him of his hours at Rightweigh and what had happened to Lou. Wilson told Ed that he was living from one paycheck to the next. He told him, too, that what he was planning was insane. "You can't break *into* Rightweigh!"

"Why not? It's the last thing they expect. They're not set up for it. Besides, look what happened to Stan."

"Goofy Stan?"

"They can't handle him, he's unpredictable. That's how you beat the bastards."

"Yeah, but they're dangerous, Ed. They believe what they're doing is right. You can't go up against people like that." Wilson rubbed the side of his head. "What the hell hit me, a sock full of quarters?"

"Something like that. Sorry. Don't forget there's all that food."

"You keep saying that. Where is all this food?"

"Trust me, there's literally more food than you can look at."

Wilson, a fat man with another fat man inside screaming to get out, was about to become a double agent, but he was confused. He wavered, looked at Ed with a glassy stare that suggested he might pass out again—and then did. But Ed believed he would be with them, at least as long as he could keep the reward of a normal life alive in Wilson's mind.

--

Milrot finally got Harry Steckle on the phone. "Did you analyze the specimen?" he asked breathlessly.

"Yep," Steckle said.

"How?"

"I cut it in half and looked at it."

"Then what?"

"Then I tasted it."

Milrot was incensed. "You *tasted* it!?"

"You were right. It's a green candied maraschino cherry sure enough."

"What did you do after *tasting* it?"

"Then I swallowed it."

"You ate the discovery of the century!?"

"Eli, calm down."

"Calm down!? Calm down!?"

"I only ate half of it. I've got the other half right here."

"Okay, okay..." Milrot tried to salvage the situation. "Is there anything strange about it?"

"Aside from the fact that it has no pit and was much too sweet for my liking? No, not really."

"No pit?"

"Yeah."

"How do you explain that?"

"I don't. You're the biologist," Steckle chuckled. "I was kind of hoping *you*'d know how these things work."

"If I could explain it, I wouldn't have sent it to you, damn it."

Steckle decided it was time to end it. "They have seedless grapes, don't they?"

"No, those grapes have seeds, their development is stunted genetically so you don't notice them." Milrot wished he'd never sent the cherry to Steckle, that he had studied it more carefully himself. "Are you sure there's nothing there?"

Harry laughed. "Eli, someone's playing a joke on you and you're falling for it."

"The thing appeared from nowhere," Milrot said, struggling to control his emotions. "Suddenly. There was a big shock wave and everyone here got a bloody nose, and Emily Milne went blind in her left eye. There's a section of brick wall missing"

"You must have an equipment malfunction."

"Harry," Milrot pleaded, "there are a lot of things we don't understand about the universe."

"Agreed, but maraschino cherries isn't among them. Look, I'll take another peek at it and think about it, but other than that..."

"I suppose that's all I can ask. Goodbye." Milrot hung up, then watched the two men who were on a scaffold outside the hole in his wall mixing mortar. As soon as the lab was back in working order, he'd run another experiment with Lou, only this time he'd set up video feeds and watch from a safe distance.

Harry Steckle went back to thinking about the Higgs boson and the origin of mass. Ironically, Eli Milrot's maraschino cherry *was* an important piece in this puzzle, but a virgin-birthed cherry spawned from the imagination of a fat farm inmate was too much for him. Nevertheless, Lou was becoming a conjurer greater than the fabled Merlin. Compared to Lou Kennedy, magicians like Doug Henning and Criss Angel were sleight-of-hand tricksters. Lou was a *real* magician. His god-like powers were a work in progress.

--

When Ed told the Fat's gang—now about twenty men and women—more about the cache of food in the basement at The Church Of The Safe Way, what information Wilson had about Rightweigh poured forth: an accurate map of the Rightweigh grounds, the number and locations of the security personnel, the key codes to many of the locked doors, and the locations of most of "those stupid weigh scales". Wilson's conversion inspired the others to accept the whole idea of breaking into the place they dreaded most. They all agreed to meet at the church first thing the next morning.

Slim should never have agreed to steal a forklift from the food terminal. They start up before 4 A.M. and so he had to get in and out with the machine well before that. He almost got caught twice. But, as the folks from Fat's stood outside the back door of the Church of the Safe Way and watched him come trundling up the drive on the machine, they became emboldened by his act of daring and courage.

--

That morning Sara had just enough juice in her phone to call from the hospital and plan her father's funeral and his final interment beside his beloved Elspeth in the Churchyard cemetery. No one mentioned her assault on the intern and the cops the day before, probably because no one wanted an investigation into the behaviour of some hospital staff and police during the incident.

Sara went home to, somehow, get on with her life.

Home.

What did that mean now?

Sara turned onto the street where the Church of the Safe Way sat nestled beyond the trees. She passed through the cemetery to stop at her mom's grave. Emotions welled up inside her again, but she refused to cry. She looked away to the church and wondered what would become of... Then she saw a large van. It looked like one of those Rightweigh vehicles, but from this angle she couldn't be sure. She focused on the figures moving back and forth, carrying heavy-looking boxes and bags from the rear doors of the Church to the van. Was that a red forklift?

She circled around the back of the property. In the heyday of the Church of the Safe Way, Sara grew up playing hide and seek on the property with the other children of the parish. She knew her way through the concealment of the bushes and trees to a spot where she could observe the strange activity.

At first she thought it was an official confiscation of the cache of food from the basement. But looking closer, she saw that the Rightweigh insignia barely covered the words "MAX AUTO WRECKER." And the men who lugged the boxes didn't wear Rightweigh uniforms, and they were big men; too big to be Rightweigh personnel. What the hell was going on?

There was someone at the wheel of the vehicle. He was a thin man, lounging in the driver's seat, picking his teeth with a matchstick. Country music blared from the van's radio loud enough to cover her approach. The only one who saw Sara was Porky, sitting bolt upright on the passenger's seat of the van. Porky had been watching Sara since she first set foot on the property.

As soon as the coast was clear Sara stepped up, threw open the van door, grabbed the driver by the shirt and pulled him out and down onto his back on the asphalt. It was Tapeworm.

"Jesus Christ, lady!" He gasped.

Sara put her foot on his chest. "If you don't tell me what you're doing here, you will know more about Jesus Christ than you'd like!"

Slim emerged from the Church on his forklift hauling a pallet of frozen Alberta prime rib steaks, followed by Tiny shouldering a frozen side of beef. Both men saw the fracas, abandoned what they were doing, and ran to their comrade's aid.

But the men were dealing with someone who could muster her entire life force. In seconds she somehow flung Slim on top of Tapeworm and was about to pull Tiny's arm from its socket when Ed came out carrying two boxes of frozen filet mignon and saw what was happening.

"Hey, hey, hey!" He pulled Tiny and Slim away from Sara. She struck out at him several times before he could wrestle her into a bear hug against the wall. "It's me, Ed," Ed said, trying to quell the commotion.

"What are you doing?" She looked around to see that others were now standing in the doorway holding crates of frigid free-range chickens and heavy sacks of Yukon Gold Potatoes.

"I've figured it out," Ed said enthusiastically. "Things aren't that bad. I've got a plan," and he waved his men back to work. "We can do your father's plan, only we don't need to break everyone out, we only need to get ourselves in. Civil disobedience, like you said. There was no one at the church so I figured..." He looked around. "Where is your father? I have to tell him."

"He's dead, that's where he is!"

"What?!" Ed's heart sank into his feet, then into the ground beneath.

"They got him. He was trying to help you and they got him."

Ed held Sara by the shoulders. "No, that can't be right." Sara didn't answer. Her face said it all. Ed struggled to take it in. "Are you sure?"

"I don't get things like that wrong."

He could see the truth in Sara's eyes. The bare fact hit Ed in the chest like a coronary. They were dealing in death now, and what he had thought of as a dangerous but kind of fun urban romp had become desperately serious.

He realized in one crushing instant that if one life could be lost, many could follow. And a strange thing happened to Ed right then. He cared, not only about Father Allen's plight or his own or Sara's or any of the poor people in Rightweigh, but of people everywhere who suffered. Suddenly he understood what the Father had been saying. By ignoring suffering, we ourselves suffer. Ed had spent his entire life concerned only for his own well-being. He ignored all the little agonies he saw around him. Suddenly he felt the planet beneath his feet. He felt the nurturing radiation of the morning sun, the breeze on his face, he heard the birds and the traffic on the street, but strangest of all, he felt tears welling in his eyes. It was a profound sadness—not only at the loss of someone who had in a very short time become an ally and a friend, but at the senseless destructive ignorance of human stupidity.

He could feel Sara's pain. She radiated grief, and it froze Ed's heart. How could it be? He'd only known these people for a day, hours really, but now he was feeling such loss. Was it the good Father's naïve wish for global well being that filled Ed with remorse? Or was it his sudden love for his daughter whose pain was so infectious? Ed didn't know. He didn't care. All he knew was that the emptiness in his gut began burning in anger.

When Ed came back to the world, he found Sara's arms around him, her head resting on his chest. She sobbed quietly.

Tony emerged from the back door of the Church carrying two fifty-pound bags of red onions and saw Ed's shattered expression. "Everything okay man?" he asked.

"Think you can get another truck like this?" Ed said.

"Shit, I don't know." Tony looked at the truck and the bad paint job.

"We're gonna need another truck," Ed said.

"Please Eddie, no more violence." Sara blubbered. "Daddy wanted to stop the hurting and the suffering."

"There won't be any violence." He thought about this for a second, then added, "I hope."

--

Aside from a few loose ends, Lardner figured the Rightweigh escape case was all but wrapped up. He issued an APB on Ed Miller. It was only a matter of time before he got himself rearrested. Lou Kennedy was back where he belonged and under the watchful eye of Dr. Milrot. The death of Father Allen had been hushed up.

He had no idea that a culinary insurrection was underway.

--

Ed kept his forces hungry, focused. Not because it was a brilliant tactical idea, but because much of the food was so deeply frozen, it would be at least twenty-four hours before they could do anything with it.

And in spite of his grief, Ed kept on working on the recruits' moral, relating stories of injustice, stories that made them angry, inspiring them to soldier on. They were not belligerent people by nature. He had to keep drawing their resentment to the surface and transforming it into raw, usable passion.

Sara knew he embellished the stories he told, but

these were the techniques of a brilliant revolutionary leader. Her sorrow at her father's death became a quest to fulfill his purpose.

Sara overheard Ed and Tiny discussing the bad paint job on the fake Rightweigh van. Ed looked at where the "Max Auto Wreckers" insignia bled through the fake Rightweigh logo and said, "This doesn't look good."

Tiny ran his hand over the area, hoping to wipe the failure away. "What about at night?"

"What about bright street lights?" Ed saw Tiny's disappointment. "Think we could redo it and maybe get another van?"

"Yeah," Tiny sighed. "But I don't know where we're gonna get another van."

Sara took out her phone and dialed. Ed and Tony cast her a strange look. She covered the phone and explained, "We're going to need more than another van," she said, then returned to the phone. "Hello, Amy? This is Sara Allen, I need to speak to your mother." She rolled her eyes. "Amy, it's me, Sara, from the Church of the Safe Way. Tell your mother I'm coming over to see her now." She pocketed the phone and muttered, "Silly girl," then said to Ed, "Let's go."

"Where?"

"To money."

Good thing there was a spare key to Father Allen's car. His personal keys were in a Ziploc bag along with the rest of his effects in a storage room in the basement at Fifty-one Division.

--

As the city fell into shadows, Lardner slouched in his car at the end of Howard St. with his radio and cell phone turned off. He watched as Bailey hefted the now full suitcases from the trunk of his car and lugged them into a three-story walk-up. Bailey lived alone in a decent little apartment on the other side of town. Could this be a girlfriend he never spoke of? And what was in those suitcases? Was it narcotics?

There were windows in the stairwell, and Lardner watched Bailey trudge to the third floor.

After a few minutes Bailey came back out with only one suitcase, now empty. He hoofed it back up the street to his car, tossed the suitcase into the trunk and drove off.

Lardner went into the building and climbed all the way to the top. Thirteen apartments. Televisions blared inside all of them. No clues. As he retraced his steps back down the stairs, a little girl peered out at him from a doorway on the second floor. He smiled and waved at her, but her little poker-face just stared at him until he left. He had spent almost an hour on this. He needed to get a life. He should be home spending quality time with his wife Joan.

--

A determined Sara wheeled the big Caddie up Church Street into Rosedale, where the rich folks lived. Tony and Tapeworm peered out from the back at the immodest dwellings swooshing by one after expensive other. "Nice houses," Tony said.

"Yes, if you enjoy crushing debt," Sara stated bluntly.

"Yeah, I guess," Tony said. He didn't really have an opinion.

Sara pulled the car into the circular drive where the huge Adams estate hunkered in a grove of impressive weeping willows.

Ed looked up at the mansion and sighed. "Sometimes I suspect everything I think is wrong."

"If *everything* you think is wrong," Sara said, "then the idea that everything you think is wrong must be wrong too. Let's go."

Sara knocked on the Adams' front door.

After a terse exchange with Gregory, the butler, Sara, Ed, Tony, and Tapeworm stood in the foyer of the Adams mansion. They looked like they were there to audition for *Les Miserables*. Gregory tried again to turn them away, but Sara cut him off. "Just tell Mrs. Adams that Sara Allen is here to see her."

Intimidated, Gregory scurried off.

"I didn't think they had butlers anymore," Tony whispered.

"They don't," Sara told him, "at least most people don't. That was the young cousin, Greg. He's their front man, the only one who can pass for a thin person."

"Why do rich people need a front man?"

"The head of this family, Alderman Adams, has been in trouble for months." Sara explained. "Tax problems. The police keep showing up unannounced." Sara wondered at the rectangular spots on the walls where large paintings used to hang.

Then, three-hundred-and-seventeen pound Amy Adams waddled into the foyer. The cavernous rooms and hallways somehow made her look even bigger.

"Can I help you people?" Her voice echoed off the blank walls.

Sara stepped forward. "Amy, where are all your family's beautiful paintings?"

"Hidden." She looked at Ed and the others with a withering sneer. "Some are sold." She noticed that not only was Tony wearing odd socks, he was wearing odd shoes. "Who are these people?"

"Hidden? Why must you hide your beautiful art?"

"You've taken everything else we have who knows what you will take next?"

"Amy, what are you talking about? It's me Sara, Sara Allen. You know all I want to do is help. Why are you treating me this way?"

Tony sniffed the air and whispered to Ed, "You smell something cooking?"

"I don't know, it's been so long." Ed said. "I can't remember."

"Is it a barbecue?" Tony said and went in search of the appetizing aroma.

"Stay where you are." Amy barked at Tony and he stopped dead in his tracks.

"Amy, stop this," Sara said firmly. "We're here to help. We want to talk with your mother."

"She's busy, she told me to get rid of whoever it was..."

"Nonsense," Sara said. "Is she, in the backyard?" She didn't wait for an answer, pushed past Amy and marched down the hall past the library and the alderman's den, down four wide stairs that branched off to the unused swimming pool to one side and the very-often-used four-car garage on the other. Past the dining room, big enough to entertain several hundred, through a kitchen that dwarfed that of most four-star hotels, and out to the backyard where Mrs. Adams was holding an intimate, secret barbecue for some close, large friends in a gazebo that was almost as big as Sid's Cabana on the beach in the Dominican Republic.

"Mrs. Adams!" Sara said loudly from the back porch overlooking the vast yard.

Mrs. Adams looked up from the large hooded stainless steel barbecue that was pumping out the seductive odours. Everyone gaped at Sara, shock and terror in their eyes.

"Oh," Mrs. Adams wiped her hands on an apron then pulled it off and stashed it under a table. "Sara? Sara Allen, is that you?"

Sara approached her. The others drew back in horror. "Who the devil do you think it is? I told Amy I was coming. Didn't Greg tell you it was me?" and she grimaced at Gregory cowering in the shadows.

"Well, yes, but we were uh, just playing cards and..."

"Oh, stop it. I know exactly what you're doing. I don't care. You're treating me as if I was one of of... *them* for goodness' sake."

Ed and Tony and Tapeworm appeared in the door behind Sara with Amy scrambling after them. "I'm sorry, Mother," Amy said. "they just barged through."

"Who are *these* people? Mrs. Adams said. "What do you all want here?"

"Mrs. Adams," Sara said patiently. "We're here to help."

"We don't need help."

Ed placed a gentle hand on Sara's arm and addressed Mrs. Adams calmly. "You have a very nice home here, Mrs. Adams."

"What do you want?" she said again.

"I was with your husband after his arrest." He said this loudly so all could hear. "You should know that he is well. He's a good, brave man who speaks eloquently for all of us."

Mrs. Adams came down a notch at the mention of her husband's courage. "Are they mistreating him?"

"Aside from a diet of overcooked, desiccated, cold vegetables, shoe leather meat and plain tofu for dessert? No, he has a nice warm place to sleep and his spirits are good."

A large middle-aged man in a jogging suit stepped forward. "You've been in Rightweigh?"

"I got the grand tour. Couldn't stand it, took a friend and got the hell out of there."

Fascinated by this bold figure, they gathered around as he told of his recent exploits. Sara smiled when she recognized his embellishments to stories she'd heard before. But she knew that this was his way, and it was working.

Mrs. Adams offered an apology. "I'm sorry, it really isn't much of a barbecue, but we'd be happy to share what we have. It will be ready soon." Ed smiled. "Thank you, Ma'am. We weren't invited. But I couldn't help notice that you *do* have other resources that could be of use to us in our quest."

"Your quest?"

Then Ed laid the zinger on them. "We're going to break your husband and a few others out with a big splash so the press covers it, and everyone gets to know what's going on in there. But we'll need a few practical things that you may help with."

In the conversation and drinks that followed, Ed made everyone laugh heartily. The group toasted Alderman Adams several times, and Mrs. Adams wrote Sara a check for ten-thousand dollars to finance Ed's plan.

On the drive back to the Church of the Safe Way, Sara concentrated on carefully manoeuvring the big Caddie through the dark narrow streets. "We must send them some groceries ASAP."

Half-cut from many toasts on an empty stomach, Ed lolled in the front seat. Tapeworm and Tony were asleep in the back. "I shouldn't have turned down the barbecue offer," he slurred.

"I shouldn't be driving," Sara said. "I'm having double vision from all the drinks and nothing to eat."

Ed smiled. "Try closing one eye. It works for me."

She closed one eye and that was an improvement until the car mounted a sidewalk in a right turn. She regained the road in a violent lurch throwing Ed against her. He kissed her on the cheek.

Sara giggled. "Stop it, I'm trying to drive here," she said and struggled to keep her open eye on the road. The thought crossed her mind that it might have been better if Tapeworm drove; he was used to this.

Ed kissed her again. She moved into it this time and the Caddie grazed a parked Volvo neatly removing a wing mirror.

No one noticed.

--

Kent Nason hadn't slept a wink. Something inside him kept telling him a story was about to break. Three TV sets monitored the headline news channels. A police scanner rattled nearby. There wasn't a single sign that something was about to happen, but *something* was brewing, he could *feel* it.

The raid on Jacque's.

The Fatman burger caper.

Lou's escape attempt.

Ruth Bracket's screamed parting threat to Nason and Sally as they drove off. What was she hiding?

Nason looked from his second-floor apartment into the quiet streets and felt he was the only person alive. He was experiencing the exhilaration and euphoria of a reporter whose hunches are adding up. The truth felt within reach. A silent war was going on out there and Kent knew a repressed minority will not submit to tyranny forever no matter who they are.

Nason went this way all night, pacing up and down, drinking too much coffee, his mind flitting from one thing to the next and back again. He had to stay awake. Alert. Something was about to happen.

Zero Hour

Sara awoke in her bed upstairs in the rectory. Daylight. A thousand birds chirping away outside as if nothing was wrong. Her head throbbed. She thought she might throw up. Then the emotions welled up again, flooding her heart with the loss of her father. It was really sinking in now that he was gone. Forever. It was a devastating emptiness and she sobbed.

But she had to move on with what her father wanted. She pulled herself from the bed and went downstairs. There was Eddie asleep, snoring on the couch, Porky in a purring little pile on his chest. She looked around the lonely den full of her father's religious artifacts and memorabilia. The framed family pictures. His bible on its wooden pedestal—open but covered with the purple velvet cloth with the little yellow tassels.

She looked again at Eddie, asleep, like a baby. Porky yawned opening up her whole head in that alarming way cats do. Sara sat down and stroked Eddie's brow just as she once had her father's. She knew she loved this man and she believed he loved her. Anyway, she wouldn't dwell on that for now. There was work to do.

She got up quietly and went to the bathroom to clean up, then returned, leaned close and said softly, "Eddie?"

Ed, in a staggering stroke of luck, unconsciously muttered "Mom?"

Sara's heart swelled. "It's Sara." Ed looked at her, focused, then smiled. "Hi there."

"Better get up. We have a lot to do. I'll make coffee."

Ed's stomach growled something fierce, but he could ignore it. Something new was happening in his life: Ed Miller was in love for the first time.

He went over to the Church hall where several of the men were asleep on pews. Goofy Stan was already awake. His voice echoed through the holy chamber. "If God exists why doesn't he say so?"

Ed laughed and called out to all, "Let's go people, coffee's on."

--

Nasty Jeannine wasn't nasty at all. She had gotten her nickname the same way as everyone in this strange "little" community got theirs; Jeannine went along with anything. She accommodated every whim of anyone who suggested any scheme whatsoever and, though it never got her into serious trouble, it made her life quite a chore. As a teenager she mowed more lawns than she could count, delivered newspapers for boyfriends and filled in at strange jobs for God knows how many girlfriends. So far in her adult life she had sewn at least a dozen wedding dresses, learned to play and deliberately lose at five-card stud, driven a box van all the way to Denver to pick up a broken down motorcycle, and, among many other things, performed more blow jobs than she could remember.

Sara and Tiny prepared a quick breakfast from what was in the rectory fridge—which wasn't much for a group this size—but everyone was up and ready to get on with the adventure.

--

Ruth Bracket felt positively fulfilled this morning. She was at once relaxed and invigorated as she sat on the edge of her bed, felt the warmth of the morning sun on her face.

She went for a brisk walk. It was a fine time of the day. Seven A.M. and the joggers were out in force.

Her people.

No unsightly fat rabble up at this fine hour.

Driving to Rightweigh, Bracket hummed what she thought was "Rain Drops Keep Fallin' on My Head." Ruth had a thing for both Robert Redford *and* Paul Newman. Ruth Bracket was in a rare good mood. But unbeknownst to her and everyone else that glorious morning, the unsightly rabble *was* up. And it was busy.

Best Laid Plans

Ed and Sara had worked things out in as much detail as possible, delegating specific jobs to each member of the team. Even Goofy Stan had a tactical role; to befuddle the dim-witted guards with his weird wisdom whenever necessary.

By three o'clock in the afternoon, everything was ready.

Ed rented two more large white vans and one of the men provided stick-on Rightweigh logos from the print shop where he worked. Tapeworm and Sara bought two large charcoal party grills and loaded them disassembled into the back of each of the vans along with folding tables. There was just enough room for four large people without popping the doors.

They loaded another van to the ceiling with slowly thawing food. There would be enough room left to cram in two passengers. The total compliment was eighteen. Without all the equipment and food, there would be room for several escapees. Fake Rightweigh Uniforms turned Sara, Tapeworm and Gregory, the Adam's butler/nephew, into Rightweigh employees. Gregory volunteered to drive the second van. He would make sure his uncle got out unscathed. Even though Alderman Adams was a compulsive gasbag, Gregory loved him.

In broad strokes, here's what this stalwart group of

activists had planned for that evening: They would drive the vehicles in a convoy to a staging point on the road just out of sight of the Rightweigh front gates. From here, Sara would call the press to tell them that a newsworthy event was happening at Rightweigh.

Getting past the guards with the first two vans, driven by Tapeworm and Gregory, would be the hardest part—and the scariest. The pretext of their late-night arrival was the delivery of air-conditioning equipment. That's what they decided the big barbecues in the back of the vans looked like in the dark, air-conditioners.

Once inside, the drivers would kill their lights and split up. Tapeworm would drive to the shadows at the main administration building and drop Sara, Ed, and Wilson off near where the power and communications cables came into the compound. While Tapeworm continued on to join the others at the jogging track where the heavy culinary gear was being set up, Wilson would climb up and cut the cables coming into the compound plunging the place into silent darkness.

While confusion set in among the staff of the facility, Wilson would make his way back to the main gate—hopefully abandoned by the confused guards—and open it for the third fake Rightweigh van, Father Allen's Caddie driven by Nasty Jeannine, and an old donated green Buick that belonged to someone, but nobody was clear who.

Sara and Ed would steal into Bracket's office in the administration building and steal or destroy as many of the inmate records as they could lay their hands on. Sara made a point of recruiting Nasty Jeannine to drive her father's car. She took care to make Jeannine understand that after dropping her passengers off at the jogging track, she was to drive the Caddie back to the administration building and leave it there unlocked with the keys in the ignition. This was important, so she repeated it several times.

They all followed Wilson's crude map.

While burgers, sausages, steaks and foil-wrapped potatoes were sizzling on the grills, the rest of the brave liberators would steal into the barracks, rouse the inmates and lead them out to the party.

By then the press should have arrived to provide free advertising of the protest barbecue. Everyone assumed that once the guards confronted the inmates en mass, they would lay down their arms and surrender, perhaps even join in the festivities. What could a few little guards, armed or not, do to stop the onslaught of hundreds of starving partyers?

However, there's no point in going into any more detail here since none of it would go as planned.

Wilson's Map

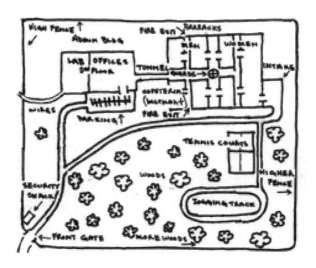

Everything was ready by mid-afternoon when Tapeworm arrived at the rectory with a stack of frozen pizzas that he'd purchased one and two at a time. Sara microwaved them. Everyone gathered around the dining room table to go over the plan one more time.

Wilson proved to be a great asset. He was the only one among them who'd had some para-military experience. He didn't mention that it came from episodic television shows, but that wasn't important. The important thing was that they were a dedicated team.

"Tonight?!" Tony exclaimed when Ed announced that the plan was to go into action immediately.

"We've got our plan. We've got the vehicles." Ed gestured to the parking lot. "The food's almost thawed. All we need is six dozen paper plates and some plastic forks. Why wait?"

They were stunned. Maybe they thought it was to be a nice barbecue picnic in the country. It was, but now they realized they were mounting an incursion into a fortified, *armed*, encampment. Ed and Sara knew the plan should go ahead before anyone developed cold feet, or worse; before they started tucking into the food reserves.

"We should have got more pizzas," Tiny said as he searched frantically through the empty boxes piled on one end of the table.

"No," Ed explained. "We have to stay sharp. Quick on our feet."

"This is no time for nervous impulse eating," Sara insisted.

"We're a lean, mean fighting machine." Ed said, then corrected himself. "Well, *mean* anyway." Everyone laughed. "There will be plenty to go around once we get set up on the inside."

Through all this, Tapeworm held onto the notion that they were about to commit a series of felonies. He knew that if things went wrong, the worst that would happen to the others would likely be stiff weight-loss sentences at Rightweigh. If they caught Tapeworm, he would go to prison. He'd visited folks in federal prison before. It wasn't a place he wanted to call home.

It is interesting to note here that collectively, through general activity, deprivation, and chronic anxiety, the group, collectively weighing 2.874 tons, had, in a single day, lost over thirty-two pounds. It was vaguely the opposite of what Lou did when he created mass from nothing. These brave folks were converting mass into pure nervous energy.

An uneasy silence permeated the rest of the preparations until it was time to board the vehicles and move out.

--

It was a slow day at police headquarters and by noon Lardner thought he might make it home for dinner for once. He even called Joan to let her know. No answer. He left a message. Idly waiting out the clock, he wondered, if after work, Bailey was planning another rendezvous on Howard Street. Curiosity got the better of him. He had to know.

Lardner parked his car a block away from the tenement on Howard Street and climbed the stairs to wait inside an alcove at the end of the hall on the third floor. It took a while, but eventually he heard the door downstairs. Soon Bailey arrived lugging two suitcases, went to room 3-C and let himself in.

Okay, this was it. Lardner no longer cared if Bailey caught him. He had to learn the truth. No point in being subtle about it either, he'd just walk down the hall, open the door and walk in. But then, if there was nothing wrong, if it was just a girlfriend or something, then he'd never regain the trust of his partner. Could he ever again rely on Bailey to have his back in a dangerous situation?

Then he heard voices. An argument. It was Bailey and a woman. Lardner moved closer but couldn't make out what they were saying. He moved closer still. Then suddenly, the door banged open, and Bailey came stomping out. Lardner was right there, next to one of those brass fire extinguishers that hang at shoulder level on the wall, and the only reason Bailey didn't see him was that he didn't expect to see him. Before the door could close behind him, Bailey turned back and said into the room, "I don't care what Edith says, she should do her share. Tell her that."

With that he turned away from the room and away from Lardner and left down the stairs and out the front door, slamming it hard behind him.

Lardner got his foot in the apartment door before it clicked shut. He took out his ID, then pulled the door open and stepped in.

It was a single room. At the far end, if you could call it far, was a queen-size bed and in the bed was the biggest, fattest woman Lardner had ever seen—and that includes photographs on the covers of the tabloid papers. This woman was so fat that Lardner had to look around her for a few seconds to sort out where her face was and where her arms and hands were. He guessed that she was so big that getting in and out of bed was a major operation, if it was possible at all. In one hand she held the remote for a big-screen TV that stood against the wall. In the other, an overloaded burger with cheese. The two looked at each other mutually stunned by the unexpected encounter, then she said, "Who the hell are you and what the fuck do you want?"

"Uh... um... uh, Lt. Bill Lardner Ma'am." He showed her his ID, then pointed after the long-gone Bailey. "I'm uh..."

"Oh yeah," she said. "You're his partner. He told me about you," and she took a big bite of the burger.

Lardner was reminded of Jabba the Hutt in Star Wars. "Uh look, I'm uh sorry if I..." He backed away.

She waved a hand the size of a pork butt. "Ah, never mind him. He'll be okay. Come on in." She downed the rest of the burger and Lardner thought she would eat the paper wrap too, but she extracted it at the last second.

"Are you his...?"

"His mom," She said without a single crumb falling from her lips. "It's not his fault, and it's not my goddamned fault either so quit looking like that." Lardner vaguely recalled Bailey mentioning that his father was one of those guys who liked to lose himself in the folds of an ample woman. "Sit down," she said and gestured to the foot of the bed. But Lardner couldn't find any place that would allow him to sit without sliding off onto the filthy floor, so he just moved closer and kind of leaned down. The place smelled like sour milk mixed with Noxzema, or something. Not exactly revolting, just weird. He noticed that dirt had accumulated in all the corners and along the baseboards.

She shovelled through the contents of one suitcase and took out a package of frozen sweet-and-sour spareribs, then leaned way over to set them carefully on top of a small steam radiator to thaw and warm. Now Lardner knew why it was so hot in the room. The rest of the contents included orders of takeout lasagne, half a dozen burgers, a big bag of French fries. A dozen neatly wrapped squares of fudge brownies fell all over the floor when she reached for them. Lardner gathered them up, and she helped with one of those long reacher/grabber devices they use for high shelves in discount stores.

"I guess he never told you he had a mom," she said with her mouth full. "I can tell by the goofy look on your face."

"Uh well, um, no. I guess it never came up." Lardner was trying to be polite. He looked for something to wipe the brownies off with, but she grabbed them from him. Headphones lay on the bed beside her and Lardner followed the cord to a DVD player on a small table and a stack of pirated DVDs, all well within reach.

"How, uh, long have you uh, lived here?"

"You mean how long have I been in this goddamn bed? Three-and-a-half years since I went down the stairs last time. Nothin' but trouble out there anyway," and she opened the second suitcase and perused its contents.

Lardner spotted a toppled chair in the debris, dragged it over, sat down and the two had a long conversation about many things. Bailey's mother's name was Sandra, and she was actually quite nice.

Lardner learned many things about his partner during the visit: That Ray Bailey only had a grade nine education meant he'd lied on his recruitment application. Lardner ignored this, but it explained his butchering of the English language. He learned that Bailey's father died in bed six years before and though she never said it happened during sex; it was the first thought that popped into Lardner's head and he had to shove the image out of his mind, through the door, down the stairs and all the way out to the street before it faded.

But as the conversation went on, Lardner thought he now knew where his partner's hostility about the fat people came from. He was in no hurry to leave, either; he was finally doing real police work. He was in his element, uncovering the facts between the lines, discovering motives, learning how and why people do the strange things they do.

--

Exhausted and aching all over, Dr. Milrot had retired early to a cot he had set up in a storage room beside his lab. He wanted to be awake before five AM.

First thing in the morning, before the sun came up, was the time when Milrot's brain worked best. He knew that the older he got the shorter that maximum brain time became. Now, at thirty-seven, he was at his peak functioning power. He was physically fit and took pride in the fact that he could put on his socks without sitting down. He had calculated that by the time he was sixty his vital peak brain time would be only a few hours each morning. By the age of eighty he would have only half an hour of intellectual capacity each day after morning coffee. At eighty-nine, he doubted he would be able to follow the Saturday morning kiddie's cartoons and he would probably have to sit down to put on his hat.

Now visions of literal sugar-plums danced in his head as he lay half-asleep on the cot he kept in a large supply closet. He envisioned vast orbiting space farms where teams of psychic farmers could manifest huge quantities of food in the near vacuum of space where shock waves couldn't propagate. The heat of re-entry could even cook the food on the way down to landing pads at supermarkets all over the planet.

Then a realization hit him, and he sat upright and stared at the wall ahead in horror. If Lou Kennedy could cause an object mimicking the pulp and skin of something as complex as a maraschino cherry to pop into existence several feet from his body, what stopped him from producing the proteins, nucleic acids and lipids that are the ingredients of a living cell? And why couldn't he will this to be on another planet? As Milrot stared at the wall, he realized that this man, this stupid,

stupid fat man, Lou Kennedy, could jeopardize the entire search for extraterrestrial life. Then another shock of realization: "My God!" Milrot said out loud in the dark, "Could this be how life on earth began? That some intelligence somewhere in the distant depths of space and time had, by sheer accident, imagined all this into being in a daydream!?"

He thought of Edgar Allan Poe who said, "All that we see or seem is but a dream within a dream," and idly thought "Isn't there some religion that contends all our reality and being is but the dream of a Creator asleep in a higher reality? The aboriginal people of Australia. Yes, that's it. My God!" And Milrot suddenly concluded, "there *is* a God!!" It didn't bother him that he was imagining a lazy, uncaring self-concerned, indolent, being far removed from the day-to-day affairs of humans and totally unaware of their condition. His mind spun with other things. He should never have sent the cherry to Harry Steckle. He should have had its DNA tested himself.

He fretted like this for the better part of an hour before he leapt up and bolted from the room. He had to get Lou back in the rig. Had to produce another cherry, a Brussels sprout. Even a single pine nut would do. Anything.

He went straight to work in the lab. Good, Gwen was working late. Milrot convinced her to stay and help set up a new experiment. It didn't bother her at all that he was in a tee-shirt and boxers; he did that often.

The two dragged a comfy chair from the first-class lounge across the hall to a corner of the rebuilt test chamber. Milrot loaded a syringe with phenobarbital solution while Gwen went to fetch Lou in his room on the second floor of the barracks. When everything was set, and they had strapped Lou into the chair in the test chamber and sedated him, Gwen left for the day.

Now Milrot could keep a close eye on Lou via monitors above his cot in the closet.

--

Ed pulled Father Allen's Caddie over to the side of the road a safe distance from the main entrance to Rightweigh. Sara was in the passenger's seat with Tiny and Wilson huddled cheek-by-jowl in the back. The three fake Rightweigh vans and the old Buick pulled in behind. They killed engines and lights and waited for silence to settle in.

Oddly, everyone was dressed up for the event. The men from Fats all wore suits and ties. Sylvie had done the women's hair, and they looked good in what evening dress they could manage. Sylvie, by the way, did look remarkably like a young, slightly plump Raquel Welch.

Ed found it sad that these poor socially starved people had become so stranded in a world that was out to get them, they thought of this dangerous, expedition as a social event. It hadn't occurred to any of them that, if they had to lie face down on the damp ground or scale a twelve-foot fence, it wouldn't be the most dignified thing they had ever done.

The next morning the entire scene would be thoroughly photographed, but it would be the aging, rusting Buick that would become known as the "Fatmobile" across North America, a large part of western Europe and, strangely, Japan. Perhaps it had something to do with Sumo wrestling. Within six months, two FATMAN manga books would hit the stands and a feature-length anime movie would be in the works. There would also be a sudden surge in

Japanese fat porn. Had Ed Miller chosen to reveal his secret identity as the original FATMAN, he would have enjoyed immediate Japanese rock-star status in that country.

It was a cool evening for early September, but everyone was sweating because they were scared rigid. This fibrillating fighting machine, this phalanx of fear, would soldier on without complaint. With the added anxiety, the the group was collectively losing weight at the steady rate of 2.43 pounds every twelve minutes. But if all went well, there would be plenty of food for everyone.

That is, if all went well.

Light from the front gates of Rightweigh, seconds away down the road, reflected in thirty-three dilated pupils as Ed and Sara got out of the Caddie and went to Tapeworm in the first van. There was no need to go over things again. Wilson got out of the Buick to join Ed and they hunched down out of sight behind a barbecue. Sara pinned her hair under her Rightweigh hat and climbed in beside Tapeworm. She wouldn't have admitted it at the time, but the whole caper invigorated her profoundly. Gregory was already at the wheel of the second van.

Command and communication functions within the group would be via toy Batman walkie-talkies from the children's room in the church basement. Cell phones didn't work inside Rightweigh.

Ed saw no movement in the guard box at the main gate up ahead and to his surprise one of the big double steel gates hung wide open. "Okay," he said into his plastic bat-cowled walkie-talkie. "Is everybody set?"

There was no answer.

Ed rolled down his window, leaned out and spoke into the device again. "Are you guys ready back there?"

and he heard his own voice squawk from the walkie-talkies inside the other vehicles. The devices were working perfectly, but the inhabitants of the vans were too scared to respond.

"You guys want to go over it again?" Ed asked across the tiny network.

"No, we're okay," someone's voice stuttered from one of the other vehicles. Someone else coughed. This was the last time the walkie-talkies would be used; they would be forgotten as fear and excitement took over.

Ed reached across a barbecue cover and patted Tapeworm on the shoulder. "Ready Tape?"

Tapeworm nodded. "Ready as I'll ever be."

Sara put a gentle hand on Ed's arm. "If something happens," she whispered, "I'll never forget you Ed Miller." Suddenly they were resistance fighters in the black-and-white universe of a World War II spy thriller. It was the first time she'd called him Ed, and right then Ed decided he preferred Eddie. They kissed deeply and Tapeworm exchanged an obscure glance with Wilson.

"Okay, let's do this," Ed said and Tapeworm released the parking brake with a loud clunk that startled everyone on that dark section of country road. Gregory revved the engine of the second van gently, put it in gear and the two vehicles crunched off the shoulder and onto the pavement.

The front gates of Rightweigh loomed ahead.

A Moveable Feast

Wilson looked around the cramped quarters in the back of the jostling van and said to Ed, "Maybe it'd be better if you were over here where I am. You know, in case the range gets too far for the walkie-talkies."

"Yeah, maybe," Ed said, and the two began exchanging places. But as soon as they did, all three of Newton's laws of motion came into effect at once and the van lurched wildly.

Tapeworm struggled to keep it on the right side of the road. "Hey, sit down back there. We're goin' in."

In the confusion, Sara made a quick secret phone call.

Two guards sat before a bank of flickering video monitors in the main gate security hut. Each display showed dark views of the exteriors of the buildings, and equally murky strategic views along the perimeter of the compound. Keeping the grounds dark at night was Milrot's idea. "If anyone wants to leave after lights out," he explained, "they will have to generate their own light to find their way making them highly visible to security staff." It hadn't occurred to anyone that someone would attempt to break *in*.

Tapeworm pulled his van up beside the guardhouse and waited, trying to swallow his heart. A guard put on his hat and came out to investigate. Fortunately, his vision didn't adapt quickly to the darkness as he peered into the first van at Tapeworm and Sara. Sara grimaced, trying unsuccessfully to look like a man.

"You guys new?" the guard asked.

"Nah." Tapeworm was a natural-born liar. "Been working downtown." He looked the guard up and down "Before your time."

"I thought the union didn't allow you to work nights."

"Oh thanks," Tapeworm mock whispered. "Shout it all over the place that we're moonlighting."

The guard leaned in and tried to get a look in the back. "What's that?"

"Air-conditioning. Just droppin' it off."

The guard looked at the other van, then made an executive decision. "Okay, take 'em in," and he waved them through the gate.

Tapeworm was so light on the throttle he could hear the tires squeak on the treated pavement of the main driveway. He couldn't believe it had been that easy. He'd been looking forward to more of a challenge. Surely they should have been more suspicious. Was it a trick to trap them inside? He glanced in the rearview mirror as he pulled the van around the first bend in the road and the guardhouse disappeared behind the trees. Ed peered out the back window and let out a sigh of relief. "So far so good," he whispered.

Right then Wilson added an unnecessary thought. "Christ Ed, if you'd told me a week ago I'd be doin' this I'da thought you was nuts!"

"Shh," Ed and Tapeworm said in unison.

Tapeworm pulled the van into the shadows beside the administration building, killed the engine and the lights. "Is the coast clear?" Ed asked.

"I don't know," Tapeworm said. "It's so fuckin' dark out here there could be a parade of deaf mutes goin' by and I wouldn't know it." Then Tapeworm remembered that Sara was with them. "Pardon my French Ma'am."

As they disembarked, the van's suspension squeaked loudly, echoing across the grounds. "Jeez," Ed said, "I thought someone oiled that."

"We did," Wilson said. "Never seemed that loud before."

Ed pulled a rope and grappling hook from under his seat and stepped from the van. The darkness was so complete it felt as if it was pushing on Ed's face. He saw the brake lights of the other van glow for an instant as it pulled up at the jogging track.

There were small pockets of light here and there from low-voltage bulbs at exits, but other than that, the grounds were perfectly dark.

Tapeworm stayed back at the van to keep an eye out, so to speak. Wilson led Ed and Sara to a corner of the administration building and snapped his flashlight on momentarily to locate the big cluster of wires high on the side of the building where power came into the facility from outside.

"Think you can climb up there, okay?" Ed whispered to Wilson, handing him the grappling iron.

"Me?" Wilson had conveniently forgotten it was part of the plan. "I thought I was going back to the front gate to let the other folks in."

"That too," Ed said. "Right after this. But you know this layout better than anyone. Here you go," and he handed Wilson a pair of heavy gardening shears.

Wilson didn't want to let down the effort, so he planted his feet firmly in the soft earth, held the grappling hook with resolve, then looked up at the heavy eaves that ran around the top of the two-story building. Ed and Sara stood back as he swung the hook around two, three, four times and launched it into the air.

It didn't even come close and now the heavy iron grapple was coming right back down at him. When Wilson tried to leap out of the way he tripped and fell and the hook missed him by inches, landing on the grass with a muffled thump.

"Jesus Chri..! I mean, uh wow man," Ed said. "You okay?"

Wilson got up, favouring his left knee. "Aw shit, it's my bad knee."

"You got a bad knee?"

"Yeah."

Ed knew he was faking it, but he helped him up and took the rope. "Okay, I'll do it. You start for the front gate. The power should be out by the time you get there." Ed clapped Wilson on the shoulder and added, "Good luck, man." Wilson fake-limped off and was swallowed by the night.

Ed looked up at the cluster of wiring. He knew that even if he could grapple the eaves, the climb would be difficult. He swung the heavy hook once, twice, three times and let it fly. This time it hooked onto the heavy eaves trough with a dull clank.

"Hey, I got it," Ed said with pride.

"Okay, up you go," Sara said giving him a gentle shove.

Ed hadn't climbed a rope since high school gym class. He stuck the rubber grip of the shears between his teeth, grasped the rope firmly, and pulled himself two inches off the ground before the eaves ripped away from the wall with the loud extraction of four-inch cement nails. Two entire lengths of eves swung away from the edge of the building and slouched onto the bundle of wires. There was a shower of sparks that almost set a nearby tree alight, then the eaves let go completely and came clattering to the ground around Ed and Sara. What few lights there were on the outside of the administration building went out.

"Jesus Christ." Ed exclaimed invisibly.

"Hallelujah!" Sara added.

A shout of confusion came from the distant darkness, then another and Sara said, "We'd better get going."

Tapeworm started the van and drove slowly off towards the jogging track. Ed flicked on his flashlight. Holding the beam to the ground, he led the way to a fire door on the side of the Administration Building. Bracket had high-tech magnetic locks installed everywhere, but since the power was out, and the contractor had skimmed the budget for the battery backup system, they would find almost every door in the place open.

It was dark and quiet inside as they made their way to the main foyer and the stairs leading to the second floor offices and Milrot's lab. Ed remembered his shocking experience in the cafeteria and correctly assumed that it was a regular source of electrical disturbances and the guards would check the main circuit breakers there first. This would put them well out of the way for the time being but what Ed didn't know was once the guards found nothing wrong at the cafeteria, they would move directly on to the main administration building to check Milrot's lab on the second floor and that meant he and Sara had less time to do their clandestine work.

Sara stopped him at the stairs. "Eddie, maybe you should use this time to find your friend Lou."

"There will be plenty of time to do that during the party."

"No, there won't. We'll have to be well away from here when the police show up.

"But they'll arrest the people who came in with us."

"What are they going to charge them with? It's not a crime to come *into* Rightweigh." Sara squeezed his arm. "Go find your friend Lou, I'll meet you out front at Daddy's car."

What she said made sense. "Can you do it alone?"

Sara smiled. "I've been here before. I'm not exactly sure what I'm looking for, but it can only be in a few places. I'll know it when I see it. It'll be fine." Ed wasn't able to say another word before she leaned in and kissed him. Then they embraced in a tight clutch that both of them knew could well be their last.

They heard footsteps.

"Okay," Ed said reluctantly, "I'll see you out in front in..." He looked at a watch that wasn't there. "In about fifteen minutes. And don't change anything else, okay?"

"I love you, Ed Miller," she said again.

Another quick kiss, then Ed headed to the dark tunnel that led to the barracks.

Sara looked after him for long seconds. Too long; the footsteps were coming closer. She sprinted up the stairs to the second floor.

--

Halfway down the basement tunnel Ed heard guards tromping toward him. Luckily they didn't suspect treachery and had no reason to be quiet. Ed found a nifty hiding spot beside a water vending machine and killed his flashlight. The two guards that came by wore military boots and key chains that jingled and echoed loudly. Ed stopped worrying about Sara. Even if these guys went all the way to the second floor, she would hear them coming a long way off and hide herself in time. Ed continued down the tunnel to spring Lou. He wasn't worried about his mom; she had gone over to the other side and would be safe for now. And Gregory would find Alderman Adams at the party.

--

As soon as the receptionist at First News got Sara's cryptic cell phone call, she knew this was right up Kent Nason's alley and called him immediately. Kent was just turning the SUV off the Parkway on his way back to the station.

"Nason," he answered.

"Kent, it's Marjorie."

"What's up?"

"I just got a call from some woman and I thought you'd want to go take a look."

"What did she say?"

"'Big barbecue at Rightweigh.'"

"That all?"

"Yeah."

"You call the boss yet?"

"No."

"You uh, gonna call him now?" Kent said in the teasing way he knew worked on Marjorie.

"It *is* late, wouldn't want to wake him or anything."

"Thanks Marjorie, I owe you." Kent pulled on the wheel. Luckily there were no cops around as he skidded across a grassy median in a wild 'U' turn. This could be the break he was waiting for.

--

Tapeworm pulled his van up beside Pete and Tiny's van at the Rightweigh jogging track. The big barbecue grills were assembled and the mesquite charcoal was already going.

Confused voices echoed from different parts of the compound as Tiny helped Tapeworm heft the barbecue grill from his van.

Powerful flashlights cut the darkness, but they were still far off near the main building. No immediate threat.

Wilson had made his way back to the front gate guardhouse where the two guards were now standing outside peering at a strange orange glow coming from the jogging track.

"What is that?" one of the guards asked.

His partner squinted at the scene and said, "Looks like a fire or somethin'". Night watchmen have a marvellous knack for stating the obvious.

Wilson made his way silently around the back of the hut to a position in the shadows. He could see through the fence and down the road outside to the other van, the Buick and the Caddie waiting quietly in the dark.

"Maybe you better call it in," one guard said to his partner.

"Me call him?" the other guard said timidly, but his partner was already heading off toward the orange glow. The guard went back inside to phone William. This was Wilson's chance. Silently, he crept into the hut to loom behind the unsuspecting man.

Wilson's cohorts waited silently in their vehicles until he emerged from the guard hut to wave them in. Tony started his engine. Jeannine at the wheel of the Caddie started her engine. Billy Eats Five Times cranked and cranked the engine of the old Buick, but it wouldn't start.

"Maybe it's flooded, try pumping it." Burrito Bill said. Ed put the three Bills together to avoid confusion.

"It's not flooded, it's fucked." Little Billy said, and without another word he, Billy Eats Five Times, and Little Billy abandoned the dead Buick to join Wilson on foot at the gate.

The brave cavalcade was in.

In a stroke of genius, Billy Eats Five Times, suggested they close and secure the front gates in case the police showed up. Wilson checked that the guard he had immobilized was securely bound with a power cable and gagged with duct tape, then they went to join the festivities.

The cell phone of the bound and gagged guard worked this close to the outside world, but it took a while for him to jostle it from the desk and dial William's number with his nose.

William's other half, Randi, couldn't make out the guard's muffled pleas from behind two layers of duct tape. William stirred awake, rolled over, squashing his face into Randi's rock hard bicep. "What time is it?"

Randi handed the phone over his shoulder. "I think this is for you."

William took the phone and groaned, "Hello?"

Nothing.

The guard on the floor of the hut at the front gate had given up, hung up, and was now laboriously dialing 911 with his nose. When the operator answered he could say nothing but knew they would trace the call.

--

Lardner had just left Bailey's mom's place when he got the call informing him of the 911 call from Rightweigh.

He called Bailey and arranged to meet him at headquarters. A nice long late-night drive would be the perfect opportunity to settle the thing about Bailey's mother. Maybe it would do Bailey good to know he had a friend and sympathizer in Lardner.

--

Sara found Bracket's office door unlocked. She moved immediately to the desk, sat in the high-backed chair and studied a group of framed photos of Ruth Bracket with different celebrities. Was that Jane Fonda Bracket had her arm around? And could that be a young Richard Simmons mugging in the background?

Sara tried the drawers. Locked. She pulled a large screwdriver from her backpack and committed her first felony of the evening.

She got lucky. Bracket had left her laptop in the top drawer of the desk. Sara knew it would be password protected by some long string of numbers and letters, so she slid the whole machine into her backpack. They'd crack the password later. She experienced a slight twinge of guilt over committing the crime of theft but then considered the greater good and moved to two filing cabinets. Original, signed paper documents spoke louder than computer files.

From the window she could see the flames from the barbecues below at the jogging track. Her emotions swelled. She thought it must have been like this the night the Berlin wall came down. She wished her dear father could be here to see the triumph of his efforts—if there was to be a triumph.

Sara's heart was going like a jackhammer as she pulled open the first filing cabinet and riffled the files looking for God knows what.

The Kraken Wakes

Ruth Bracket opened one eye and peered at the digital clock on the bedside table. Twelve forty-one A.M.

Click.

Twelve forty-two.

It was strange for her to wake at this time of the morning. Ruth didn't believe in the supernatural, but she had a feeling that something was up. She sat on the edge of the bed. Picked up her phone and speed-dialed the Rightweigh security office. No answer. Probably making the rounds. She speed-dialed the office at the front gate and waited as the bound and gagged guard watched it helplessly from his place on the floor.

Something *was* up. She dressed, washed her face and hands and brushed her teeth. For once she would beat William to the punch and get there before him. She threw on her green jacket from the front hall closet, grabbed her car keys and left.

--

Ed flattened himself against a wall and peered around a corner. In the confusion, security had left the central barracks security desk unattended.

Good.

He would wake Lou and lead him out through the rear fire exit, hustle the half-asleep Lou down the side of the building to meet Sara at the parking lot.

Simple.

He could hear the men's snoring chorus from here. Soon they would be awake and on the move. He had to get Lou out of there before the rush.

In minutes, he was in the sleeping hall and looking down at Lou's bunk. It was empty.

Now what?

He hoped the guards were still fumbling with fuses in the basement as he made his way to Lou's private room upstairs. He wasn't there either. Ed recalled Lou's vague description of Milrot's experiments. Milrot's lab was all the way back through the tunnel, to the administration building, up the stairs, to the second floor. And he had to get there without being spotted.

Lou *was* in Milrot's lab, but Ed would never know that. He would never make it all the way there and, even if he did, he would have found it locked tight with the mechanical locks that Milrot, in his paranoia, had installed foreseeing this very situation.

Lou lay asleep, strapped to the comfy chair and wired to every bio-monitoring device Milrot could lay his hands on. Two video cameras coolly watched Lou as Milrot lay on his cot in the closet watching via CCTV. He would continue this vigil twenty-four/seven if necessary.

Milrot wondered what Lou was dreaming about and if he could manifest anything without being hooked up to the electronic equipment. He wondered if Lou's dreams posed any immediate danger to the building or to himself. Probably not.

Wrong!

--

Gregory hefted a fifty pound box of beautifully marbled T-Bone steaks from the van. Pete slapped ten of them onto the coals and a big cloud of smoke and a shower of glowing embers flew up into the night. Tiny sprinkled them with Montreal Steak Spice.

The guard in the front gate office wriggled free of his bonds and made his way to investigate the festivities. He tried to figure out what to do next when he saw his partner wolfing down a loaded hot dog and fraternizing with the inmates. He didn't know Burrito Bill was standing directly behind him.

Burrito Bill wasn't a violent man, usually his sheer size was intimidating enough to get him out of a tight spot. He carefully reached down, enfolded the guard in a gentle bear hug and lifted him off the ground.

"How would you like your steak done?" Bill asked.

The guard squawked a faint reply. "We'll uh, I uh, I uh, medium uh, rare I s'pose."

"Good man." Bill said, and released him, but not before he relieved him of his walkie-talkie and key ring.

Goofy Stan came to the confused guard wiping tears from his eyes and advised, "Careful with that hot Peri-Peri sauce, though. Looks just like butterscotch."

--

Ed made his way back past the cafeteria and was about to head into the tunnel when he heard a man's voice. The sound echoed about so he couldn't tell exactly where it was coming from. He turned off his flashlight and became invisible in a dark corner at the cafeteria entrance, then peered carefully around the corner. He could see two guards standing at the far end of the eating hall. One of them was talking to William on the phone. "Yes, well, we seem to have a situation here... No sir, nothing seems to be wrong, it's just that the power's out and... I'm calling on my cell phone. Yes, they're working but... Okay, Yes sir. Okay."

Ed slid to a position behind one of the long food serving counters. When he leaned against the flat stainless steel surface, it popped inward creating a dull sound that echoed about the place.

"What was that?" one of the guards said and both of them swung their flashlights Ed's way. Ed froze. The guards began searching the area.

--

William climbed out of his bed. If cell phones were working at Rightweigh, something *was* wrong.

Soon he and Randi were going well over the speed limit in Randi's Hummer on their way to investigate. He hadn't called Bracket yet. No point in incurring *her* wrath. The guard on the phone said it was a simple technical issue. You didn't wake Bracket in the middle of the night over a simple power failure.

William relaxed, then realized that in his haste he had thrown his jacket over his elephant-motif pyjama top. He buttoned his jacket covering as many elephants as possible and hoped there was a spare shirt in his office closet.

--

The Rightweigh security force was slowly getting itself organized and Pete's barbecue had become the focus of their attention. The tough little man in charge of the night patrol marched across the parking lot to Pete methodically laying hamburger patties out on a large grill. But before he could get a word out Pete turned to him and said, "Onions? Pickles? Mustard?"

"I want to see you in my office right now!" the head guard barked.

"Sorry sir, can't do room service, too busy."

"You can't make a barbecue here," the man said and raised his baton. Goofy Stan stepped up with a hand on his shoulder. "It is a far, far better thing I do than is dreamt of in your philosophy, my son."

"What the fuck's that supposed to mean?"

But before Stan could explain, Tapeworm stepped up behind the guard and gave him a solid forty-minute dose of his trusty blackjack. The lump that rose on his head was the only injury that would be intentionally inflicted that evening.

--

Bracket drove her Mercedes like hell through town. She arrived moments before William and realized immediately that something untoward was going on. The guard box was empty and in her haste, she'd forgotten her phone. She saw the glow from the fracas at the jogging track and pulled on the gate.

Locked.

She sat in her car and tried to think things through methodically. Something told her the guards had their hands full.

Most of them did have their hands full—full of hot dogs, hamburgers and soon, piping-hot baked potatoes topped with sour cream, chives and bacon bits.

William and Randi arrived to see Bracket's car parked outside the front gate. How the hell had she gotten here before him? Why did she leave her car out here? William saw signs of activity at the jogging track but couldn't see any guards anywhere. Bracket watched in her rearview mirror as William got out of the

Hummer and walked right past to the gate without noticing her. He wasn't aware that his pyjama top collar, showing one large yellow elephant, was sticking out.

Bracket continued to watch as Randi sidled up beside him, slipping an arm around his waist. "Looks like a party," he said seductively.

"I thought I asked you to stay in the car." William tried to push him away, but Randi bit his ear. "Stop it." William moaned, half-succumbing.

Bracket hated surprises like this. She leaned out her window, speaking in an even tone. "Are you two just going to stand there nuzzling or are you going to get these damned gates open?"

William almost jumped right out of his jammies. His secret was out. Quickly removing Randi's arm he turned to Bracket and plastered a shaky smile on his ashen face. "Miz Bracket, I didn't see you there..."

"Obviously." Bracket got out of the car and sneered at Randi as she joined William at the gate.

"Could you wait in the car, please Randi?" William whispered.

Bracket held out her hand. "Gimme your phone," she said to William but glaring at Randi.

William patted himself all over, but he already knew he'd forgotten it in the rush.

"Do *you* have a phone?" Bracket said coldly to Randi.

Randi gave her a sexy smile as he took the Bluetooth from his ear and held it out to her. "Yes'm."

She took the device from him, holding it between two fingers as if it were radioactive, and passed it to William. "Get someone out here to open this damn gate, NOW!"

Randi quietly made his way back to the Hummer

and for a moment Bracket thought she glimpsed him going into a major giggle fit, but she couldn't be sure. William spoke the main security number to the voice-activated dialer. "There's no answer Ma'am."

Randi leaned out of the Hummer and called out to Bracket. "I guess you wanna get in there huh Ma'am?"

Bracket gave Randi a sharp look. "Ya think?"

The Hummer roared to life and Randi manoeuvred it up to within a few feet of the gate, got out and removed the designer leather bag from a large winch on the front of the behemoth.

"Where did you find him?" Bracket asked William. "At the wild west rodeo show?"

"Oh, uh, he's um, Randi, Ma'am."

"Yes, I'll bet he is."

William blushed furiously as Randi grabbed the thirty-pound winch hook in one hand and hauled out the thick steel cable. William caught Bracket eyeing Randi's ass while he attached the winch hook to the bottom of one of the heavy gates. He wondered if he still had a job as they watched Randi return to the Hummer and rev it several times. The gate screamed as it wrenched free of the stonework, Bracket looked up at the administration building. At first it was hard to see, but there was no doubt. Someone was inside her office moving about with a flashlight.

Randi threw the big truck into reverse and backed away, pulling the entire gate clean off its hinges. Just the sort of work for which the ridiculous civilian vehicle was designed.

When silence returned Bracket said calmly to William "Where are the cattle prods?"

"The what?"

"The crowd control devices that came by Fed Ex last week."

"Oh, of course. They're in the closet, in my office."

Bracket shot William a wry smirk. "Good, I guess there's plenty of room in there for them now, isn't there?" William didn't get it. Randi did. "Get them," Bracket croaked. She got into her car, over-revving the engine furiously and squealed out disappearing down the road toward the administration building.

"Jesus," Randi observed, "you're right."

"About what?"

"She *is* quite the harridan little cunt, isn't she?"

--

A woman, sleeping under a small partly opened window in the woman's barracks, snorted, rolled over, sniffed the air, then sat bolt upright in bed. Sniffed the air again. Is that...? No, No.... just dreaming.

She was trying to return to a troubled sleep when another woman sat up. "A barbecue!"

Another woman called out. "There's a barbecue!?"

Others woke. "What? Where?"

Outside, things were just about ready and Wilson and the three Bills were preparing to enter the barracks and go to the Men's area to start the call to party. The strategy was to raise the men first so there could be no trampling of women in the rush. Louise, Jeannine and Sylvie were getting ready to make their appointed rounds when, without warning, the women emerged cautiously following the incredible scent.

"Hey look," Bill said and pointed.

It was the Night of the Large Living Dead. The women came forth in disbelief, as in a dream, one at a time, slowly gathering at Pete's glowing, crackling burger pit.

--

A thin, delectable tendril whiff of mesquite-grilled sirloin continued on, drifting up the side of the building, making its way through a ventilation grill to the halls where the men slept.

Suddenly the snoring stopped as if someone had thrown a switch. Long seconds passed then, as though twenty feet were cut from the film, suddenly and at once everyone in the room was crowding toward the exit. The stampeding tsunami of giant men surged into the hall. Thoroughly programmed by rigorous routine, they turned en masse towards where they knew the food to be: the cafeteria.

Not one man in this bizarre onslaught was fully awake.

The two guards were still snooping around the main eating room and Ed was still trying to avoid them when he heard the rumble of the grunting and mumbling bare-footed herd approaching.

--

Lou snoozed comfortably in Milrot's lab while Milrot lay awake on his cot watching him on the TV monitor. What Milrot couldn't know was that at that moment the faintest invisible wisp of burning mesquite was snaking its way down the hallway outside the lab. Soon it would find the ventilation grill above the door, pass through and make its way across the lab ceiling, then sink slowly downward to caress Lou Kennedy's senses.

One important thing that Milrot had failed to understand while experimenting with Lou was that the stimulus that brought Lou's new talent to life had to be subtle. It had to evoke strong imaginings. Rather than induce appetite, it had to provoke fantasy—fantasy so strong that the object being thought about popped into existence in the real world.

The tantalizing, lilting wisp of barbecue fragrances reaching out to Lou were just the right thing to conjure a major manifestation.

Another thing: Lou no longer needed the apparatus of Milrot's lab to fabricate matter from thin air. All he needed was the stimulus and the unconscious desire and it would happen.

Lou Kennedy was a bomb primed to go off.

--

Sara's search of Bracket's filing cabinets was going slowly. Not only did Ruth Bracket have detailed personal information on past and present inmates, but she'd been scouring newspapers from dozens of major U.S. cities, collecting articles and photos of prominent obese Americans. Too much to carry and no time to sort through it. Besides, Sara had a different plan.

From another drawer, Sara pulled out a folder marked FINANCING and stuffed it into her backpack. This file would later prove to be evidence of the fraudulent purchase of the Rightweigh property. Then she spotted a file folder marked "JC." Why would Bracket have a file on Jesus Christ? She opened it.

Judge Conroy.

The file contained four documents, both personal letters from the Judge to Ruth Bracket thanking her for her support and there, stapled in their top right-hand corners of each, precisely what Sara was looking for: photocopies of cancelled checks payable to Conroy, drawn on Bracket's personal bank account. One was for twelve thousand dollars and the other, dated two months later, was for twenty thousand. This was it. Proof that Rightweigh and the courts were working in collusion to exploit and suppress an innocent minority.

She heard laughter in the yard outside and looked to see that the party was on. A fair amount of fraternizing between inmates and guards was going on. This was good. Exactly as she wanted it.

Sara folded the precious documents carefully and was sliding them into her backpack when a sharp woman's voice rang through the room.

"Well, isn't *this* just perfect?"

Sara turned, swinging her flashlight beam onto Ruth Bracket leaning in the doorway. "Yes," Sara said, recovering fearlessly. "We're here to put things right."

"We?" Bracket came to Sara and looked down at the melee in the yard. "Who else is in on this?"

Had she seen Sara take the Conroy file? Sara played dumb. "I'm here with a small group of brave souls to make sure you can't continue to victimize innocent people…"

"Small?!" Bracket laughed, cutting her off.

"Yes, and brave."

Bracket waved a dismissive hand at the window and the commotion in the yard below. "The only thing those people are concerned about is getting large quantities of fattening food into their bellies. You know that as well as anyone." She looked around. "I suppose your round friend Edward Miller is here too, somewhere."

"We're *all* here."

"The police are on their way," Bracket lied, "and now I've discovered you committing a felony." Bracket softened, placing a kind arm across Sara's shoulder. "My dear girl, all my sympathies are with you in the loss of your father. I don't mean to be unkind, but perhaps if he'd done more to mitigate his health situation..."

"He would have been fine if he wasn't trying to help the people you persecute..."

"Oh, stop. I help people get better."

"You break their will."

"I help people *find* the will to get fit, to become happy, functioning..."

"How can you expect to help when all you do is create oppression, sadness and fear? Happiness is not something you can enforce."

"My clients are here of their own free will... well, many of them are. The rest are criminals," she smirked. "Like you."

"Most of these people are here because of callous and thoughtless family interventions or an unjust and cruel judicial system," Sara said.

"Come now, you don't really believe that." It was then Bracket noticed her laptop in the backpack.

Sara went on. "What free will can a person have when they're constantly told they are no good? That society hates them and discriminates against them everywhere they go?"

"That's cute. What were you planning to do with whatever you thought you could find on the computer you've stolen?"

Good, Bracket didn't know Sara had the incriminating Conroy file. Sara was emboldened. "I will use the contract you force people to sign and expose the deceptive practices of your..."

Bracket smiled. "You didn't have to break in here for that, all that material is on our website. All legal and above board."

Sara so wanted to slam Bracket with the damning evidence she had, but she kept quiet. Instead, she launched into another diversion. "Research has proven conclusively that a moderately overweight person can still be healthy." She glanced down into the yard. The crowd had almost doubled. Gas lamps cast bright circles on the grass. People were standing in groups, talking and laughing. It was a glowing green garden party in the pit of hell.

"These people aren't sick, they're unhappy."

"Oh, you poor naïve child." Bracket said. "Don't you see? I would like nothing better than to be shut down by world fitness. There are better ways of making money than trying to save these pathetic souls."

"My father and I have saved hundreds of people and it hasn't cost a dime."

"Oh, and did they lose the excess weight?"

"Some did. Some learned to love themselves for who they are and became immune to the harassment and ridicule."

"How sweet. What about their weight?"

"Some of them didn't lose weight. So what?"

Bracket moved to one of the filing cabinets and slid the bottom drawer open—the very drawer where Sara had discovered the Conroy file. "Let me show you something." Sara held her breath. Would she notice that the file was missing?

Bracket took out a file she'd laid flat, out of sight, in the bottom of the drawer. She pulled out a dog-eared photo and handed it to Sara. Sara illuminated it with her flashlight. It was a faded colour shot of a two-hundred-plus pound teenage girl in a black one-piece bathing suit frowning beside a kiddies' wading pool.

"Who's this?" she asked.

"Look closely. That's me. I was sixteen. I keep it to remind myself of who I *really* am."

Sara studied the picture. Could it be? It looked a

little like Ruth Bracket, but Sara couldn't believe she could ever have been this big.

Bracket gazed wistfully down into the yard. "I understand what it's like for a six-year-old to wake up every morning and know that all day people will call you cruel names," Bracket said. "Miss Piggy this and cowgirl that. Rumble Buns—that was a good one. To not be able to go into a restaurant without people making you feel you don't belong there. An embarrassment to your parents. Parents who plunk you down in front of the television where you find comfort in the promise of Cocoa Puffs or a package of Oreo cookies or..." Bracket choked up slightly and Sara noticed that her eyes were welling with tears. The revelation impressed Sara, but she had to be careful. None of what she was saying explained or justified the brutal treatment of the people under her care.

Bracket pressed her sympathy attack. "Children are entitled to a loving environment. When the family is indifferent, when the community rejects the child because they are less than perfect..." She choked again. "You may disagree with the way I do certain things, but Sara, imagine if we were to work together. Imagine the power we could have to make these innocent lives whole again."

Flashlights flashed in the outer office and William and Randi appeared in the doorway followed by two security guards lugging Fed Ex boxes. "Ma'am," William said, "aside from the disturbance occurring in the yard there is an incident in the cafeteria..."

But Bracket raised a bony finger, silencing him, and turned back to Sara. "Is it our Mister Miller?"

"I uh, don't know, it could be," Sara said.

Bracket cast her the softest look she could muster. "Maybe you're right. Perhaps we should make some changes around here. But right now it seems Mister Miller has gotten himself into an untenable situation. I'd appreciate it if you would come along and help me to help him."

Sara was sure she had what she came for. It was time to see what was happening. She took the laptop from her backpack and put it on the desk.

"Good girl." Bracket said. "Now let's go see what we can do for your friend."

As Bracket passed by William, she leaned in close and quietly said, "Bring Ed Miller's file and uh..." she gave him a nod that he interpreted correctly; he was to bring along the Fed Ex shipping boxes full of cattle prods.

The Standoff

Kent Nason drove straight into Rightweigh through the broken front gate. Halfway to the jogging track, he stopped to survey the scene with binoculars and plan a strategy. It would be best to get straight to where the real story was. He scanned the big party at the jogging track. Interesting, but things seemed calm there. He panned over to the administration building to see Bracket's car and Randi's Hummer parked askew. A light in Bracket's office window. This was where the story was.

He intercepted Bracket, Sara, William, Randi and the guards in the lobby on their way to the cafeteria.

"Ms. Bracket," he said, fumbling with the camera, and wishing he'd woken his partner Sally. "Ms. Bracket," Nason said again, "could you fill our viewers in on a few of the details about what is going on here tonight?"

Bracket kept moving, trying to stay ahead of him. It gave her time to think. Things were happening fast now. She took a chance.

"Have your camera ready, Kent. Now perhaps you and everyone else will see what we're up against here and the resistance we encounter as we try to help these people."

"What bullshit," Sara mused, surprising herself with the tiny, profane thought crime.

Kent was making brilliant cinéma vérité as he ran ahead of Bracket, turning and skipping backwards, holding her in the shot. "Is this an uprising, a revolt?"

"I don't know Kent, you can evaluate that for yourself in a few moments. I'm sure you've seen a patient fighting off a paramedic who is trying to save his life." He hadn't, but he knew what she meant. "Sometimes that happens when you help." Bracket went on, "They resist, sometimes violently."

Sara remained silent. 'Play it out, stay calm,' she kept saying to herself.

At the entrance to the cafeteria they stopped short at a wall of backs of large male inmates. The blockage was impenetrable. The action, whatever it was, was beyond the human barricade.

Bracket turned back. "This way," and she and her little group went back the way they had come, around another corner to a small locked door marked EMPLOYEES ONLY. Suddenly the lights flickered and came on. Good, they'd restored power. Bracket took out a card key, and they filed into the cafeteria supervisor's office, then straight through to where Ed Miller was now holed up.

--

Here's what had happened: The two guards searching the cafeteria area confronted the surge of semi-conscious men, and what would have been a fairly normal situation at noon had, in the middle of the night, immobilized the guards with fear.

As for the inmates, all they knew was that someone, somewhere was cooking up a mess of burgers, steaks, ribs and baked potatoes and they were eager to learn if there was an option to partake. No one said anything. It was a silent standoff.

From his hiding place behind the serving counter,

Ed could see the situation was not good. He'd armed himself with a broken ceramic turkey leg left unnoticed under the counter from the earlier incident. If he stood they would see him. If he so much as coughed, they'd know he was there. In a reflection of a stainless steel back splash he could see that the guards and the inmates transfixed upon each other. He decided his only chance was to make a break for a small door at the back.

He went for it.

He made it to a long steel table and crouched under it. No one noticed. Quickly, he moved out to cross the open space to the exit door.

Suddenly it opened and there stood Bracket, Sara, Kent Nason, William, Randi and two guards. It was over. Or was it?

Bracket. took charge. "Well, Mr. Miller," she said calmly, "here we are."

Ed held up the turkey leg just in case no one had noticed he was armed.

William eyed the makeshift weapon and wondered if they'd charged the cattle prods up before shipping them. Luckily, they had not.

No one moved. Bracket tried to block Nason's camera, but he jockeyed his way around to get a bead on Ed.

With the press now in attendance, things might shift in Ed's favour. He took a chance and called out to the assemblage. "Who's hungry?"

The mob looked vacantly from Ed to Bracket.

"It's over," Bracket said calmly to Ed. "Accept it." Then, in a miraculous effort of self control, Bracket softened. "Mister Miller, we are not at odds here. It isn't my concern what laws you are in violation of..."

"I broke no law," Ed said, "and I bet most of these

people here didn't either."

Sara bit her lip, remained quiet, waiting to see where this all would lead. Ed was holding his own.

"I believe you're confused." Bracket said as she came right up to Ed, braved the threat of the broken turkey leg, and stared him straight in the eye.

"I will make it simple for you to understand. You are in contempt of a court order. If you don't like the law, then do the democratic thing and endeavour to have it changed. Meanwhile, you will comply with the ruling made against you and remain in our care here at Rightweigh until you have lost..." she held her hand out to William for Ed's file.

William advanced ever so carefully, eyeing the turkey leg and imagining long nasty sessions of reconstructive facial surgery. He held the file out to her at extreme arm's length.

Bracket snatched the file and scanned it. "The court convicted you of disorderly conduct and creating a public disturbance. Rather than send you to jail, they placed you in our care at Rightweigh until you have lost twelve kilos." She snapped the file shut and smiled at Ed. "You may disagree with these rulings but I can tell you right now Mr. Miller, there are worse consequences to this kind of conviction than the treatment and attention you receive here with us."

Sara had to step in. "I thought you wanted to help these people." She squeezed forward. "What about what you said upstairs? What about that poor girl from your past? Do you want the world to know about that?"

"Why not?" Bracket flashed her a grotesque smile. "She's my *big* sister Rumble Buns. She lives *alone* in a bungalow in Santa Monica. If you can call that living."

--

Lardner, Bailey, and four cops in two cruisers pulled in through the front gates. During the drive, the subject of Bailey's mom didn't come up. Ray Bailey just couldn't shut up about how no one listened when he warned them there would be trouble with these "fat fucks".

They arrived to see Tiny singing opera in public for the first time, his gargantuan aspect, for once, entirely appropriate as he rendered an a Capella solo from *I Pagliacci*. No one knew Tiny was an opera buff, let alone an accomplished bathroom baritone.

Bailey tried in vain to corral the shindig until someone thrust a burger overflowing with fixings into his hand. Lardner waved him and the other men over to one side to organize a plan. When Bailey placed the hamburger on a table, it disappeared in less than four seconds.

"Whatever happened here has already happened." Lardner said to Bailey. "Let's try to find out what it is exactly." He led the men through the empty barracks toward the cafeteria where Ed was stating his demands.

"We want redress for the abuse!" Ed said to Bracket and Kent's camera.

A small tentative applause rose from the crowd.

The accusation offended Bracket. "What abuse?"

Now Alderman Adams stepped forward. "Serving nothing but leafy greens for dessert is undeniable abuse!" There was a muffled, hesitant cheer from the men.

"You're here to diet Sir." Bracket reprimanded the alderman as if he were a child.

"And no more torture." Ed said.

"Torture! What torture?"

"Electric shocks." Ed said.

"What about those awful turmeric milkshakes?"

someone in the back called out.

"That's all recognized aversion therapy," Bracket asserted. "You men will all return to your rooms."

Another unidentified inmate yelled. "What about the kielbasa beatings?"

This pronouncement took Nason by surprise, and he searched with his camera for the speaker.

Suddenly a loud klaxon sounded in the hallway outside. Lights flashed, and the gruff mechanical voice of one of the ubiquitous weight scales boomed out. **"SHAME ON YOU! YOU NOW WEIGH SEVEN HUNDRED AND EIGHTY-FOUR POUNDS AND NINE OUNCES!"**

"Wow," Sidney the human metric converter said from somewhere in the crowd, "that's almost three hundred and fifty-six kilos!"

Everyone spun around to see that Lardner, Bailey, and the cops were caught frozen in the red glare of a weight-scale warning light. Bailey pulled his gun.

"Good, the police are finally here." Bracket said. She pointed at Ed.

"Arrest this man."

Lardner was confused. Bailey spotted Ed's turkey weapon and levelled his gun at him. Taking their cue from Bailey, two of the uniformed cops covered Ed with their weapons.

"Hold on, hold on, hold it now," Lardner lowered his partner's gun with a benign hand and waved to the other cops. "Come on, come on, put them away." Lardner approached Ed. "Care to tell me what the problem is here?"

Bracket moved in, handing Lardner the court order from Ed's file. "Please take this man into custody."

Kent rolled on the tense scene as Lardner scanned the document. He realized there was only one way to go. "Mister Miller, it appears, according to this, that you are to remain here until you lose…"

Bracket grabbed the file. "Twelve kilograms." She called to her men. "Escort all these men back to their rooms."

When no one moved, one guard tentatively held his prod against a man and pressed the button. Nothing happened.

The guards looked at Bracket, then at Lardner. It was up to Bracket to break the stalemate. "It's over, Mr. Miller." She looked at Sara but spoke to Ed. "Comply now and I won't press any charges. We will add nothing to your sentence."

"No," Ed said. "The police will arrest me and take me to jail. I'd rather be there than here, anyway." He put down the turkey leg and walked over to the cops.

Nason moved like a phantom, working his camera in to record Bailey snapping the cuffs on Ed.

Sara dropped her head.

"That's wise of you, Mr. Miller." Lardner said and he and Bailey and their men led Ed away, out through the cafeteria entrance where they all stepped, once more, onto the treadle of the weigh scale. The klaxon wailed, the red lights flashed and a deep male voice boomed, "**YOU SWINE! YOU STILL WEIGH ONE THOUSAND AND TWENTY-ONE POUNDS AND SEVEN OUNCES!**"

The startled men leapt from the treadle at once. From somewhere in the back of the crowd the calculating Sidney said, "that's four hundred and sixty-three and a half kilos."

Sara lost all hope. But… wait a minute! She scanned the crowd. "Who said that?" A hand appeared, then Sidney stepped forward. Sara asked him, "What did it say the police weighed when they came in?"

"Seven hundred and eighty-four pounds and nine ounces," Sidney announced.

Sara snatched Ed's file from Bracket, flipped through to his induction report and examined it.

Ed saw what Sara was trying to do and grinned at Bailey. A warm feeling flooded through him and he stepped back onto the treadle alone.

A far more sympathetic female voice announced, "YOU NOW WEIGH TWO HUNDRED AND THIRTY-SIX POUNDS AND FOUR OUNCES."

"That's a net loss of twenty-six point two seven pounds," Sara said before anyone else could work it out. She turned on Bracket, "Your own equipment says Edward Miller has completed his sentence!" Sara held up Ed's file for all to see.

Bracket wasn't prepared to accept any of this. "No, no, no. That's not how it works." She grabbed the papers from Sara.

Sara went to Ed and placed her arm proudly over his shoulder.

"YOU FOOL, YOU STILL WEIGH THREE HUNDRED AND SIXTY POUNDS AND ONE OUNCE!"

Ed whispered to Sara, "but I couldn't have lost..."

"Shhh, go with it," she said then smiled at Bracket. "According to the court order and your own records, he's lost the weight. You can't keep him here."

"No, no, no, no, no, no, no!" Bracket protested, "Something's wrong with the machine." She held out her hand to William. "Gimme your calculator."

"I don't have a calculator," William sputtered.

"Well, give me a pen, a pencil, anything."

William unbuttoned his jacket, revealing his elephant pyjama top which had no pockets.

"Oh, for Christ's sake." Bracket, panting with

frustration, struggled to do the math in her head.

Lardner removed Ed's handcuffs. Sara and Ed embraced to tumultuous applause. Ed addressed the men. "Everybody. Everybody, we're in the wrong place. The party's out in the yard, by the jogging track. No hurry, there's plenty of food for everyone."

Inmates of Rightweigh had never moved so fast.

Lardner rubbed his face with both hands. Nason swung his camera onto Bracket as she finished her mental calculations. She grinned at Ed. "Mister Miller, you are short! You owe me another three ounces."

Ed and Sara ignored her and walked away. Ed whispered, "I'm pretty sure I owe more than three ounces."

Sara quoted her father. "The weak of mind are easily swayed."

Lardner wanted to leave but Bailey stopped him. "How do you want to handle this?"

"I will go home, say hello to my wife, make us a couple of stiff drinks, and we'll stay in for a week."

"Don't we have to arrest someone?"

"For what? Sleepwalking?" He took Bailey by the arm. "Come on."

"Wait a minute!" Bracket called out to no one. "What about my three ounces?"

But it was over.

"Edward Miller!" Bracket was screaming now. "You owe me three ounces!" She grabbed the nearest guard. "Get him!" but the man just stood there. The guards looked at each other blankly but did not move. Someone's stomach growled.

"You're all fired!" Bracket screamed. Nason got it all.

--

Out in the yard the horde of men joined the others in anticipation of the midnight breaking of the fast. Laughter was heard. Tiny gave a lively rendition of the "Drinking Song" from Ambroise Thomas's opera *Hamlet*. Someone produced a battered guitar. Sylvie did a sexy dance and all were entranced by her beauty.

Strangely, no one had ventured to escape. Guards and inmates partied together as if they'd just met. All seemed forgiven.

Goofy Stan had his arm draped over the shoulder of a guard. Both of them were eating burgers and sipping cola. "If the enemy of my enemy is my friend," Stan said "then why isn't the friend of my friend my enemy?"

Sidney the human calculator came up to Pete to lodge a jocular complaint about his burger. "You call this a quarter-pounder?"

Pete grinned. "Something wrong?"

"Wrong? No." He hefted the burger up and down, estimating its weight. "My good man, I'd say this is more like a half-pounder you've made here."

They both laughed.

As Sara and Ed drove out through the front gates, they had their first lover's spat. "I've already let Lou down twice." Ed said.

Sara respected and admired his loyalty, but there were priorities. "If we take him with us now, we'll be giving her ammunition in her defence." She stroked his cheek gently then checked her watch. "I can file for an injunction in four hours. They will have to release everyone then."

Ed looked back at the festivities and saw that for once in a long while, his people were happy. Sara was probably right about Lou. "Okay, I guess." he said quietly.

The Accidental Tourist

Poor Lou had slept through the entire episode but now, finally, the scent of burning mesquite had made it all the way to him, slowly entered his left nostril, then passed on to his olfactory sensors.

Lou's previous encounter with burning mesquite was not at some steak house or at any rowdy backyard barbecue. It was during a bus ride three years earlier along the Farrington Highway at Black Rock Beach in the southwest of Oahu, an island in the Hawaiian chain.

His ex-wife, Fran, a compulsive participant in any contest she came across, had won the trip to Hawaii and she and Lou were on their way from the standard tour of Pearl Harbour, headed for a scenic turn through the Ka'ena State Park. The USS Arizona WWII Memorial had so affected Lou emotionally that he was silent for almost the entire trip.

As chance would have it, near Black Rock Beach that week, farmers were busy burning off the wild mesquite trees that were sapping precious groundwater in the area. It was an activity that was expensive and useless since the mesquite's twenty foot tap-root can regenerate a new tree in a few weeks.

It was this experience that Lou dreamed of when the smell from Pete's barbecue hit his mid-brain. At that same moment Milrot was lying on his cot in the storage room idly watching Lou on the monitor.

Lou came half awake, had no idea where he was and, in his confusion, his mysterious new ability manifested itself again. But instead of producing a small forest of smouldering mesquite there in the lab, this time Lou made every atom in his body vanish at once from that hemisphere of planet Earth and reappear at the very same instant on the side of the Farrington Highway in Oahu at 5:38 PM local time.

Lou's immediate disappearance from Milrot's lab had an exactly opposite but similar effect as the manifestation of the maraschino cherry had earlier, only bigger. In the implosion, most of the atoms within a forty foot radius were abruptly stripped of their energy and everything in the immediate environment rushed in to fill the void left by the sudden absence of the billions of molecules that used to be Lou. Shelves, equipment, doors, walls and one of the building's critical supporting beams were all slammed together to fill the momentary black hole that formed, and Milrot was looking straight at it when it happened. In fact, he even got sucked out of his room along with a large slab of the wall and found himself clinging to a sloping section of floor that now yawned perilously outside into the warm night air.

Startled by the concussion, the partyers in the yard below turned at once to see that a whole corner of the administration building was destroyed. Reaching the safety of a level section of floor, Milrot stood and turned to look back down at the gathering. The crowd burst into applause as if were the climax of some strange and wonderfully surreal stage show.

--

It was only lucky that there were no fatalities when Lou

appeared in Oahu that afternoon. Two cars were thrown off the road into a shallow ditch, and a truck loaded with raw sugar was overturned. It could have been worse; had he appeared only half-a-mile south along the highway, he would have forever changed the lives of at least twenty people who were sitting at tables in front of a roadside diner at the time.

The whole teleportation experience made Lou feel weird. No normal person could have survived the abrupt relocation as his tissues and organs strained to push away the new environment at supersonic speeds. But Lou regenerated damaged cells instantaneously, and though it made his bones hurt and upset his stomach in a way that he didn't like, he survived.

--

Always on the lookout for a snappy headline that might help sagging circulation, the local print press dubbed the events of that night the Rightweigh Hamburger Riot and featured a blurry photo of the moment of the implosion as it appeared in the background of a selfie of Tapeworm and Pete high-fiving each other. But Nason's brilliant video scoop blew the cheesy print coverage out of the water with its expose of the hypocrisy at the heart of Rightweigh. His follow-up piece featuring interviews with people incarcerated there against their will was seen around the world.

Sara presented the letters and checks between Bracket and Judge Conroy to a federal prosecutor, and an arrest warrant was issued for Ruth Bracket, but she had vanished. In return for retiring from the bench, no charges were brought against Judge Conroy. All his Rightweigh judgments were quietly overturned.

In Memoriam

The service for Father Allen took place at the Church of the Safe Way. His full congregation attended along with hundreds of new followers. Sara gave the eulogy, which included the thirteenth draft of her Father's last sermon. It borrowed heavily from Dr. Martin Luther King's famous "I have a dream" speech.

> *"... it is time to rise from the dark and desolate valley of discrimination and hate to the sunlit path of justice. Those who hope we will just go away, who hope we will stay in our rooms and never venture out into their streets, will have a rude awakening. As we stand on the warm threshold which leads into the palace of justice, let us not seek to satisfy our thirst for freedom by drinking from the cup of bitterness and hatred. Now is the time to make justice a reality for all of God's children."*

It was the first time there was applause in a Sunday service of the Church of the Safe Way. Everyone hailed Father Allen as a spiritual hero since it was essentially his life's work and his martyr's death that precipitated the great liberation.

--

Sara and Ed closed the Church for renovations and reopened it as a restaurant called THE CHURCH. (They wanted to keep calling it The Church Of The Safe Way, but after their story hit the media, a large American grocery corporation threatened them with charges of trademark infringement.)

In partnership with Jacque, and with an investment campaign organized by Alderman Adams, The Church offered an array of exotic cuisine creations at affordable prices. On the side, Sara gave free seminars on practical health management. "If you don't feel the personal need to lose weight, then don't. No one here will think badly of you," she explained. "But if you chose to lose some weight, we will help."

As the organization's accountant, Ed's mom didn't like the non-profit aspect one bit, but she gave in to the new pride she took in her son. She even put on about twenty-five pounds and regained a decent complexion.

Ed and Sara never saw Lou again, and Ed deeply regretted his failure to save his friend. Sara had never met Lou and sometimes late at night, she would look at Ed asleep beside her and wonder if Lou Kennedy ever really existed.

--

Milrot knew damned well Lou existed, but no matter what he did, he never found a single trace of him in the rubble of Rightweigh. Not so much as a single hair. There should have been *something*. Obscure clues to Lou's whereabouts did eventually emerge, but the news went unnoticed half a world away.

Lou endeared himself with the Hawaiian natives quickly. Occasionally, he would rent a bomb-disposal suit and seclude himself inside a cave deep in the Makaha Valley, near Wahiawa. Here he would blow whole smorgasbords into being for the enjoyment of the locals. He learned to manifest large buffets on the seaward side of volcanic cliffs, where the surrounding rock directed the strange quantum blast effects harmlessly away. Seismographs as far away as Tokyo and San Francisco detected the shock waves from these preparations, but since the signals originated in one of the most geologically active places on Earth, the data was invisible in a sea of tectonic noise.

--

Ed brought Carlito from The Dominican Republic to take over the bar-tending duties at Fat's from Tapeworm, who died of intestinal cancer three months after the fall of Rightweigh. At the reading of Tapeworm's will, and to everyone's surprise, it turned out he owned both Fat's and the Kingston Hotel next door outright. The second surprise came when they learned that he'd left his entire estate to Porky, Ed's mom's cat. Tapeworm wasn't crazy or stupid. He identified with the animal, and he had confidence in his customers. He knew that the entire group had taken to Porky and that they would look after his bar. It was his way of leaving Fat's to them all. He also knew that the strange bequest would generate a huge amount of publicity for the establishment.

It did.

Tapeworm told no one of his condition. His single final ambition was to see Fat's returned to its former glory. This he knew he had done, and so he decided it was finally time to let go. It amazed Ed to realize that as Tapeworm confronted the guard that evening at the front gates of Rightweigh, he was probably in excruciating pain. No one knew. Ed made sure that his small nervous friend was immortalized as a hero of the uprising.

--

Bill Lardner was promoted to homicide. His very first case was a nasty little killing in the east end of the city. Detectives canvassed absolutely every person in a twelve-block radius. Not a single witness was brave enough to talk.

When Lardner came in, he discreetly interviewed all the same people, even had dinner with a few of the witness families. Finally, without revealing a single informant to his superiors, the community or to the press, he pieced together enough evidence to identify and arrest a suspect within six days. It was an exquisite masterpiece of detective work. Despite an affair that Joan tearfully confessed to, their marriage survived, and they eventually had two children.

Wilson took over security for The Church and he and Sylvie moved in together. No one saw that one coming.

Bailey's mom suffered a stroke while construction contractors were attempting her extraction from the third-floor flat so they could transport her to a clinic to receive a gastric bypass and psychiatric care. But she never came out of the coma and they called Bailey in to "pull the plug." Bailey eventually became a high-up in the Specialized Operations Command of the Toronto Police Service with an office of his own. He cleverly developed the strategy of maintaining perfectly manicured nails on each of his index fingers so he could point to things on desks and computer screens without showing that the rest of his fingernails were gnawed down and mangled past the quick.

William and Randi moved to the suburbs and got married. They had two children by adoption—one of whom would grow up to become the first Senegalese female Prime Minister of Canada.

Invasion Of The Body Snatcher

The report, that aired in the U.S. two days after the Rightweigh debacle, went like this: "There was a bloodless coup this week in, of all places, Toronto, Canada," the newsreader said. "Seems the big folk up there are revolting," Everyone in the studio had a good laugh about the quip. The footage for the CNN report was credited to Kent Nason. The report was roundly criticized by The National Association to Advance Fat Acceptance. Fox News offered Nason a field reporter position and he accepted on the condition that he could bring along Sally Bean. They agreed.

Ruth Bracket watched Nason's report on her iPad in an airport limousine making its way up FDR Drive, fighting the morning traffic to Fifth Avenue and 56th St..

Soon she stood at the window of her emergency escape condo on the twenty-sixth floor of the Trump Tower and revelled in the dull grey roar of the city. There was Armani across the street. A Gucci shop right in the building. She scanned the bustling obese throngs in the street far below. "So many lost souls. So many willing subjects," she thought. "Fuck it. This is the great United States of America. This is where I belong, anyway."

***

About the author

Rex Bromfield worked in the film business as a screenwriter and director for many years. His first feature film, '*Love At First Sight*', Dan Aykroyd's first film, was invited to *Filmex* in Los Angeles by the American Film Institute. He directed many children's TV episodes in British Columbia, Canada. (Full film and TV credits: IMDB.com)

In the 1990s, his Vancouver software company: The Funny Face SoftBook Company produced a musical painting app for preschoolers entitled '*Paint 'N' Play*' which won *The Newmedia Invision Award*, *Newsweek's Editor's Choice Award* and *Parenting Magazine's Magic Software Award*.

His short stories have been published in various journals and his creepy story *Hearing the Meat* won first place in the *2015 Plymouth Writer's Group International Short Story Competition* in the U.K.. His hard science fiction novel, *Visitor*, is available on Amazon.

Thanks to: Charlotte Gough for finding all the bad things. And to Fred Gonder for his cover art. Also Jytte Allen who told me three drafts ago that it wasn't good enough and explained why. If you liked *At Large*, please consider leaving a review on Amazon.com

Hell, leave one even if you didn't like it; constructive criticism is more valuable than praise, anyway.

Made in the USA
Columbia, SC
23 November 2020